SPOILS OF WAR

A MARGARET OF SCOTLAND MEDIEVAL MYSTERY

J. G. LEWIS

DEDICATION

For my son, Jordan Lewis, an excellent brainstorming partner.

ACKNOWLEDGMENTS

Many thanks to the lovely people who read this story in various stages, including Betsy van der Hoek, Dan Rothman, Kenneth Allen, Alys M. Montgomery, Viktor Steiner, and Daniel Smith-Rowsey. All remaining errors are mine.

"Then was the land of Jordan overwhelmed by armed men and hostile enemies. Many a frightened, white-cheeked lady had to go trembling into a foreigner's embrace."

Old English version of Genesis, *Junius 11*, Bodleian Library

CHAPTER 1

unfermline, December 1070
        The royal procession to bless the king's new tower marched uphill through the rocky woods in a narrow line, led by the bishop, who held his golden staff aloft. Queen Margaret walked steadily beside her husband, fighting the urge to pull her fur-lined robe tight about her neck in the icy winter air.

"Red sky in the morning," whispered Agatha, her mother, behind her. "Shepherd's warning." The sky behind the bare, black branches held a tinge of pink.

"We're in the land of the Scots, Mother, it's always about to rain," replied Margaret's sister Christina. Margaret wanted to turn and tell her to hold her tongue but managed to maintain her composure. Her mother had brought them all this far—alive and still together—from exile in Hungary to the court of King Edward the Confessor and through the bloody upheaval of the Norman invasion, and she could indulge their fussing.

"There she is, my love," said Malcolm, in his low sonorous tones. "Your tower." The gray stones of the new tower, two tall stories high and topped by a steep-pitched roof, rose above the trees.

"It's your tower, my king," said Margaret softly. "And will always be known as such."

"I built it for you. My wife won't have to live in a cowshed." The humor in his voice reassured her.

"I never said anything about a cowshed," whispered Margaret. She suspected her mother had started that rumor. "But a stone castle is more fitting for a king than a low, wooden..."

"Barn," said Malcolm cheerfully. "And you're right. This tower sends a message to the thanes and mormaers, to the King of the Isles, the Earl of Orkney and even to William himself...don't mess with the King of the Scots."

He was joking. Malcolm was always joking. And somehow his good humor, backed by his great height and imposing demeanor, his razor-sharp mind, and his loyal force of vicious fighting men, managed to defuse most of the storms that rose up in and around his court.

At least during the year and a few months she'd spent in it so far.

A carved stone arch framed great wooden doors that opened as they approached. "The carvers did fine work," said Margaret approvingly. The chiseled chevrons around the doorway were as fine as anything she'd seen at Westminster. Stonemasons who fled conquered London had worked at all hours to create them.

"I dare anyone to try these doors," said Malcolm. "Reinforced with iron straps and studs on both sides."

"A fitting abode for a king and his court," whispered Margaret. "And I'll feel safer sleeping behind stone walls if you're away without me."

"I know what exile and uncertainty do to the soul," said Malcolm under his breath. "I wish my bride to sleep easy for the rest of her life—and may it be a long and happy one."

Margaret felt tears rise and quickly drew in a breath to banish them. Her new pregnancy made emotions spring to the surface more often than she liked. She avoided her husband's loving gaze in an effort to maintain her royal composure. She'd come to this land driven by dread and duty and to her immense surprise found a kind and clever man behind Malcolm's fearsome facade and reputation.

The doors opened slowly as the procession reached them. They stopped and the bishop raised his staff and intoned a Latin blessing on the building. He prayed that the king's new tower be filled with the spirit of God and pleasing in his eyes and a fitting home for his will to be done on earth.

Margaret had written this speech for him and planned a feast that would put truth in his words. At the rear of the procession, behind the local nobles and the clerics, but before the servants of the household, marched fifty paupers gathered by the abbey almoner, who would enjoy their feast alongside them.

The sun rose up behind the hills as they entered through the great double doors. Fires roared in hearths on each side, with vents that channeled smoke out through the thick stone walls above them. These filled the air with welcome warmth and were far less smoky than a central hearth. They crossed the stone floors to where carved wooden stairs rose up against the wall and ascended to the second floor. A matching staircase on the opposite wall allowed servants to run up and down unimpeded by the procession.

"It's nice and warm up here with no drafts from the door opening and closing," said Agatha with a smile. "A great hall should always be on the upper floor." Long trestle tables already groaned with food and drink.

"I'm so glad it meets with your approval, Mother," said

Malcolm, turning to face her. His stern expression warred with his jovial tone. "I shall endeavor to always follow your advice on matters of comfort."

"Oh, stop, you're embarrassing me." Agatha waved her hand, beaming. She adored Malcolm and congratulated herself every day on arranging such a fine match for her daughter. "Some painted decoration on the walls would be a nice touch, of course."

"Mother! Stop it," whispered Christina. Margaret's sister was easily mortified by almost anything.

"Malcolm doesn't mind my kidding, do you, darling?"

"I revel in it," said Malcolm calmly. "Will you sit next to me?" He took Agatha's hand and led her to the middle of the high table, raised on a low dais, where he waited until Margaret and her mother were seated on either side of him before he took his own chair.

Margaret watched with approval as the paupers were seated at separate tables and served with bread and wine and pottage and fish as if they were lords and ladies. Some of them stared up at the great roof beams above them as if they might collapse at any moment.

"There's even another floor above us, if you count the attic." said Malcolm, looking up at the beams himself. "Does the tower meet with your approval, my love?"

"It does," said Margaret, keeping emotion out of her voice.

"It is as sturdy as the towers of Hungary?"

"Sturdier, I think."

"As comfortable as the palace at Westminster?" He watched her face, and she saw humor glimmer in his eyes. With its bare plastered stone walls and uncarpeted wood floors, it still looked more like a fortress than a royal palace. They'd both spent time at the court of Edward the Confessor, who, with his wife Edith, had maintained one of the grandest and best appointed courts in Europe. "No, it isn't, but it will be when it's furnished and fitted by my queen."

"We could commission wall paintings with scenes from the Bible," said Margaret, looking at the plain white walls. "And perhaps paint decorative borders along the high walls to make the space more intimate."

"And embroidered cushions for the chairs," cut in Agatha.

"Then we shall have those brought at once," said Malcolm indulgently. He raised his tooled silver cup. "To my beautiful family, which is about to grow with the arrival of our little one."

"God willing," said Margaret nervously. Even though she had many months to go, she grew wary of the rigors of child-birth. "May he protect us and shine his face upon us." Malcolm's first wife, Ingibiorg, had died in childbirth some years earlier, and her two young sons were now in Margaret's care.

"God will give us many sons to continue our dynasty here in Alba!" Malcolm spoke loud enough for the assembled throng to hear his words above the chatter of conversation.

Margaret prayed that he was right, and also that her sons would never find themselves at war with their older half-brothers, or with Malcolm's brother Donald Ban who was conspicuous by his absence this morning.

A cheer rose up and everyone turned to stare at Margaret, who managed a grateful smile.

"We really shouldn't be eating fish during Advent," said Christina, refusing a servant's offer of some jellied eel. "The better to celebrate the Lord's birth with it at the end of the fasting period."

"It's hard enough going without meat for many of us," said Malcolm pushing a plump piece of trout onto his spoon, along with some roasted parsnip. Our growing season is short here in the north and vegetables not abundant enough to get us through the winter."

Margaret agreed with her sister and thought that deprivation forged character. But she was learning to pick her battles with her forceful husband, who did have considerably more flesh to maintain than she did. And even the bishop had begged her to eat heartily during her pregnancy when she'd tried to convince him that she preferred not to eat at all on Fridays in memory of the Lord's privations.

As a queen she was learning to accept that her life was not entirely her own and that even her body was property of the Kingdom of Alba and a vessel for its heirs. If God wished it to be one, which he apparently did.

She had to admit that the jellied eels and baked trout and smoked salmon of the Scots were well and simply prepared and more pleasing to her palate than the spiced foods of the English court or her Hungarian birthplace.

After the main course had been eaten, the servants brought out pies and cakes and steamed puddings that elicited approval from the assembled paupers.

"I do find that inviting the needy to dine increases my appreciation of the gifts before us," said Malcolm, cutting into a hearty slice of fruit cake. "I doubt William of England has a host of paupers in his great hall."

"They say he's a godly man," said Margaret, tamping down her sinful hatred of him. "He credits prayer with his conquest of King Harold at the battle of Hastings." She steeled herself to remind him what was coming next. "When the food is cleared away, we shall wash all of their feet." She said it quietly, hoping for as little opposition as possible.

Malcolm turned his steely stare on her. "Such exertion is not good for the digestion."

"You've not overindulged, dear husband. It takes no more energy than the hunt you likely intend for this afternoon."

She'd planned this event with care, arranging for many jars and bowls of water and folded linen cloths to be at the ready so that everyone at the high table could participate in humbling themselves before the lowest.

Even Christina didn't look too thrilled.

"I will go pray in a quiet corner instead, darling," said Agatha, wiping her hands on a napkin. "The icy cold water here makes my hands ache so at my great age."

"Mother, you're barely forty and your hands are as youthful as mine," said Margaret.

"I think it's a wonderful thing that you're doing…I'd just rather not."

"The road to hell is paved with good intentions, Mother," said Margaret sharply.

"Then I suppose it's better than the road to Dunfermline which isn't paved at all." Agatha looked around brightly, hoping for a laugh; which emerged from her son-in-law Malcolm in a bold guffaw.

"You speak as if there was a road to Dunfermline, Agatha," he said jovially. "We don't hold much with roads here. We prefer to make a new track across the countryside each time we travel."

Margaret wasn't smiling. It was hard enough to arrange these bold acts of charity and get her husband on board. The last thing she needed was her mother undermining all her plans. "Let's have the servants bring the bowls and water before our guests get bored and try to leave."

As it turned out, many of the guests preferred not to have their feet washed in icy water and had to be persuaded with reminders of the feast they'd just enjoyed. Servants then ushered them to four stations in the corners of the room, one each for Margaret, Malcolm, Agatha and Christina. The family then attended—with the help of servants—to removing their shoes and washing and anointing their feet.

Margaret greeted each person with a blessing in her halting Gaelic as they sat in the chair for her attentions. She quickly realized that many present—most even—did not have shoes and had walked up the icy wooded hillside barefoot. Surprisingly, most of their feet were tough and rosy. One older man explained to her that leather shoes only got wet and uncomfortable and took a long time to dry off and then were stiff.

Margaret reflected that servants rubbed lanolin into her shoes almost nightly to keep them soft and supple. Another blessing to be grateful for. The last guest of the day, however, presented a very different pair of feet. The woman seemed reluctant to rise. She apologized profusely for the state of her feet, which—once the wrapping of rags was removed—were in a lamentable state unlike any Margaret had seen.

"We need healing ointment," she told her servant Grizel. She peered up at the woman's face, which hid in the shadow under a hood. "Your feet are not hard like all the others."

"I'm not used to walking on bare ground," said the woman cautiously.

"You speak English?" asked Margaret. Everyone else had spoken the local dialect.

"I need your help," said the woman softly. "To save my daughter."

"To save her from what?"

The woman glanced over her shoulder. "I've run away. Will your men take me back?"

Margaret looked around in alarm. "Back to where?" Her concern about the raw and blistered state of the woman's feet darkened into fears for her safety.

"Will you promise me that I won't be returned to captivity?" She spoke in a low whisper that Margaret could barely hear over the din of the celebration.

Margaret blinked. She was still finding her way in the

Scottish court, which had a lot of unfamiliar rules and customs.

She whispered back. "I'll try to help you."

She took the ointment that Grizel brought and, as gently as possible, pressed it onto the inflamed and damaged skin. "Where were you being held?"

The woman glanced about, her lips trembling. "I'm afraid to speak openly of my troubles in this great room. Could I talk to you in private?"

Margaret's shock at her audacious request was compounded by her observation that the woman's speech was refined—the speech of King Edward's court at Westminster, not the rustic tones of a peasant.

She wrapped fresh bandages over the bruised and broken skin. This strange bold woman with her bleeding feet and familiar accent felt almost like a messenger from God...a summons.

Margaret drew in a steadying breath and glanced at her husband, who'd now risen from his appointed duties and walked back to the high table, with her mother and sister close behind him. Then she tied the bandages securely and dried her hands on a clean linen cloth. "The feast won't go on much longer. Stay here until everyone leaves and I'll speak to you alone."

The other paupers—now well-fed and content—were being gathered up to file out. Margaret told Grizel to take the woman from the main hall and sit her downstairs near the fire.

Back at the table, the family washed their hands in a silver bowl of scented water and dried them on soft cloths. Agatha griped about the coldness of the water and the need to warm her hands before the fire. Christina observed that the paupers weren't poor enough and were taking advantage of Margaret's generosity and goodness of heart.

Malcolm kissed her warmly on the cheek. "Only the prettiest woman in existence could convince the rugged and warlike King of the Scots to wash his subjects' feet."

"You don't need a pretty face to lure you into doing what is right since you have a good heart," said Margaret. Her husband's lavish compliments still unnerved her. They were at odds with the praising of good deeds over good looks that had characterized her convent education. "Your work this afternoon will serve to protect your immortal soul and atone for any misdeeds that you've committed in your role as a leader of men."

Now the guests were gone, servants brought comfortable chairs and arranged them near the hearth. The family sat down to relax and enjoy the day. Malcolm's young sons played with his hunting dogs and fed them scraps. Malcolm serenaded Margaret on his small harp with a fast-paced tune. "My wife is the loveliest woman in the land, and possibly the most eccentric…"

"That is not a compliment, my husband," said Margaret quickly. "No woman wishes to be called odd."

"Not many women insist that their husbands wash strangers' feet."

"It was quite customary in biblical times for a host to wash their guests' feet."

"Do we live in biblical times?" His eyes twinkled.

"We live in a time of great upheaval and unrest and all we can do is try to create the Kingdom of God here on earth as best we can," said Margaret.

"Was she like this as a small child?" he asked Agatha.

"Yes, she was," said Agatha. "I'm sure I must credit her constant prayers to our survival in these turbulent times and that we've washed safely ashore in your court during our hour of need."

Agatha loved to pretend that a storm had tossed them

onto Malcolm's rocky shores as they tried to escape the clutches of William the Bastard—when in fact their arrival had been heralded by a series of letters and promises dating back to when Margaret and Malcolm had first met at West-minster ten years earlier under the avuncular gaze of King Edward.

"You've lifted me from the sorrow of widowhood," said Malcolm. "And brought life and light back to my court. And kept fifty masons very busy constructing this tower in just a few months."

"I shall sleep like a babe within these strong walls," said Agatha, her fingers busy embroidering a ribbon with gold thread.

"Do excuse me," said Margaret. She rose as if going to the garderobe, beckoned Grizel to follow her, and headed down the stairs.

In the room below there was no sign of the woman with her newly bandaged feet. A bench sat empty by the fire as servants bustled about their duties.

"Where did she go? Did you ask her to wait here? Did you see her leave?"

"I don't know, my lady," said Grizel, panic spreading over her usually placid features. "I asked her to wait here and settled her on the bench to rest her feet."

Where had she gone, and why? The woman was English —like herself—but was she a spy for William? Had she unwittingly introduced an enemy into their midst and now let her loose in the royal household?

CHAPTER 2

The ground level had flagstone floors and a warren of rooms divided up by portable wooden screens. Along one wall was a great hearth used for the final stages of cooking and roasting food brought from the kitchen in a nearby building. Behind the screens lay a maze of pantries and butteries and sleeping quarters and cloakrooms. Margaret and Grizel darted around from one room to the next, looking for the mysterious woman.

Should I alert the guards or tell my husband there's a strange woman loose in the castle?

No.

He'd never let her invite paupers here to feast with them again.

She realized she hadn't even taken a good look at the stranger. Her cloak had cast her face into shadow. Her hands looked like those of a middle-aged woman. With feet like that she was not a spy for the conquering King William but likely one of his victims. If she was here to poison the food or plunge a dagger into the king, she'd hardly have sat at the feast for such a long time and sought an audience with his queen.

She needs my help and I must find her.

Having exhausted their search of the ground floor, Grizel whisked Margaret's cloak from its peg and wrapped it around her shoulders. Margaret pulled the fur-lined wool around herself and allowed Grizel to place the hood carefully over her veiled head, bracing herself against the cold outside.

"Don't forget your cloak!" Sometimes the girl was so attentive to Margaret's needs that she forgot her own. She was only sixteen and still fairly new in her role, and very anxious to please since her late father had been one of Malcolm's most trusted gillies.

Well-clad against the winter winds, they waited for the porter to open a smaller door built into the great double doors, and allow them out into the neat courtyard arranged in front of the tower. An icy gust brought a flurry of tiny flakes that dashed against her skin. She closed her eyes against the sudden onslaught.

"She won't go into the kitchens. Too many people, and she just ate. Might she be keeping warm in the laundry?" She looked into the newly built wooden shed, where a big kettle of water boiled over a roaring fire. Two women were already at work scrubbing the linens from today's feast. They started at the sight of her and she told them she had no wish to interrupt their good work and to keep going. The intense heat of the fire and steam stung her cheeks almost as much as the cold as she wished them a good afternoon.

In the spring shed a boy of about fourteen pulled water from a shallow well built over a natural spring. The tower and its outbuildings had been located here to take advantage of the spring as much as the defensive advantages of the high, hilly, wooded terrain. Buckets of water—some of them already bearing a skin of ice—sat waiting for anyone who needed them in the kitchen or the laundry or to water the many horses that came and went from the royal household.

A small brazier burned in the corner for the boy to warm his hands.

Margaret asked the boy if he'd enjoyed any of the delicacies from today's feast and he said that he had, and thanked her sweetly. Her husband helped her daily in her efforts to learn the Gaelic language because none of these people spoke a word of English or Latin and she didn't expect they'd be learning any time soon.

"Let's walk through the woods," she said to Grizel, once they were back outside in the dusk. She did relish the open air and the sight of birds and small beasts—scarce though they were at this time of year. And she clung to the hope that the woman was still nearby waiting to speak to her.

Ice glittered high in the bare branches as they rounded the top of a small hill.

"My lady."

Margaret spun around at the whispered words. She saw no one. Then she heard a scuffling of dead leaves and high above her, from the crest of the little hill, she saw a cloaked figure emerge from behind a tree.

ALARM THAT SOMEONE was able to hide themselves in the woods right here in the royal demesne warred with relief that they'd found her. Margaret stepped off the path and ascended the hill as the woman scrambled down the steep, leaf-littered slope.

"Who are you?" she asked the woman. "What's your name."

"Who was I?" said the woman gravely. "I was once Aelgith of Milton in Hampshire." She pushed back her hood and for the first time Margaret got a good look at her features. Her skin, dry as parchment, stretched taut across bony features.

Her blue eyes shone behind pale-lashed eyes. Her hair, tightly pulled behind her ears into two long braids, was a mousy brown color flecked with strands of silver...except the bottom half, which shone bright gold like hair skillfully lightened with herbs.

"You were displaced by the Norman invasion?" There was scarcely a person in England who wasn't, herself included.

"My husband fought with Harold at Hastings and perished that fateful day more than four years ago. My son as well." Her eyes glittered for a moment.

"I'm so sorry," whispered Margaret. "May God rest their souls."

"I doubt they can rest if they are able to look down on the piteous state I find myself in. When a local man who'd fought alongside them brought me the terrible news of their deaths I stayed on at our manor with my daughter. We hoped the foreigners would leave us unmolested deep in the country-side. For a time we managed as best we could, though most of the men were gone and we were left unprotected."

"That sounds terrifying."

"It was nothing to what was to come. Eventually the soldiers arrived. My daughter and I hid for days in a grain shed with nothing to eat or drink except water from a nearby stream while the ruffians feasted and laughed and sang their foreign songs under the roof my great-grandfathers built. On the third day they were so drunk they started burning every-thing, and when they set fire to the granary we were forced to run outside."

The woman's hands shook violently at the memory, and Margaret took them in hers. Her fingers were so cold. Margaret noticed how thin her cloak and gown were and vowed to find her something warmer to wear.

"We tried to hide in the woods but they found us there and seized us. They bound our hands and feet and threw us

onto a cart they'd stolen from our barn. We couldn't understand anything they said. I can't describe the terror we felt as
their horses pulled us away from the place where we'd lived
our whole lives, as flames engulfed the manor and even the
woods around it."

Margaret swallowed. It was only with God's grace that
she and her family had managed to avoid a similar fate.

"After we were taken from our home, we were kept
alongside a gang of other miserable souls, forced to walk
through our own countryside, driven like cattle, by these
foreign scoundrels. At night they'd herd us into someone's
barn, and often that unfortunate owner would be added to
our number. Some people they left unmolested, perhaps in
return for sums of money or valuable goods."

The woman steadied herself on the trunk of a nearby
tree. "Eventually we arrived in York. By then I'd picked up
enough of their foreign speech to ascertain that. After a few
days there with pitiful food and drink we were—as far as I
could understand it—sold in the market square as slaves."

"I'm so sorry." Margaret's heart ached for her suffering.
War was often hardest on the women and children who
didn't have the mercy of being killed as heroes in the heat of
battle.

"We were put to doing embroidery in a large household.
My daughter and I are highly skilled at it—working with
silver and gold thread to create vestments fit for a bishop. We
counted our blessings and kept quiet and for a time life was
relatively peaceful. Then invading Scots stormed their manor
and my daughter was seized and taken away." She stopped
and her lip quivered. "I begged to go with her but they kicked
me away. Too old, they said. Another mouth to feed."

"How old is your daughter?"

"She turned fourteen this summer."

A very dangerous age for a girl. A ten-year-old would be left unmolested by all but the most monstrous of men, but a fourteen-year-old girl was seen as a fruit ripe for the plucking. That was about the age she'd been when King Edward first promised her as a bride for Malcolm, and she still remembered how she'd begged and pleaded to remain in the cloister at Wilton Abbey with her mother and sister.

"You think she's in the land of the Scots?"

"The man who took her spoke the Gaelic tongue. So I came here to find her." She glanced over Margaret's shoulder. "I ran away from the household in Northumbria, which was burned and destroyed almost to nothing anyway. Without my daughter I have no reason to live, so I've come here in the hope of finding her and helping her escape her bondage. Or at least of joining her in it."

Tears filled her eyes. "Now that I'm here I can't understand a word anyone says. There are no roads and it seems that every tiny hamlet is a day's journey apart. I have no idea where she is and I suspect I'll die on some windy hilltop and abandon my daughter to her miserable fate with no help of escape." The tears rolled down her withered cheeks and her head drooped.

Margaret's heart sank. How would you even try to find one young girl in this vast and almost trackless country?

"Do you have any idea of the name of the man who took her?"

"I heard his men use the word *Beithir*, behind his back. I asked someone in Northumbria what that meant and they said it's the word for dragon in Scots so I doubt it's his name." She pressed her face into her hands. "The ruffians showed him deference to his face, obeying orders he barked at them, so he's some kind of leader or noble. A very tall man with dark reddish hair. Not orange, but a much deeper color." She looked up. "And he had a great beard as well, darker than the hair on his head."

Was this enough information to identify him? A tiny spark of hope lit in Margaret's heart. Her husband had led the ill-starred expedition into Northumbria and might well know the man.

The woman's hands shook and tears now flowed freely from her eyes. "When I learned that the King of the Scots had an English queen and that ordinary people were given alms at her table, I seized this chance...perhaps my last chance..." her words faltered. "For I doubt I can survive much longer in this biting cold and with so little hope of finding my dear daughter. Her name is Osgifu." She inhaled on a shaky sob. "Do you think you can help me find her?"

"I'll help you find her." She spoke with sudden resolve. This woman was her kin. They were both refugees from the collapse of the great Anglo-Saxon kingdom that her grandfather had ruled and that her father was supposed to inherit. Their people had ruled England for hundreds of years and it was still inconceivable that had ended in just a few short days in 1066. "First we must keep you safe. Let's get you inside."

Margaret wasn't sure that Malcolm would be thrilled by her harboring a fugitive from one of his Northumbrian enemies. Nor yet hunting a captive seized by one of his nobles. Perhaps it would be good to keep Aelgith somewhere quiet for the time being. She needed her husband's help to determine the identity of her daughter's captor.

She turned to Grizel, who'd been standing silently beside her. "Grizel, do you think your mother would let Aelgith stay in her house?"

"Oh yes, my lady. She's always complaining about how empty the place is now we've all grown and gone." Then she hesitated. "But she might gripe about another mouth to feed."

"You can bring food from the kitchens, and for your

mother as well, as payment for her kindness. Will she be home if we go there now?"

"I dare say, my lady," said Grizel. "She's probably spinning away as usual."

After ascertaining that Aelgith was able to walk a distance on her injured but bandaged feet, they set out down the hill from the new tower toward the town of Dunfermline.

The new tower sat up above the town on a high rocky knoll, shrouded with trees and ringed by a brook. As they emerged from the woods they saw smoke rising toward the white sky from the heavy thatched roofs of the dwellings clustered on the plain below.

Sheep and cattle grazed around the settlement and a group of small children shrieked and ran as they played a game of chase among the sheep. Margaret knew that Grizel's mother lived in one of these houses, but she wasn't sure which one.

Grizel led them down a frozen path toward a small, low-slung thatched dwelling. The walls looked to be made of turf brick but barely came to knee height, so the thick thatch descended almost to the ground. A battered wood door pierced the heavy thatch, and Grizel approached it ahead of them.

"Ma, it's your daughter."

"No need for an announcement," called a bold voice from inside. "Come on in, will you."

Grizel hesitated. "I have the queen with me."

Silence was followed by rustling sounds and the scraping of a chair on the ground. A face appeared in the crack and then the door opened, revealing a small middle-aged woman with dark eyes. Her bare head revealed dark hair flecked with silver wound into a knot at the nape of her neck. She wore a long tunic of a yellowish color with a woven belt at the waist.

"Come in out of the cold, my lady," she stammered, pulling the door back for Margaret to enter. Margaret saw her glance past her to Grizel with questions written all over her face.

"It's a pleasure to meet you..." Margaret realized she had no idea what Grizel's mother was called. Grizel always referred to her as "Ma."

"Beathag," she said quickly. "And it's my pleasure, I'm sure." Now she glanced at Aelgith, who stood silent, with her ragged cloak pulled tight about her face by a hand holding it under her chin.

Margaret brought forth her Gaelic, knowing that Grizel would gently prompt her if it was somehow incomprehensible. "This is Aelgith of Milton, who finds herself alone and friendless in our midst. She's seeking her daughter who was abducted in Northumbria. I wonder if she might take shelter with you while we try to find the girl."

"Yes, my lady. I've all the space in the world, as you can see." She gestured around the soot-blackened interior of her smoky cottage. Margaret couldn't see anything at all as her eyes hadn't yet adjusted from the bright daylight outside. The fire flickered in the center of the room, with an iron pot on a tripod over it bubbling and sending steam rising along with the smoke.

"That's wonderful. Thank you so much," said Margaret with relief. She'd hardly thought that Grizel's mother would say no, but it was always a possibility. "Grizel will bring good provisions for both of you from the castle for you to cook her meals, and I'll make sure you're compensated for your time and trouble."

Beathag brightened considerably. She turned her inquisitive gaze on her new guest, looking her up and down several times. "Come close to the fire, my dear, you look half frozen."

Aelgith shuffled forward, picking her way past a basket of

kindling and a wooden tool that Margaret didn't recognize. Beathag disappeared into the shadowy blackness of a corner and pulled out a second three-legged wooden stool for her to sit on and placed it by the fire next to her own. Margaret could see her long spindle and the spun thread in one basket on the ground, and a fluffy pile of un-spun wool in another basket next to it.

"I shall ask my husband which men might fit the description you gave me of the man who took your daughter," said Margaret.

"I know everyone around here," cut in Beathag. "What did he look like?"

"Ma!" Grizel looked appalled by her mother's interjection.

"What? I do. You know that."

Margaret felt her first twinge of apprehension about this arrangement. She hoped Beathag wouldn't be a gossip. Grizel was the soul of discretion and already trusted with many potentially embarrassing secrets despite her young age.

Beathag gestured again for Aelgith to take a seat in front of the fire. Aelgith hesitated, her noble upbringing probably preventing her from wanting to take a seat while Margaret was still standing.

"He was a very tall man with dark red hair. I think he had some gray at the temples," said Aelgith, looking at Margaret as if to ask her permission to speak. "I'm not sure of his eye color. They could be brown or hazel or even a darker blue or gray. Dark brows. A big man."

Beathag frowned. "Well, that does narrow it down but also excludes any of the men I can think of off the top of my head. Dark red hair, you say?"

"Yes, it was a distinctive color," said Aelgith quietly. "Like aged copper."

"But not so aged that it turned blue, I'll wager," said Beathag with a wink.

"Ma!" Grizel shot a mortified glance at Margaret.

"Your hospitality and graciousness is much appreciated," said Margaret. "And I would like to rely on your discretion as well. It's important that the person keeping her daughter captive not learn of our search for her, so please don't tell anyone why Aelgith is here. In fact, if you can keep her presence here something of a secret, that would probably be best."

Beathag's brown eyes widened. "Goodness. Yes. I won't breathe a word of it to a soul."

CHAPTER 3

*M*argaret and Grizel left Aelgith and Beathag in the dark cottage with promises that she'd make urgent inquiries into the identity of the tall chestnut-haired stranger. She suspected he was one of her husband's allies who'd accompanied him on the last incursion into Northumbria.

"Before we go back to the tower, let's step into the church to pray for her daughter's safety," she said to Grizel as they blinked in the bright white afternoon light. The quiet sacred atmosphere of a church had been her sanctuary for as long as she could remember, and her place of refuge during the years of tumult and upheaval she'd known since her family left their exile in Hungary.

The rectangular wood building rose above the squat thatched huts of the village, its peaked roof covered with tiles. Grizel opened the crudely carved wood door and admitted her to the chilly interior. The church was heated by two small braziers—which often went out—near the altar, Two high windows contained glass—very rare in Scotland, as she was learning—to keep out the bitter winds. A sturdy new church would soon replace this drafty edifice, but this one must suffice since she had urgent business with God.

The church was empty, between the services of Nones and Vespers, except for the sacristan who bowed to her slightly before fussing over the braziers. She knelt before the altar and offered up prayers for all the blessings of her life—her mother and sister and brother still at her side despite all they'd been through, her kind husband, the baby growing in her belly. Then she offered a prayer for all those who'd lost loved ones and homes and who were hungry and cold and she promised to do everything in her power to help those less fortunate than herself.

Dusk cloaked the land in shadow by the time they emerged. A guard stood there carrying a lit torch as if waiting for them.

"How fortunate," said Margaret. "Where did you come from?"

"Your husband asked me to escort you home, my lady."

"And how did you know I was here?"

He looked awkward.

"Were you following me the whole time?"

"Oh no, my lady."

She wasn't sure she believed him. Not that there was any hope of privacy in the royal enclave of Dunfermline. Likely half the people in the town knew exactly where she was at any given moment. She envied those who could just head out for a walk in the fields all alone without anyone knowing or caring where they'd gone.

"I'm glad of your company and your light, please lead us back to the tower."

DARKNESS FELL, heralding their first night in the new tower. Servants had carried all furniture, bedding, clothing, washing bowls, hair combs and other necessities up the wooded hillside like a column of ants bearing breadcrumbs. Now everything sat, dusted and ready, in its new place.

The tower interior glowed with the warmth of the fires in its large stone hearths and candles flickered in holders fixed to the stone walls.

Inside the entrance, Grizel took her cloak and removed Margaret's sturdy leather boots, replacing them with a more delicate pair of shoes with punched leather decoration.

She climbed the stairs to the hall with eager anticipation of quizzing her husband about his auburn-haired cronies, only to find that Malcolm was deep in conversation with his younger brother Donald Ban.

A twinge of apprehension slowed her steps. Donald's tousled blond curls likely contributed to his nickname of Donald the Handsome. Almost as tall as her husband, he carried himself with imposing dignity and heads turned toward him wherever he went, which was how he liked it. She knew it rankled him that her husband was King of the Scots…and he wasn't.

Just as her brother Edgar, grandson of Edmund Ironside, rankled that William of Normandy—or William the Bastard as his enemies still called him—ruled all of England and he didn't. Bitter men in their midst were like the bitter poisons tucked away on a shelf in the cook's pantry. Harmless as long as they stayed in their place, and even useful if they were needed to help subdue a rebellion or kill a plague of rats—yet always brimming with dangerous potential.

"My dear wife!" Malcolm stood and ushered her to his side, where a servant quickly placed one of the more comfortable chairs. "This fine fortress was my wife's grand vision."

"I'm sure it wasn't," said Margaret. Her mother had schooled her at an early age that the best way to get anything done was to let someone else take credit for it.

Donald Ban's pale blue eyes flashed a warning at her before he greeted her through tight lips. "Now you've got my brother hiding in a tower. Scottish warriors don't need stone walls to crouch behind. Our men are the bravest fighters in Christendom. We could live out in an open plain without a hint of a roof or wall or a fear in our hearts."

"I have no doubt about that," she said with a careful smile. "But your womenfolk do enjoy a wall to keep out the winds blowing in from the sea. And if you're away fighting we have another layer of protection."

"You speak as if the Vikings might sweep up the Forth at any moment," said Donald slowly, picking up his engraved cup and taking a swig of wine.

"They wouldn't dare," said Margaret evenly. Donald Ban liked to toy with her like a cat with a mouse but she wouldn't fall into his trap. Her husband didn't even seem to notice. Perhaps because she was usually able to handle him deftly.

Impatience to pursue her new quest tugged at her. Margaret hesitated. How best to ask her question without revealing too much about the circumstances? "I've heard there's a noble…a thane or mormaer perhaps…who's a tall man with dark red hair. Do you have any idea who that might be?"

Her husband stared at her, curious. "Where did you hear that?"

"Just the women talking." She had no intention of telling her husband a lie, but he didn't need to know the whole truth, either. "It's an unusual color. I can't say I've seen anyone with dark red hair." She decided to keep the beard detail for later.

26

Malcolm looked at his brother, Donald. "One springs to mind."

"I can think of three," said Donald. "Oengus Mac Ruaidrí, called The Pigeon, Gille Mac Lochlann, also known as The Fat. And the one you're thinking of."

Margaret waited for the third name. Malcolm shook his head as if he'd like to shed the very thought of the third one from his mind. At last she despaired of him ever saying it without a prompt. "Who's the third one?"

Donald Ban laughed. "Mac Duff—the Mormaer of Fife. The man who'd like to see himself on the throne instead of you."

"Oh. So you're enemies?" That would mean he hadn't accompanied Malcolm on his foray into Northumbria and could be eliminated from her list of suspects.

"I have no enemies," said Malcolm. "Only a foolish man has enemies."

Margaret knew that subtlety was a great strength—one that her husband perhaps possessed more than she did. Her impatience got the best of her. "Do people call him a dragon?"

Malcolm and Donald Ban looked at each other and burst into a laugh.

A bell rang to announce the readiness of the evening meal. Servants had spread a linen tablecloth and now laid plates and bowls and jugs of wine and ale along it. Margaret's mother and sister arrived, along with Donald and Duncan, Malcolm's two young sons from his first marriage. Margaret's brother Edgar—who lived on a nearby manor and who had been scarce all day—also arrived and they all took seats at the table.

"Well, do they?" Margaret burned for the answer to her question. Her brother Edgar now sat next to her, opposite Malcolm and Donald Ban.

"Did who what, sister dearest?" asked Edgar. His golden good looks rivaled Donald Ban's, though his hair was straight rather than curly.

Margaret swallowed. She didn't really want her brother involved in this. He had an odd way of taking offense at the strangest things. "I was asking if the Mormaer of Fife is ever referred to as a dragon."

"How do you know anything about the Mormaer of Fife?" asked Edgar, staring at her while a servant filled his jewel-encrusted cup with wine. "Besides, isn't he called the Earl of Fife now?"

"I don't know anything about him," said Margaret simply. "Except that he apparently has dark red hair." She began to despair of getting a useful answer. And it would be awkward to bring up the subject again without revealing how important it was to her. She picked up a jug of wine and poured her husband's cup, which she'd learned was a noble wife's duty here.

"They do call him the dragon," said Malcolm, helping himself to a piece of bread. "But not to his face. Perhaps the foul fire of his breath stirs the name." He and Donald Ban guffawed again and Edgar joined them.

He's the one. Encouraged, Margaret pressed on. "Did he come along with you on your last foray into Northumbria?"

"Yes, he did," said Malcolm. "And was very happy with the treasure he brought back with him by all accounts. That's what I like to do, make people happy." He smiled and lifted his cup. "Sláinte."

So Malcolm had invited his nobles and their mustered armies to invade Northumbria with him for the express purpose of enriching them with ill-gotten gains, in order to keep them content and supportive. Her heart sank. One of these men had seized the girl and taken her home as if she were a silver chalice or a good horse.

A servant brought around a platter of poached fish and sliced eggs garnished with springs of something green. How they got anything green to grow in Dunfermline at this time of year was beyond her. Given the baby growing in her belly, she decided not to make a fuss over the rich fare as the servant spooned some fish and egg onto her plate.

The men were already murmuring about a hunt that they planned to organize early in the morning, with the pursuit of a particular stag in mind. Margaret decided on one last attempt tonight to further her pursuit of the captured girl. "When you take a raiding party into Northumbria, what exactly are people looking to bring back with them?"

"All moveable goods," said Malcolm. "If it will fit on the back of a pack horse it's fair game."

"It doesn't need to fit on a horse," said Donald with a sly grin. "We steal their carts and load them on those as well."

"So you seize jewels and livestock, but do you ever take —" She found it hard to even say the words. "Young girls?"

Donald Ban let out a throaty laugh so loud that nearly everyone at the table stopped talking.

"What's he laughing about, dear?" asked her mother.

"I'm not sure," said Margaret truthfully. She turned to Malcolm. "Well, do they?"

"Yes, my love. They do."

"That's barbaric."

"We live in barbaric times, in case you hadn't noticed," said her brother Edgar, who she didn't realize was still listening.

"What do they do with them? Are they married or kept as slaves of some kind?" The idea of marriage by force appalled her but it was worse if they didn't have even the protections of legal marriage.

"I'm not sure I know, my love."

"Have you ever removed a young girl or woman from her

29

home and brought her back to Scotland?" asked Margaret, staring her husband in the face.

"I have not. As you know, I was raised in the court of Edward the Confessor, who taught me respect for God and all his creations, especially the fairer sex." He said it with a perfectly straight face and she could tell he meant it. Then a brow lifted. "My dear brother, however, was raised by Irish savages and might feel differently."

Donald Ban sipped his ale. "Now, brother, my upbringing was also in a royal household and founded on Christian principles."

"Are you trying to tell me the Irish don't keep slaves?"

"I wish I could, but I can't. Besides, there are so many refugees everywhere right now, like beetles crawling out of diseased wood. If they weren't made slaves what would become of them?"

Margaret's plate of fish and eggs now looked as inedible as the table it sat on. "We must stop this horror."

"I'll be sure to write a missive to the kings of Ireland to that effect," said Malcolm wryly.

"Never mind about the Irish," said Margaret. "From what I'm gathering, innocent men and women—even young girls —have been abducted and stolen into our own dear Kingdom of Alba where they're being held against their will. We must return them to their homes."

Donald Ban let out another laugh. "And let's gather up all the gold cups and jeweled scabbards and return them home as well as an act of Christian charity."

Sometimes Margaret really hated her husband's brother. Luckily he didn't live at court and wasn't here that often. Still, he was an important ally and she had to bite her tongue more than she liked.

"Husband, surely you agree with me." She looked hard at Malcolm.

"I don't like the taking of…captives, but it is a part of our culture, just like it's part of the culture of our neighboring nations."

"It's not against the law?"

"No." Malcolm seemed unruffled by this appalling situation.

"But we are literate and educated, not savages."

"So were the Greeks and Romans," said Donald Ban brightly. "They kept slaves. And surely you've heard of the time Pope Gregory saw one of your fellow golden-haired Angles in a market and marveled that they did indeed look like angels."

Margaret felt physically ill. "It's ungodly. It's cruel and evil and—" She felt tears rising to her eyes and stopped herself before her words came out on a sob. Her determination to find and rescue the missing girl—and any others like her—grew with each passing moment. "They must be set free."

"Sometimes one must learn to leave well enough alone," said Malcolm softly. "Maintaining the peace with our allies is hard enough sometimes, let alone maintaining peace with our enemies."

"But you agree with me that it's wrong?" she asked him earnestly.

"Morally wrong, yes. But not entirely avoidable."

This shall not continue. But she could tell she'd said enough for one night. Since arriving in Scotland she'd found many things in need of reform, not least of which was the church itself, which had some very strange habits and customs which would cause jaws to drop in Rome.

She decided not to mention Aelgith's daughter for fear of making her a target or alerting her captors to tuck her away somewhere she'd never be found. She'd need to pursue the investigation herself.

CHAPTER 4

*M*argaret retired before her husband. Her pregnancy made her sleepy and somehow noises—even the music of minstrels—grated on her senses more than usual. A warm fire already burned in the newly built chamber just off the great hall. She could still hear the music, but it was muffled by thick wooden walls.

"I'm grateful to your mother for providing shelter for Aelgith," she said as Grizel unpinned her veil and shook it out. "I shall go visit her first thing in the morning."

"My ma doesn't usually rise until sun-up, my lady."

Margaret laughed. "I promise I won't visit her before dawn." Grizel knew her too well. She liked to rise while all the others were asleep and seize the time to pray and think in peace. Even during times of war, disruption and displacement the hours before dawn were usually a lull in the tumult of life. Grizel brushed out her hair, which glowed gold in the candlelight.

Servants had dismantled the great carved wooden bed from the old palace and put it back together here. Fine new curtains hung from its sturdy timbers and one of the ladies had sewn her a new quilt made of linen stuffed with goose down. Dyed a rich red, it looked as warm as glowing embers as she lifted it and climbed under it.

"I feel fortunate indeed to inhabit this comfortable bed in this sturdy new tower," she said to Grizel. She didn't want the girl to think she took the great advantages God had given her for granted.

"Yes, my lady. It is a blessing indeed." Grizel plumped up the pillow where her husband's head would lie after a few more cups of ale and laughing conversations with his men.

Grizel herself would sleep downstairs with the other servants so that she and her husband could enjoy privacy in their chamber. Her mother found this quite odd as she didn't consider the servants to have eyes and ears. She'd thought nothing of one sleeping at the foot of the bed in which she lay with her husband.

Grizel used bellows to build the fire and snuffed out two candles before retiring. Despite her new worries, Margaret drifted off to sleep, lulled by the sounds of merriment in the hall and glad that her husband seemed so happy with his new tower.

She awoke when Malcolm lifted the covers to climb in and a rush of cool air swept in through the opening in the curtains. "Go back to sleep, my love," he whispered.

Margaret reached for him. She enjoyed the warm bulk of him against her under the covers. Something she would never have known if she'd taken the veil as she'd wanted to so badly. Sometimes she had to remind herself that loving her husband, even cherishing his handsome face and his tall, well-muscled form, was not a sin in God's eyes. Even the carnal acts she'd dreaded—but now welcomed—were an opportunity to fill his world with godly men and women that she could raise from the cradle to lead this nation one day—God willing.

"What was the meaning of the question about red-haired men?" he whispered, his breath warm on her ear. "You piqued my brother's curiosity."

Margaret sighed inwardly. The last thing she wanted was Donald Ban following her endeavors and sticking his interfering oar in. "Your brother thinks I should stick to pouring the wine and hold my tongue."

Malcolm chuckled and kissed her gently. "He doesn't like you any better than he likes me, but we both do a good job of managing him."

A question burned in her mind, and she suddenly had to ask it. "Aren't you afraid he'll try to kill you to seize the crown?"

For a moment she thought he'd laugh. He answered so many deadly serious questions with a quiet chuckle. But he didn't laugh. "He wouldn't dare. He knows my men are loyal and he wouldn't live to see another sunrise if he was even suspected of harming me. Keeping them loyal is my real work here—It's more important even than fighting battles with skill."

"Is that why you married the widow of the Earl of Orkney?"

"You understand it perfectly. Her first two sons are now the rulers of Orkney, and her second two sons are asleep under my roof. Peace through shared blood."

"Is that why you married me? To have blood ties to the great and ancient house of Wessex that ruled England for so long?"

Again, he didn't laugh. "I can't deny that's one reason, but you must admit that marrying into English royalty doesn't do me much good right now, since the entire nation has been overthrown by the Normans. The truth is your beauty and sharp mind caught my eye when I first met you many years ago."

"I know, you've said that many times. But King Edward planned the alliance, not you."

"And you refused it, begging for more years to mature."

"And I'm grateful for them. Now, at twenty-five, I'm ready to be your wife. As a silly girl of fourteen I would have been quite challenging to deal with, I suspect."

Now he did laugh. "I don't think you've ever had a silly bone in your body. I've never known a woman more deadly serious and with the knowledge of the royal library stored inside that pretty head ready to cut a man like a freshly sharpened knife."

Margaret stiffened. "I certainly hope I shall never do that." She sometimes wasn't able to hold her tongue when a man was spouting nonsense. And she had to ask one more time about the red-haired warrior. "Did any of the men who went to Northumbria with you last year bring any captured women home with them?"

"I dare say they all did," said Malcolm.

"You didn't."

He stroked her cheek with his thumb. "The thanes and mormaers that I trust to defend me as king are mostly a rougher sort who've never entertained a thought that wasn't passed down by their father and his father and a long train of mountain-dwelling warriors with habits stretching back to the ancient days."

"But you could instruct them that taking slaves is cruel and immoral."

"I could and I should, my love. And now that you've put the idea in my head I shall share it before our next excursion."

"God forbid!" Margaret couldn't help the outburst. "You have no need to invade anywhere at all. And your last efforts drew the wrath of England's new king with such force that they say Northumbria was laid to waste so fiercely that it may never recover."

"Yes. He's a different one, to be sure. I'll have to manage him carefully."

~

THE NEXT DAY, after her morning prayers and breaking her fast, Margaret donned her cloak and she and Grizel hurried down one of the wooded paths that led from the tower into the town. Smoke rose against the pale dawn sky and she could hear the cows lowing as they waited to be milked and the sheep bleating in their enclosures, perhaps hoping to be herded out to grazing despite the wintry weather.

They approached Beathag's house and Grizel called from outside the door, "Mam, I'm here with the queen."

The door opened and Beathag ushered them into the smoky darkness of her small house. Aelgith had risen to her bandaged feet and stood anxiously clasping her hands.

Margaret murmured a greeting to both of them. "Aelgith, I've been praying for guidance and trying to come up with a plan."

"Thank you, my lady." Aelgith shuffled forward. Beathag moved behind her and stoked the fire in the center of the room. "I'm so grateful for your help."

"I inquired of my husband and his brother who campaigned with him, which Scots noblemen have dark red hair and if any of them is called the Dragon. They knew of one who fit that description. I can't be sure it's the same man, or even that he still has your daughter, but we have a place to start."

"He had three of his men seize her and bind her and throw her over the back of a horse before she disappeared from my sight." She pressed her hands to her face at the awful memory as a sob rose inside her.

"It's something no mother should ever have to see. As God is my witness, we will search the land until we find her." Her resolve had strengthened every minute since last night's conversation with her husband and his brother. The idea that such cruelty was a typical custom in her new land boiled her blood. Jesus had said it was every man's duty to care for and protect the weakest among us. She hadn't wanted to be a queen but God had made her one and she would use her role to do His work.

Margaret hesitated. Should she tell Aelgith his name? If she knew it, might Aelgith run away and try to find her daughter herself? Or would she start saying his name in town and stirring up interest that might bring trouble on herself or even on the royal house?

"This man called the Dragon is a powerful one. He must be handled with care."

"Who is he?" asked Aelgith through her tears.

The Mormaer of Fife.

Her instincts, which she trusted, told her to keep his name to herself for now. "I think it's better if you don't know. If you can keep your own counsel—and Beathag the same—it will bode better for us. We don't want to alert anyone to our search or they may move your daughter to hide her from us."

Aelgith's face crumpled. "I wish to start out toward her today, if you know where she might be. God only knows what those cruel brutes are doing to her right now."

Margaret drew in a breath. The baby in her belly was too new and small for her to even feel its movements, but already she felt protective of her future son or daughter. If someone stole her child she knew she wouldn't be able to rest—she'd want to chase them across the whole earth if needed.

"I must make a plan. I promise to do it with all due haste. As queen, I can't just get on a horse and go riding across the countryside without a word of where or why I'm going. I need a pretext and trust me I shall find one."

"Is my dear Osgifu far from here?"

"Not so far, I believe." She really didn't know how far it was. Everywhere in this kingdom seemed to be a day's ride—or more—from everything else. She would have to make careful inquiries and look at what maps she could find. Studying the terrain of her new homeland was well within a queen's purview, so that much shouldn't be so hard.

"When can we go?" Poor Aelgith clasped her hands together in a pleading gesture. Margaret reflected that there was good reason to bring Aelgith with her. She'd recognize her daughter, for one. And no one would know who she was. She had the speech of a noblewoman and would know how to comport herself in company. Margaret could claim her as a friend from England. But could Aelgith control herself well enough not to reveal their true purpose?

"If you're to come with me you must become mistress of your emotions, Aelgith. Our stated purpose will be something very different from a search for your daughter. You must promise not to betray our true goal or I can't take you. You'd endanger your own life and possibly even mine."

Aelgith crossed herself. "As God is my witness I shall be as quiet and discreet as the dead."

"Good." Margaret looked at Beathag. "And your silence and secrecy are essential as well."

"Yes, my lady." Beathag glanced at her daughter, no doubt wondering what she'd been roped into. "I'll be as silent as my cat." Since Margaret hadn't yet noticed a cat in or around the house, she hoped that was a promising sign.

"Have you been outside?" asked Margaret of Aelgith.

She shook her head. "It's so cold I've been sitting here by the fire helping Beathag with her spinning."

"Good. Keep yourself hidden inside if you can," said Margaret to Aelgith. "So no one asks who you are or why you're here. We don't want people asking questions or even thinking them. I'll be back as soon as I have a plan."

CHAPTER 5

argaret had brought her book collection with her from England as her family fled the conqueror. Her books were her most prized possessions. Her favorite book was a gift made for her that contained passages from the gospels and paintings of the apostles. She read from it every day and the familiar passages steered her soul and soothed her heart even in the most difficult times.

At first, she'd thought Malcolm had no books at all and was concerned about the state of her betrothed's mind and her own future sanity. It later emerged that he was multilingual and well-read and had a collection almost the size of her own, just carefully tucked away in leather-bound wooden trunks with iron bands and heavy locks on them.

"It won't do to have these burly warriors knowing their king likes to bend his head to study the letters of dead men," he'd joked when showing her his books for the first time. "It's best to show people the side of you that they need to see—that they want to see. My men want to know I'm a fearsome fighter, brave in battle, deft with a sword and skilled with a horse." His mastery of the warlike arts was indeed much discussed around the scarred wood table they ate their meals at. "That I enjoy the poetry of Virgil is none of their business and would not impress them if they were to learn of it."

"I understand." Margaret's love for her husband, a slow trickle at first, had swelled to a flood when she learned of his keen intellect and love of learning.

"I shall learn from you, dear husband. I shall strive to be all things to all people—but perhaps not all at the same time."

Malcolm chuckled. His easy humor helped him navigate the stony and winding path life had brought him on. She did not possess such winsome charm, being of a naturally more serious disposition. Her mother had found her too earnest and bookish as a girl, while the sisters at Wilton Abbey had praised her steady faith and devotion to the scriptures.

As queen she hoped to keep a foot in both worlds: the quiet contemplation of the cloister and the boisterous world of court where men argued and fought over tracts of land and the people living on them.

And she intended to use both feet to walk into the territory of the Mormaer of Fife to look for Osgifu.

Alone in their chamber, she opened Malcolm's chest of books with the key he'd given her. Several scrolls sat on top and she recognized one tied with a green ribbon that he'd shown her when she first arrived. Malcolm had a collection of maps of his territory, and the ones around it. They varied in age and—according to him—in accuracy, but would give her a sense of the journey required to take her where she needed to go.

She unfurled the well-thumbed scroll of vellum and spread it out on the top of the chest. This map showed the almost impossibly jagged coastline of Scotland—where many ships wrecked every year—and also the locations of settlements important enough to be on the annual pilgrimage they called The King's Progress.

Almost every year Malcolm would travel around his kingdom with a large retinue of fighting men, servants and horses, and visit the thanes and mormaers whose favor and loyalty were essential to his own power. The progress generally took place during the summer months—such as they were in this rainy and windy land—and he would enjoy the hospitality of each noble family for weeks at a time.

The hosts were required to provide housing and sustenance for the entire retinue. They were also expected to kill the fatted calf and provide a steady flow of strong drink and a bevy of musicians and bards and jugglers and tumblers to entertain the king during his visit.

Malcolm cheerfully observed that it was an excellent way to conserve the contents of his own coffers, while draining the resources of those who might try to gather strength against him.

They'd made a journey that summer but had not visited the Mormaer of Fife. She thought rather that they had gone in the opposite direction, to Scone and Dunkeld and other ancient seats of the Kingdom of Alba.

She saw the word Fife written in faded ink the color of dried blood. But where was the mormaer's hall, and how would she get there? And what kind of terrain lay between here and there? The weather was cold and wet enough in her husband's kingdom that being caught in the wrong location at the wrong time could cause death from exposure to the elements even during the less frigid times of the year.

Travel by carriage—which would provide at least some protection from wind and driving rain—was impossible in most parts of the kingdom due to the hilly or even mountainous terrain, which was also veined with deep bogs and rushing rivers and the almost total lack of anything resembling a road.

What was poor Osgifu doing right now? Was she shivering while cutting peat in the icy wind and carrying it on her back in a basket over miles of terrain in bare feet? Or worse, was she falling victim to the cruel and evil lusts of her captor?

A mark on the map drew her attention. An X shaped cross on the coast marked the church dedicated to St. Andrew, an important pilgrimage site that she'd learned of even before coming to Scotland. Relics of the saint—who'd been one of Christ's twelve apostles—were supposedly contained in the church.

Her fingers prickled with excitement at the prospect of visiting such a holy place. And it was on the far side of the territory of the Mormaer of Fife. To get there she could pass right by one or more of his strongholds. Could she use a visit —a pilgrimage, even—as her pretext for a journey at a time when most people didn't leave their hearth unless war was declared?

THAT AFTERNOON, Margaret attended the church for confession. Should she confess that she intended to hood-wink her husband and his court by venturing on a holy pilgrimage that included a detour to steal an important noble's "property"?

The old wood church would soon be overshadowed by the new stone abbey slowly rising from the earth near it, on the exact spot where their marriage took place. She'd wanted the abbey to be built before her husband's new tower, but her mother had begged for the security stone walls around their bedchambers and had prevailed.

With Grizel beside her, she walked past the building site to the much smaller and rather ancient church behind it. The clang of chisels on stone rang in the air as masons chipped away at blocks dragged from the nearby quarry.

Since she confessed at much the same time every afternoon, Bishop Causantin waited for her just inside the battered wood door. Charcoal burning in an ancient brazier nearby was probably the only reason he didn't freeze solid. A very old man, he had snow-white hair and a craggy, weathered face whose lower half disappeared into a great white beard. His tonsure seemed trimmed more by age than by the work of a blade. His eyes had a more youthful aspect: brown and beady, with a look of constant disapproval that she tried not to take personally.

"Good afternoon, Bishop." She crossed herself, with her eyes on the altar.

"God be with you, my child." He made the same gesture, though it was somewhat vestigial due to a chronic stiffness in his right shoulder.

Grizel quietly crossed herself and took up her usual position at a prie-dieu on one side of the church. Margaret hoped she used the time for prayer but didn't badger the girl about it.

Margaret followed Bishop Causantin up the aisle—which was really just a path between some ancient, scarred wooden furniture. The altar was a carved table with an embroidered cloth on it and—happily—a tooled gold chalice encrusted with gems that her family had brought from Hungary. A fine gold paten, made by the goldsmiths of Constantinople, sat next to it. Soon these holy objects would have a home worthy of their workmanship and also worthy of the glory of God. Their current one was so drafty that candles struggled to stay lit.

Bishop Causantin took her behind a wooden screen, where she'd installed a padded prie dieu to provide her knees some respite from the icy stone floor. She knelt at it and apologized for her many sins and launched into a litany of the usual ones: pride, willfulness and impatience.

Should she go into more detail? She'd had this discussion many times with her mother and sister over the years. Agatha—who'd lived her life in several royal households at this point—insisted that God understood the need for discretion and subtlety. "They're only men, darling, for all their robes and supposed piety. One must guard against giving them too much to hold against you."

A younger Margaret had revolted against this worldly view. They were men of God and trusted with upholding God's kingdom on earth. But after a decade among the sisters of Wilton Abbey—some of whom were godly in name only—she'd realized that even men and women of God were frail humans vulnerable to the sins of spite and jealousy and capable of causing considerable damage without necessarily even meaning to.

"Your duty is first to God, of course, my dear," her mother had said softly. Margaret was weeping bitterly after being scolded by a cruel older nun who'd somehow learned that she didn't know all the Latin words of a particular canticle and used to mouth along instead of singing. She'd confessed her failing to the priest but told no one else. "But also to your family. Royal blood and royal birth come with great responsibility. The royal family is a ship that must survive rough seas and buffeting winds of circumstance. Don't give anyone —even your confessor—tools to drive holes in it." She'd preached vagueness: knowing one's detailed sin in one's heart and showing it to God, while asking forgiveness for a version with the edges filed off.

After her confession had ended and the bishop offered her absolution, she rose to her feet.

"How long does it take to travel to the shrine of St. Andrew?"

A frown creased his brow. "Kilrymont, where it lies, is right on the coast. Would you travel by horse or boat?"

"By horse." A boat would whisk them there in an hour with no chance to visit her true destination.

"A good horse can get a man there the same day."

Having seen the map, Margaret suspected that this good horse was probably trotting and cantering most of the way, not being led while carrying a pregnant woman. Still, her heart swelled with hope.

Her inability to make the entire journey in one day would be a blessing. She could travel to Kilrymont and on the way there and the way back make a detour into the territory of the Mormaer of Fife to seek hospitality. He could hardly refuse comfort and shelter to the wife of the King of the Scots.

Margaret realized her brain was embroidering the future so fast that she now stared at the bishop in a silence that seemed to perturb him. He rubbed his sore hip. Would he be up to the journey? Could he even ride a horse at his age?

"Have you made the pilgrimage there, your grace?"

"Many times, dear lady. Many times."

"Recently?"

He frowned again. "No, not recently."

She thought as much. Still, if a pregnant woman could make the journey an elderly cleric could be provided for. He could sit sidesaddle and be led like herself. "I would like you to accompany me on a pilgrimage to the shrine. I would like to see the relics and pray there. It fills my heart with joy that a companion of Our Lord—a man who knew him and broke bread with him—now rests on the windswept shores of our kingdom."

"It is a blessing indeed, but a pilgrimage is a man's business."

Margaret felt her mouth fall open. She closed it. "What did you say?"

"That a pilgrimage is not a journey for a woman." He now had the decency to look slightly uncomfortable. Perhaps her shocked expression had penetrated his self-assurance.

"I am not just a woman, I am Queen of the Scots."

Her conviction surprised her. She'd been Queen of the Scots for barely a year. She'd donned the identity with considerable uncertainty and reluctance but it now felt like her own skin.

"I did not mean to offend, my lady, but it's not customary for women to go on pilgrimages. What would happen to their families and their husbands if…" his voice trailed off.

"My husband is hardly likely to go without sustenance if I make a holy pilgrimage for a few days." She realized her eyes had narrowed. Her stomach had also clenched into a knot and her heart was pounding.

She'd spent her teenage years in the company of nuns who were the daughters of the most powerful families in the nation. They lived under the watchful eye of a brilliant and accomplished abbess who enriched their lives with knowledge of the scriptures and the wisdom of its teachings that rivaled any man's. The idea that women should be denied access to the sacred relics of one of Jesus's apostles—one of his holy martyrs—shocked her to the core.

A strongly worded letter to the Archbishop of Canterbury formed in her mind as she stared at Bishop Causantin's aged and weathered face with its ludicrous sheep's wool beard.

"I intend to make a holy pilgrimage to each of the blessed sites in this land. I wish to walk in the steps of St. Columba, St. Ninian and St. Cuthbert. And I intend to start with a pilgrimage to the shrine of St. Andrew." Resolve formed inside her like a steel blade.

47

"Next summer, perhaps." His conviction had shriveled and his voice had a reedy tone.

Not next summer. Now. At once! But she'd already decided that Bishop Causantin would be entirely unwelcome on her holy pilgrimage.

She turned to the altar and crossed herself then wished the bishop a brisk good day. Grizel rose and opened the door for her. A biting wind slapped her face as they emerged into the gray afternoon. She tugged her fur-lined cloak about her.

"I suspect the bishop is getting too old for his tiring position," she said softly, as much to herself as to Grizel. "The church is so cold and drafty and a most unsuitable environment for a man with crippling arthritis. He should be tucked away in a comfortable retirement."

"Yes, my lady."

CHAPTER 6

"I wish to make a pilgrimage this Advent," said Margaret during dinner in the hall that night.

"A pilgrimage?" Malcolm looked up from his bowl of hot soup.

"To the shrine of St. Andrew. He was one of Jesus's dearest companions and a martyr in his name. His remains lie but a few hours ride away."

"I'm aware of the shrine, my love." He smiled. "It's one of the most popular sites in my kingdom. We have a veritable nuisance of pilgrims drowning trying to cross the Forth to reach it every year. The monastery near the crossing complains about the expense of all the unexpected burials."

"God forbid!" Margaret crossed herself. This news of untimely deaths—and on a holy pilgrimage—appalled her. But it was a subject for another day. Christmas was fast approaching and she needed to make her pilgrimage before the festivities started.

The sounds of a stringed instrument being plucked swirled around them. Malcolm enjoyed music greatly and sometimes Margaret wished there was slightly less of it. "It will be a short journey. I wish to travel to Kilrymont, to the shrine to St. Andrew, and stay somewhere suitable for one night on the way there and the way back."

"It's not so far. The journey can be done inside a day, even in winter."

"By a man on a fast horse, perhaps. But you forget that I must travel more slowly." She placed a hand on her belly.

"I don't think you should be traveling at all."

"I still have many months left before I'll deliver. If women did nothing during pregnancy they'd spend their entire lives sitting by the hearth, waiting."

"And what's wrong with that?" asked Malcolm. "I'm sure there are many women in the land who'd be grateful to sit by a nice warm hearth in the dead of winter instead of milking cows or going on pilgrimages across the frozen countryside."

"My sister is not an ordinary woman," said Christina drily. Christina never seemed to be listening to conversations, so her interjections were often a surprise.

"That much I know," said Malcolm with a smile. "She's an extraordinary woman."

Now Margaret felt embarrassed. "I certainly don't want to be odd or unusual, but the Lord has put it in my heart to make this pilgrimage during this Advent season." She spoke the truth. The Lord had summoned her to rescue a young girl being held against her will by a violent stranger. Her fervent prayers had only deepened her conviction that it was God's will for her to find and rescue Osgifu and return her to her desperate mother.

There but for the grace of God go I.

"I was thinking perhaps I could rest my head under the roof of the Mormaer of Fife. Is his seat not somewhere along the way?" She tried to sound casual.

"I wouldn't say it is, no," said Malcolm thoughtfully. "He

stays inland at Cupar this time of year. It's about an hour's ride to the north of the way to Kilrymont."

"That's not so far, if a bed may be had there."

"I dare say Mac Duff would offer hospitality if he were called upon." He spooned some soup into his mouth. "And if you wish to make the journey during Advent and be back before Christmas we must make it at once. I shall send a messenger to him in the morning"

Margaret found herself speechless. Was he really going to make it this easy? Sudden emotion choked her. She fought the urge to clasp his hand, which would have been awkward since one rested on his soup spoon and the other around his golden goblet. *What did I do to deserve such a kind and generous husband?* She felt guilty that she'd wanted to be a nun so badly, when others craved nothing more than a loving marriage.

"You've made so many of my wishes come true, dear husband," she said softly, trying to keep emotion out of her voice. "Building this tower to make my family feel safe after our tribulations. The new cathedral...." Her voice trailed off as tears tugged at it. "I'm sorry, I'm not sure why I'm so emotional."

"It's the child growing inside you, my darling," said her mother. "I burst into tears over nothing during my pregnancies with you and your sister and brother." She looked at Malcolm. "She was never like this before."

"She was never married to me before either." His eyes crinkled with amusement.

Margaret took a sip of her tisane. She didn't want to lose momentum. "Can we leave tomorrow?"

Now Malcolm laughed. "That will hardly give the messenger time to arrive before us."

"To ask the mormaer's permission to come?" she asked.

He laughed again. "Ask his permission...that's a good one.

No, just to tell him that we're on our way so he'll know to crack open a cask of good Burgundy wine and fluff up the feather beds."

Margaret's family, though royal, had never been in a position where they could descend upon others without begging forbearance first. "And how long will that take?"

"We can leave the day after tomorrow. I'll instruct my steward to choose the horses and tack for the trip so we can keep you comfortable in the winter weather. I shall lead your horse myself."

THE NEXT MORNING Margaret's prayers were especially fervent. Her excitement about visiting the sacred resting place of St. Andrew almost eclipsed her yearning to search for Osgifu.

Once her prayers were said, and she'd eaten an egg and a honey cake, she and Grizel headed down to the village again. The paths down the hill from the tower were slippery and a mist of rain still fell on them as they hurried through the woods.

"My lady, I can barely keep up with you."

"The faster we move, the drier our shoes will be."

Aelgith rose and rushed to the door of Beathag's house when they arrived. Her red-rimmed eyes spoke of a night of worry and tears.

"I've arranged a journey into the very hall of the red-haired man I suspect may have taken your daughter."

Aelgith's eyes widened. "Truly? When?"

"As soon as tomorrow, I hope. And you must come with me. We need to come up with a reason for your presence that isn't the absolute truth but isn't a lie either. I propose we say that you are a friend from London, visiting on your way to…somewhere."

"But surely any friend of yours would have a retinue? Servants and guards and horses and—"

"We don't have to pretend that it's still five years ago. My husband and everyone else know what happened to our people. We can honestly tell them that you were driven from your home. We just don't want them to know exactly who you are or where you're from since the Mormaer of Fife may well have extracted that same information from your daughter."

"I understand. But I've never been to London."

"Then we'll say you're from Wiltshire, near Wilton Abbey where I lived for some years. No one here knows anything about the countryside there and Hampshire is near enough. No need to talk about it. You can even start to weep if anyone asks too many questions."

"That won't be difficult." Aelgith's face was so lined with worry that she looked years older than her age. "But what shall I wear?"

"I shall find you suitable clothing."

Now Aelgith lifted her chapped and reddened hands. "But who would believe that these are the hands of a well-born lady?"

Margaret stared. This was more of a problem. But for every problem, God would provide a solution. "You shall wear gloves. Tell them you have chilblains and don't remove them even to eat. It's not so unusual for older people to wear gloves all the time here, because of the cold."

"I'm so grateful for your help, my lady." Aelgith's eyes filled with tears. "I shall pray fervently for our success and your health and happiness."

"God will decide how much health and happiness I enjoy in this life, but I too shall pray for our success."

～

THAT EVENING MARGARET enlisted Christina to help her prepare Aelgith for the trip. They sat in the bedchamber that Christina shared with Agatha and two ladies in waiting, who were all in the hall embroidering by the fire.

Christina unpinned her veil, revealing her thick dark hair in its two plain braids that fell to her chest. "You wish me to give my gown to one of your paupers?"

"She's not really a pauper." Margaret wasn't sure how many details to share. "I mean, she is now, but before the invasion she was a high born lady from Hampshire."

"How much I despise William the Bastard. No matter how much I pray I can't purge the hatred of him from my heart."

"I feel the same," said Margaret. "I pray daily that my anger over what he's done to our people won't poison my soul and keep it from Heaven. Now we have a chance to help two of the most needy. Aelgith's daughter was seized and abducted by a Scot and I mean to find her."

"Is that what all those questions about red-haired men and dragons were about?"

"You won't tell anyone, will you?"

"Not even my confessor." Christina's eyes twinkled. Margaret cheered. Her once spirited sister seemed to have lost all sense of joy and hope for the future since the invasion and their flight to Scotland. "But why my gown and not one of yours?"

"Mine will be too long for her."

Christina looked down at her dark green gown that pooled on the floor at her feet. "Oh, she's short and plump?"

"You're not short or plump!" Margaret hated the way her sister criticized herself. Though unfortunately some of it came from their mother's unthinking comments. "Besides, she's a rack of bones due to starvation. I hope to fatten her up a little."

"Will she need a veil and a cloak?" Christina opened her wooden chest.

"She will. Do you have extra?" Christina's chest was hardly brimming. She didn't love finery the way Margaret did.

"You know I do. And she can have my embroidered hair ribbons." She pulled out a pair of long yellow ribbons, embroidered with tiny pink and green flowers. "I don't need to wear anything like that now I've decided to become a nun."

"You haven't decided any such thing," protested Margaret, taking the ribbons. "It's me that always wanted to be a nun, not you. And look how happy I am with my husband. We'll find you a good husband."

"God forbid I be married to one of these brutes and packed off to live in a windswept hovel on some remote mountain. I'd much rather be back in my cell in Wilton."

"Well, when you put it that way I do understand." Margaret smiled. "But look how comfortable we are here." She gestured around the cozy room, warmed by a brazier. "It's a little plain right now, but that's just because it's new. Soon the walls will be painted with decorations and we'll buy some pretty new rugs for the floors. This new tower is living proof that you can bring civilization to the wilderness."

Christina laughed. "Your husband wouldn't be happy to hear you call his precious kingdom the wilderness. Besides, it's not as if thanes and mormaers are breaking the door down asking for my hand in marriage."

"They're intimidated by you! You're a princess of England. Only a very great man would be worthy of your hand and they know that. Malcolm will choose the right one for you."

"Perish the thought." Christina inhaled deeply. "I haven't seen a single man here who doesn't pick fowl out of his teeth with his own fingernails."

"You may find that their brutishness is an act. My husband would have people believe he can't read!"

"If their behavior at his table is any guide, I doubt most have a thought beyond hunting and raiding." Christina pulled a gray cloak out of the chest and handed it to Margaret. The thick, tightly woven wool and fine fur lining would keep Aelgith warm on the journey.

"This is perfect, thank you."

"And she can have this red dress that mother insisted on. I never wear it."

"That color would complement your rosy cheeks," said Margaret, taking the dress with some reluctance. Lately Christina seemed to be trying to make herself invisible. "Are you sure you don't want to part with something more worn."

"You want her to look like a noble lady, don't you."

"You're right, and this dress and the ribbons will be perfect." She leaned in and kissed Christina on the cheek. "Thank God I have a confidant and ally in you. I'd never dare reveal my plans to mother. She's far too cautious."

"Her caution and cunning is the reason we're still alive." Christina folded up the pinkish-red dress.

"And I thank her for it. Still, don't tell her of my plans!"

"Your secret is safe with me."

TRUE TO HIS WORD, her beloved husband notified the Earl of Fife of their imminent arrival and arranged for a retinue to accompany them. Unbeknownst to her, he'd also invited old

Bishop Causantin—who had mercifully begged off due to his infirmities—and they would thus be traveling without a cleric. But no matter. Her main goal was to find Osgifu. The pilgrimage to Kilrymont to see St Andrew's relics was an added blessing and would hopefully be made many times during the course of her life here.

Their breath smoked against the thin dawn light as they mounted their horses early the next morning. Margaret was helped into a very padded sidesaddle on a kind gray mare called Snowy. Her husband had eschewed his usual spirited black charger for a sturdy bay palfrey, insisting that the intelligent and agile mare would rise to the challenge of remaining calm and steady enough to lead Margaret's horse.

As a child Margaret had ridden astride, holding the reins for her own mount, and even galloped across the fields of Hungary. She'd since learned that in any formal situation— such as a pilgrimage or the Royal Progress—it was considered appropriate for an English or Scots noblewoman to sit sidesaddle in an un-split gown and be led by a man. All the more so now she was carrying a royal baby.

She did still insist on a bridle that gave her some reins to hold, in case of accidental separation from the leading horse. The sidesaddle was comfortable enough and even had a wooden handle to hold onto for extra support. She doubted that anyone could manage to stay steady in it for long during a big trot or a rolling canter, but it served well enough at a brisk walk and at the smooth, fast, four-beat gait that was Snowy's natural pace.

The rope connecting her horse's bridle to her husband's gloved hand was made of dark red twisted silk and looked almost like a baby's umbilical cord.

"Are you sure you'll be warm enough," asked Malcolm, turning to her. "The winds come in off the sea something fierce on the coast near Kilrymont."

"My cloak and hood and boots are lined with fur, I'm wearing two layers of gloves, and my gown is of tightly woven wool and made for travel. I'll be as comfortable as a cat by the hearth." His thoughtfulness impressed her every day. Unlike many men, he had the ability to put effort into many things at once.

She glanced back at Aelgith who was coming as her friend and attendant, swathed in Christina's gray cloak, with a crisp white veil, green leather gloves and a pair of Margaret's spare boots. Underneath the cloak, Christina's red dress draped her slender figure and the pretty yellow ribbons wrapped her long braids. As long as no one examined her battered feet or worn hands, she looked every inch the noble lady. Malcolm had been pleased for her to entertain a friend from her old life and had welcomed her warmly. Margaret felt only a small twinge of guilt at the deception.

They set out from Dunfermline before the sun was even fully up behind the dark wooded hills, harness jangling and horses' hooves crunching on the hard semi-frozen soil.

"It's a good time of year for travel," remarked Malcolm. "Not boggy, not too much snow, the ground is firm but not as hard as it will be in February."

"And Advent is an excellent time for a holy pilgrimage," said Margaret with enthusiasm. "We shall celebrate Christ's birth with even more joy when we've been blessed by seeing the relics of a man he knew and loved."

She prayed that St. Andrew himself would bless their journey, and guide them to Osgifu. She hadn't yet come up with a plan for how to extract the girl, but God would surely provide her with one when they found her.

THE LANDSCAPE between Dunfermline and the Mormaer of Fife's winter seat was a mix of woods and scrubby fields. Happily the tracks were well beaten and their horses could move at a faster gait for much of the time. The weather was cold, but not too windy. There wasn't even a spit of rain in the air, which was a blessing as the cold bit so much harder through damp clothing.

They stopped several times to water their horses at rushing streams.

"In Hungary everything would be frozen at this time of year," said Margaret, grateful for the easy journey. "We'd have to dismount to break a hole in the ice."

"That can happen here, but we get more snow and ice up in the mountains. There's a reason the kings of the Scots live in the lowlands."

Woods provided welcome shelter from the winds, and the tracks revealed that men had been taking these routes since very ancient times.

"Does someone maintain these chases?" She wondered if the nobles kept these trails open for hunting.

"Mother nature does it for us, helped by the deer. The cold and wind doesn't encourage weeds to spring up head-high as they do in the south of England."

"I must thank her for that. I suppose that's why no one has bothered to lay roads."

"The Romans tried. Why would we give foreign soldiers an easy journey over our land? Let them pick their way through the woods and up the hills."

Aelgith rode astride on an easy mount and looked the happiest that Margaret had seen her. For once she had hope in her heart. She had no trouble keeping up with Margaret and Malcolm's fast horses.

"I'm grateful that Mac Duff winters inland at Cupar," said Malcolm, as they headed into another tract of relatively open woods. "His summer seat is at Wemyss, right on the coast, savaged by wind and rain at this time of year."

They passed some small settlements on the way, with their grazing sheep and cows and fires rising from the low thatched dwellings. They were few and far between, though. Margaret was intrigued by the emptiness of the countryside.

"It's not an easy place to live," said Malcolm, when she inquired about the absence of settlements. "The soil is sour, the winters are long, and the days short. It takes a special breed of man and woman to survive let alone thrive here."

"I suppose that means there are less people trying to invade and conquer."

"You'd think, but the lands of Norway and Sweden make our gorse covered hillsides look like the paradise of Eden."

"Do they raid regularly?"

"We must always be ready, especially along the coast, but for the most part we maintain an armed peace. The Earls of Orkney and the vikings of Ireland between them rule all of the islands and the northernmost and least habitable part of this land. I rule the most fertile and least frostbitten part of Alba and have no urgent desire to start new wars over the wettest and windiest parts of it."

THEY ARRIVED in Cupar shortly before dusk. Margaret wasn't sure what to expect at the seat of the Mormaer of Fife, who was apparently one of the most important men in the kingdom. "His family has an ancient claim to the throne," said Malcolm. "So I've taken pains to cultivate his loyalty. What's good for me is good for Mac Duff."

"I can't get over expecting a castle," said Margaret, at the sight of yet another collection of low thatched roofs. With smoke rising from them into the purpling sky, they almost looked like steaming mounds of dung. "It's so strange to me that there aren't stone fortresses in Scotland."

"There are," said Malcolm with a smile. "I slept in one last night. And there are round stone forts around the northern coast that were built by some long-dead ancient people."

Malcolm's harness jangled as they rose up a bank toward the enclosure. A wooden bridge led them over a wide defensive dry ditch. "As my brother told you, the Scots don't need stone walls to keep ourselves safe. Our keen eyes, strong backs and fighting spirit do that."

"I suppose the strong winds would knock down a stone wall if it wasn't built just right." They'd built the new stone tower amidst the protective woods for that reason. The hill and its surrounding brook provided natural protection, and the trees broke the gusts blowing in from the east.

They crossed over the ditch into the enclosure, which was fenced only by the banked spoil from the ditch. There were pens for cattle and sheep but she couldn't even tell what the walls were made from. The thatched roofs of the houses descended almost to the ground, with very little standing wall at all. These steep roofs shed the rain and resisted the buffeting winds.

She glanced behind her at Aelgith, whose eyes hungrily searched the scene before them, scanning the shadowy figures moving to and fro in the last of the light. Margaret wished she could squeeze her hand and reassure her, but she turned her head back to the large group of men, swathed in thick wool plaids, now surrounding them inside the enclosure.

Margaret couldn't really understand what Malcolm said to them due to their rapid speech but she did catch that it was a friendly greeting.

The men held their horses while they dismounted and Margaret embraced Aelgith, taking the opportunity to whisper in her ear. "If you meet Osgifu, tell her to keep her head down and continue her daily life. We're going to visit the shrine to St. Andrew and return here on our way home. If she's here we'll come up with a plan to take her with us when we leave for Dunfermline."

CHAPTER 7

"What are you two ladies whispering about?" asked Malcolm, beckoning Margaret to enter the mormaer's large home.

A door had opened into a long, rectangular hall with a fire blazing in the middle. Margaret hurried forward to accompany Malcolm through the door.

"My dear friend was anxious about not knowing the customs. She's new to Scotland and, as you know, manners can be quite different here. I told her not to worry."

"We don't bite people's heads off," said Malcolm with a grin.

"Who's biting people's heads off?" came a loud male voice. A big, burly man, with a great deal of dark red hair, with gray patches at the temples and a big dark beard, strode forward and embraced Malcolm.

Margaret stiffened. Such a gesture would be the perfect time for one man to plunge a dagger into the other. She didn't trust any of the mormaers and thanes in this power-hungry and pugnacious land. But Malcolm pulled back, still alive and showering him with more incomprehensibly rapid Gaelic speech.

"And your lovely wife," the mormaer spoke in heavily accented English. "Who is even more beautiful than the rumors had led me to believe."

Margaret found it odd that she hadn't met this man before, given that his territory was so close to Dunfermline. A horse really could leave at dawn and arrive here before Nones without even galloping.

Two women came forward to take their cloaks. Margaret peered at their faces. Both were too old to be Aelgith's daughter. She fought the urge to scan the hall for a girl in her teen years and tried to focus on their host.

Their cloaks were whisked away out of sight. She watched the women leave the hall with them, which left her feeling strangely vulnerable. Without a cloak, there could be no hasty escape in the dead of winter so she had an uneasy feeling of being held hostage.

Malcolm seemed to feel no such compunction as he greeted several other men, some of them almost as tall as himself. She detected a hint of wariness, a stiffness in his posture, that deepened her sense of unease.

The men gathered together at a large table near the fire. Margaret was surprised to find herself shuttled off to a different table on the other side of the fire, with Aelgith and several other ladies. Initially piqued and somewhat alarmed at being parted from her husband, she realized that this separation would give her a better chance to observe the room and perhaps even gain useful information from these local ladies.

The hall had no windows at all. The fire burned in the center of the room, like an ancient longhouse, with smoke rising through a hole in the thatch. The ladies' table sat just as close to the fire as the men's but on the other side.

As her gaze adjusted to the dark, smoky interior, lit by only the fire and candles burning on the tables, she could make out at least three score people sitting or standing within the hall.

"The journey went as well as could be expected," she said to Aelgith, trying to look as normal as possible.

"Yes," managed Aelgith, who wasn't looking normal at all. Margaret prayed that she'd be able to hide her emotions.

Is that him? Are we in the right place? She longed to ask Aelgith but didn't dare. The other women at the table stared at them in silence. Margaret managed a greeting in the local language, which elicited smiles and returned greetings.

She'd learned many of the words but found that her accent was hard for Scots to understand, and she didn't yet speak fast enough for an easy conversation.

"My husband tells me that you're making a pilgrimage to the shrine of St. Andrew." A woman with pale gray eyes and white-blonde eyebrows startled her with perfect English speech.

"Yes! We are. Advent seemed an auspicious time for such a journey. I've been longing to visit the relics of the saint since I arrived in Scotland." Was it rude to ask someone where they were from? "You're English?"

"I'm from Northumbria. My father held a settlement near Bamburgh."

Margaret saw Aelgith's hand tremble as she took an offered cup of ale.

"Have you lived in Scotland for long?" asked Margaret, trying to sound casual.

"Eleven years," said the woman with a smile. "I was married to my husband when I was but twelve years old."

The woman didn't look a day over twenty right now. "Which man is your husband?" asked Margaret, hoping the question wasn't offensive.

"The Earl of Fife," said the woman stiffly, as if that should have been obvious. Margaret now noticed the fine embroidery around the neck and cuffs of her dark wool gown. She also wore a large gold cross studded with precious gems hanging from a chain around her neck.

"I beg forgiveness for my ignorance," said Margaret quickly. She should have noticed the woman's fine raiment, but no one had introduced them, so she hadn't really looked at her until now.

"You must never beg for anything," said the lady calmly. "You are the queen."

"I suppose you're right," said Margaret, relaxing a little. "Do you miss your homeland?"

"That would serve no purpose," said the pale-eyed lady, with only a hint of sadness in her voice. "My home is here now. My name is Enfleda."

"I know exactly what you mean. My home is here too." She hesitated, and glanced at Aelgith, hoping she was mistress of her emotions. Aelgith's white veil and the dim fire-lit interior cast her face into merciful shadow. "This is my friend Aelgith, from the south of England." They made polite greeting noises.

"All three of us English women here in the land of the Scots," mused Margaret. Did Enfleda's Scots husband return to Northumbria to raid the lands of his wife's family? Or did they marry her off to him to prevent that? Or was she taken by force, like Aelgith's daughter? These were not polite questions one could ask. She decided to change the subject. "Have you been to Kilrymont to visit the shrine to St. Andrew?"

"No. I've never had the opportunity."

"Oh." Margaret thought this odd when she lived only a few hours ride from it. "Do you wish to?"

"Only if my husband wishes it." Enfleda smiled as if this was perfectly acceptable. "I'm busy managing my household."

Margaret wished she could be so easily satisfied with the domestic realm. It would make her life easier. "How many people live here in your household?"

"I've never counted them." Enfleda smiled again. "Enough to keep meals on the table and linens clean and the settlement defended."

Another conversational dead end. Margaret steeled herself to forge ahead. *We're here for a purpose.* Was Osgifu one of the countless people beneath the thatched roofs of Mac Duff's settlement? "Have most of them lived with you their entire lives?"

"Some have, and some haven't." Another beatific smile, as if she didn't have a thought behind her pretty face. Margaret wanted to ask if there were any English captives amongst them, but didn't quite dare. She didn't want to alert Enfleda —or any of the other ladies who sat at the table watching them—to her true purpose.

Margaret turned to Aelgith to read her expression, and found she was staring hard at a small doorway on the side of the hall. "Are you comfortable?" she asked her, to jerk her back to the present.

"Oh yes, very," stammered Aelgith.

She's seen her.

Margaret's watched the doorway as it opened and three girls came in, each carrying a platter of steaming food. The girls were all young, their heads bare with long plaits hanging, and their faces clearly visible. One of them stared at Aelgith with a look of utter astonishment. A pretty girl with light brown hair, she stood an inch or two shorter than the other servants.

It's Osgifu.

Margaret didn't want the mother and daughter to betray their kinship so she quickly created a distraction by spilling half of her cup of ale on the table. A flurry of activity, with one of the girls rushing to get a cloth to wipe it up, helped break the tension in the air.

The girl had now mastered her face and placed her platter on the table and stood nearby, looking directly at the table.

"Would you like a capon?" asked Enfleda, gesturing at a fragrant plate of steaming roasted birds.

Margaret's stomach—pregnant and very hungry—recoiled at the sight with horror. "It's Advent."

"Oh, my husband insists that birds are not meat. He says men can't survive on eggs and fish alone for weeks at a time."

Malcolm had made a similar argument at first. She convinced him that fasting in solidarity with the rest of Christendom was no great hardship, and would bring him closer to God. He'd since developed a taste for well-prepared eels and perch and pies made with eggs and vegetables wrapped in pastry.

"Birds are most certainly meat," said Margaret. "Even seabirds." She found it hilarious that some people insisted that gannets and gulls were sea creatures. "I don't wish to be inhospitable but I'm afraid I can't eat them." She reached out and helped herself to something that looked like an oatcake.

One of the girls, not Osgifu, ladled a thick soup into a carved wooden bowl and placed it before her. The soup, with barley pearls floating in it, steamed with welcome warmth and smelled delicious. Margaret felt a swell of relief that she'd be able to eat anything at all in this household. Then she realized that the rich aroma of the soup came from bone broth.

She quieted the protest that rose to her lips. This was not her household and she'd come here as a guest. She thanked Enfleda and lifted a spoonful of the meaty broth to her lips. Four other ladies sat around the table, silent as their inscrutable host as they ate their capons with delicate fingers.

"Perhaps you should take your gloves off?" said Enfleda to Aelgith, as she broke bread with her leather-gloved fingers.

Aelgith shot Margaret a panicked glance, and started to stammer something about the cold. Which wasn't going to be very convincing since they sat so close to the blazing fire that it was almost hot.

"She has a rash," said Margaret brightly. "Better to keep it covered."

Enfleda peered for a moment Aelgith as if she smelled bad, then pushed another smile to her mouth and agreed.

Margaret felt herself trapped in an enemy kingdom almost as much as poor Osgifu. She prayed Aelgith could keep herself together long enough to make it through this meal. She also wished she sat with Malcolm, not exiled here among these silent ladies. She could hear him and the other men roaring with laughter on the other side of the fire, but could barely make out their outlines in the smoky gloom of the dark hall.

At last she could stand the suspense no longer, and desperately wanted to speak with Aelgith alone. "Could someone show me the way to...." She didn't want to mention the unmentionable in words, especially over food. She glanced at the girl she believed to be Osgifu—who looked panicked.

"Yes, of course." Enfleda signaled for one of the other girls to take her. Margaret asked Aelgith if she wanted to come with her, and she rose from her chair rather too fast and almost tipped it over.

Osgifu could barely take her eyes off her mother, and Margaret prayed that no one would notice. She bundled Aelgith away out of the hall to a small and malodorous building with only one purpose. Once inside, Margaret grabbed her gloved hands. "It's her, isn't it?"

"Yes, and she looks healthy, praise God."

"No one must realize that she's your daughter. You must do your best not to look at her."

"How can we get her out of here?"

"I'll have to tell my husband about the situation. Perhaps he can offer to buy her. But I haven't spoken to him yet and he has no idea that's why we're here. As far as he knows we're on a pilgrimage to St. Andrews."

"Will he be angry?"

I don't know. She'd been married a full year but was still uncovering the many facets of her husband's personality. He was quick to good cheer but also to anger. So far his anger had always been directed at others, but she'd not yet done anything to provoke it. In this situation she was almost certain he'd be sympathetic and helpful, but she couldn't be entirely sure. Especially since this Earl of Fife was clearly an important ally and a powerful man in his own right.

"Since I'm pregnant I have an excuse to come out here more often than is customary. If I need to talk to you I'll summon you to come with me." She spoke in a low whisper since the servant girl waited outside. "Otherwise do your best to make conversation and act like nothing is out of the ordinary."

"It's very hard. My emotions are on a knife edge. I want to cry every second."

"You must grit your teeth and battle through it. You've survived many trials and here you are, still alive and your daughter well and healthy. Have faith."

Margaret squeezed her hand and they headed out into the icy night air.

On the way back to the hall, which was only about three score steps, she summoned her Gaelic to ask the servant girl if she was lucky enough to sleep in the warm hall with their masters.

She nodded and said that she was. Margaret, still holding

Aelgith's hand, squeezed it. The mother and daughter would sleep under the same roof tonight for the first time in many months.

Back at the table Margaret made another attempt at conversation with Enfleda. "They say English refugees are everywhere these days. Does your husband give them shelter?"

"Only if they're willing to work for it. Unfortunately, most of the refugees are people who've never lifted a finger in their lives."

"Like you and me," said Margaret carefully.

"You and I have married into our position with all the safeguards that implies. If they are begging for a roof over their heads they must do as they're told or feel the sting of a switch."

Margaret felt Aelgith twitch beside her. She prayed that her face wouldn't reveal her feelings.

"Surely you don't beat your servants when a word of correction would do?" asked Margaret.

"I don't do it myself, of course," said Enfleda, with another cool smile. "But discipline must be maintained, as you can imagine. Some of my husband's men seem to enjoy it. And those who can't learn from their mistakes are sold to Norway or Ireland. Young English girls fetch a pretty price."

Margaret could feel Aelgith shaking, her knee vibrating against her own. She decided that she'd better change the subject quickly. "That's a lovely gown. Do you spin and weave your own wool?"

SOMEHOW, they made it through the rest of the dinner without Aelgith bursting into tears. She then sat through the tweeting and squawking of a piper and watched as the ladies of Fife attended to their embroidery. Her hands sat empty as, in the scramble to plan this rescue mission, it had not occurred to her to bring any of her own sewing.

In England, she was used to traveling in a comfortable carriage, shaded from the sun and sheltered from the rain and with plenty of room for fripperies such as needlework and pet lap dogs. Here in Scotland one brought only the bare necessities for the journey.

Finally, she was shown to her sleeping place. Set back in an alcove similar to the apse in a cathedral, the curtained bed promised a measure of privacy. Far from the central fire, it was dark and private. For the same reason it was also unpleasantly cold. "Would it be possible to have a small brazier nearby?" she asked of the same girl who'd taken her outside.

The girl said she'd ask her mistress.

"You don't need a brazier, my love. You have a husband to keep you warm." Malcolm's deep voice right behind her ear made her jump.

His arms closed around her waist from behind, his hands resting on her belly. Relief flooded through her. She always felt safe in his arms, at least for a moment. "You're right, of course," she whispered. She told the girl that she would be fine, with no need for a brazier. "Though I do hope the bedding is quilted," she whispered to Malcolm.

"I'm the King of the Scots, my love. The bedding had better be fur or he'll be hearing from me."

Margaret opened the curtains and peered inside the bed. Since it was too dark to see the bedding, she felt around with her hand and discovered a feather pillow covered in soft linen and—"You're right, my love. Fox fur, I think."

"Do the strictures of Advent prevent us from sleeping amidst the luxurious skins of animals?"

"Not that I'm aware of." She couldn't help smiling. He

loved to tease her but rarely tried to change her mind about anything she held dear.

Once they were both comfortably settled under the covers, Margaret knew it was time to confide in her husband. Many women would have to worry that their partner was likely too drunk to remember a word they said after a long night of feasting. Malcolm, however, could down ale with the best of them and keep his wits about him.

Still, her stomach clenched as she wondered how he'd react to her proposal.

"What's wrong my love?" he asked.

"I have a confession," she said softly. It was too dark to see even the gleam in his eyes. "My friend Aelgith is here with me because her daughter was stolen away from Northumbria. She's being kept here in this house."

Malcolm tensed. He rose up on his elbow. "What do you mean?"

"Her daughter is a slave, I suppose. Of our host. She was one of the girls who served us dinner."

"Ah. That's why we're here." He settled back down again.

Guilt tugged at Margaret's heartstrings. Should she have confided in him from the start? He didn't seem angry. "I didn't want to bother you, in case she wasn't here and he wasn't the one who took her...." She trailed off, ashamed of her lack of transparency.

"Now I understand your mysterious questions about red-haired men."

"When you said that Mac Duff is called the Dragon I was almost sure this must be the place, and it is. The girl served us our dinner while our hostess talked about how they beat refugees and sell them overseas if they don't work hard enough. How can we rescue her?"

Malcolm leaned forward and pressed his head into her shoulder. She felt him rock with something that might be laughter or might be sobbing. "Oh, wife of mine. You never seem to run out of surprises. I suppose the Lord called upon you to save the girl from captivity?"

"Indeed he did." Was he teasing her? "Aelgith came to me when we were washing the people's feet last Sunday."

He propped himself up on his elbow again. "So she's not your old friend at all?"

"She is my friend," protested Margaret. "Her plight could easily have been my own. She's an English noblewoman whose husband and son were killed and her home burned. All she had left was her daughter and now even she's been torn from her arms."

She felt Malcolm's chest rise and fall against her own. "How old is the girl?"

"Fourteen. Ripe for exploitation. She should be safely married to a good man not—" Horrible images crowded her mind.

"You saw her. Does she seem in good health?"

"She has flesh on her bones and, thank God, not yet in the places that entice men. I could tell no more than that."

"Where is her mother right now?"

"Sharing a bed with our hostess, I believe."

"Is she likely to do anything rash?" Malcolm tensed. "Like try to steal away with the girl or club our host with an iron poker?"

Margaret blinked in the thick darkness. "I don't think so." The possibility hadn't occurred to her. Now that it did, tendrils of unease curled all the way to her toes. Surely Aelgith wouldn't try to steal away with the girl on a frosty winter's night into unfamiliar territory?

As for the other…. No. Aelgith was a frightened mouse, not a ferocious avenger.

"Can you ask Mac Duff to return the girl to her mother?"

"No."

"Why not?"

"I would have to buy her."

Her heart quickened. "How much would that cost? I'd gladly part with my gold rings to pay for it." She could feel them burning into her fingers right now.

Malcolm sighed again. "The price would depend on the girl's value to him. And he can't know that her mother is here. What kind of a fool would I look like to bring an angry enemy into his household?"

"She's hardly that," protested Margaret. "She's a desperate mother. I'm to be a mother myself soon. My heart breaks for her."

They'd kept their whispers very low, but Margaret noticed that the entire hall had fallen into a deep silence. The piper had gone to bed, the company disassembled, and now you could hear a pin drop.

She pulled the covers up high over their heads. "We must take her with us, one way or another."

CHAPTER 8

*I*n the morning, Margaret rose early to pray. At least she hoped it was morning. In the pitch black of the lightless hall she couldn't see any moon or stars so she relied on her body's internal hourglass. She slipped out of her husband's warm embrace and donned her gown and shoes.

Shivering in the frigid air—her cloak somewhere unknown—she was about to kneel on the floor when something told her to determine what it was made of first...a quick grope with her hand revealed damp, gritty stone that might stain her gown.

The Lord will understand if I pray standing up. She offered up several familiar prayers and was beginning an entreaty to the Lord to allow them easy passage away with Osgifu, when she heard a bone-chilling scream.

She groped to find her veil on the hook where Grizel had left it and tugged it over her sleep-tousled braids. Then she darted out of the dark alcove into the open hall. The fire burned low in the center, kept alive overnight—but just barely—and she could make out the shadowy forms of other people emerging from their sleeping places.

"Husband!" she called back to where Malcolm lay behind the bed curtains, then ventured further into the hall. Someone had lit a candle and another two were stoking the fire with bellows and a poker.

"What was that scream?" asked Margaret, of the first dark faceless person she approached.

"She's stolen my cross!" screamed a woman. Margaret squinted, trying to adjust her gaze to the dark. More candles filled the air and Margaret's heart almost stopped beating as her features became visible in the growing firelight. It was Enfleda.

Margaret hurried over to her. "What's amiss, my friend?"

"She's gone, your lady in waiting has disappeared in the night and my gold cross set with precious stones is missing!"

Panic flashed through her. *Where was Aelgith?* She didn't dare ask that question. "Where was it?"

"It was hanging on a hook right next to my bed. No one here would dare to touch it. They know my husband would have their head! It must be that stranger you brought with you. She shared my bed with me then stole my treasure."

"Are you sure she didn't venture outside to relieve herself?"

"I already looked. There's no sign of her and her cloak is gone."

Margaret wanted to argue and protest that her dear friend couldn't possibly have committed such a monstrous crime as to steal her jeweled cross. But she couldn't. She barely knew Aelgith and really had no idea what she was capable of. Who knew what she'd done to survive the cruel years since her husband was killed and she was driven from her home?

"Find the thief! She can't have gone far!"

Still shivering in the frigid hall, Margaret looked around for Grizel. The girl rushed up to her, panic in her eyes. "She's gone," she whispered.

"The girl, too?"

"I think so. I haven't seen her."

"Could you fetch me my cloak? The servants will know where to find it." At least Aelgith had taken her own cloak before fleeing into the icy darkness with her daughter. She surely wouldn't be alive for long if she hadn't.

Malcolm appeared and observed the commotion in the hall. He came over to her and whispered into her ear. "What's amiss, my dove?"

She turned her head and whispered back into his. "It seems Aelgith has fled, taking a valuable item."

"And her daughter?"

He spoke softly, but still Margaret clutched his hand and nodded. And silently pleaded with him not to say more since she fervently hoped that no one had discovered the relationship between mother and daughter.

Grizel returned with Margaret's cloak and wrapped her in it. Clutching the fur-lined wool about her, Margaret hurried to the main door of the hall that now stood open, inviting a chilling blast of wind. Dawn was only the faintest pale glow in the far distance. The moon and stars hid behind a thick bank of clouds, so darkness still cloaked the land around the settlement.

A rooster crowed nearby and made Margaret jump. People milled about, horses now appearing, fully tacked up, and men jumping onto them in the near-darkness.

Margaret's heart ached for poor, desperate Aelgith. Her escape attempt could not be more foolhardy. The geography of this land, with its long bodies of deep, frigid water and far distances, made travel of any sort challenging at the best of times.

Barking dogs ran around the camp, then followed at the heels of the horses as they set off into the darkness. Hunting dogs. Trained to follow the scent of game. Margaret closed her eyes for a moment as horrible visions swarmed her mind.

Malcolm stood at Margaret's side, peering into the darkness. Shame soaked through her. Malcolm would be blamed for this and it was her fault. She'd kept a secret from her husband—who trusted her. "I'm so sorry."

"It's not your fault, though it will go hard with her when they find her."

"Why would your friend steal from us?" asked Enfleda, who'd rushed up to her, pale eyes flashing in the first glow of dawn.

"I can't imagine," said Margaret, hoping the half-lie wasn't a sin. She decided to follow it with pure truth. "I admit I don't know her well. She arrived on my doorstep as a stranger but as my sister in exile from our English homeland, as you are, too." She hoped to appeal to Enfleda's heart, for she, if anyone, might be able to plead for Aelgith's life.

"She'll be found and she'll feel the sharp sting of retribution—if she isn't torn to pieces by the hounds when they catch her."

Margaret swallowed. The massive hounds were trained to take down stags and wild boar, they'd likely have little trouble with an undernourished middle-aged woman.

But what of Osgifu? No one had yet mentioned the girl except Grizel. Surely another had noticed that she was missing, too?

The bitter cold drove them back inside the hall, where the fire now roared. Servants brought them each a warm posset of herbs and berries boiled in water. Margaret was startled by the unfamiliar taste and wondered for a brief instant if it might be poisoned—then decided that if it was she half deserved it. She noted with relief that the men drank small ale instead. *My husband can find a third wife if needed. He deserves better than me.*

She was still alive when the servants brought bowls of steaming oat porridge mixed with half-frozen cream.

She whispered in Grizel's ear. "What of the girl?"

"Her cloak is gone and there's no sign of her," whispered Grizel. People surrounded them, going about their morning duties, so there was no way she could extract more information.

"All is prepared for us to leave for St. Andrews," announced Malcolm after consulting with one of his men. "The horses are packed and provisioned and the sun's up. Let's make haste so we can settle there before nightfall."

Panic clawed at Margaret's gut. "Should we not stay to—"

"Our hosts will handle our guest when she is found. We will be back tomorrow night and can make restitution to them if needed at that time."

His voice brooked no contradiction and she couldn't argue with him in front of the company. Panic surged inside her. Who would plead for Aelgith's life if she was gone?

Bright early morning light shone down on the fire through the hole in the roof over it. Shafts of low sunlight blasted through the eastern-facing door each time it opened. Was there a chance that Aelgith had left hours ago and had time to put distance between herself and Mac Duff's men?

She had to leave now with her husband and resume their pilgrimage. She really had no choice.

Margaret offered a wordy mix of both thanks and apologies to Enfleda, and promised that all would be made good on their return. She vowed to pray to the saint for the safe return of the missing cross.

Enfleda was barely civil, but Margaret understood her anger. As the mormaer's wife, it was her duty to keep order in her household and Margaret had brought a criminal to her hearth and home.

A guard helped Margaret up onto her padded sidesaddle and she settled herself into it as well as she could and took up the reins. As they rode away, up one frost-dusted hill and down another, she fought the urge to glance back.

"Will they kill her?" she asked, once they were thoroughly out of earshot of the settlement.

"If she was a man, she'd be in considerable danger. I doubt they'll kill a woman, at least not without something that passes for a trial."

She could only speak but so frankly, since she didn't want the men around them to know the full extent of what had happened—which included her deceiving her husband into a wintry pilgrimage. "I hear a servant girl is also missing."

"Perhaps she seized the girl to be a guide to her," said Malcolm, taking her hint to be mysterious.

"It's possible that the girl would know the country well." This thought hadn't occurred to her before. Osgifu had been there some months and might know places to hide and even the routes to other settlements.

A tiny glimmer of hope flickered alive in Margaret's heart. "I shall pray to St. Andrew for both of their safety."

"They'll need all the prayers they can get in this winter cold. Especially if it snows or rains and their clothing becomes soaked. They can't light a fire if they're trying to escape notice."

The ember of hope guttered. "May God go with them."

Malcolm turned and stared at her. "With a thief? I wonder at your loyalty to this friend of yours. She stole from our hosts."

"I can't imagine what got into her."

She didn't trust me.

"She's a fool at best. A criminal at worst."

A sigh rose in Margaret's chest and escaped slowly. He was right, of course. But still…. "I felt so much sympathy for her as a refugee from the ravages of William's invasion. She's just one of thousands—tens of thousands—of people driven from the only homes they've ever known to be starved or enslaved far from home."

She didn't feel any compunction about speaking this truth in front of the entire mounted company. They all knew the circumstances under which she and her family had arrived in Scotland. If they hadn't left England when they did, they might all be dead or imprisoned, since her brother was a known claimant to the English throne and had already run afoul of William.

Malcolm had saved them from exile and ignominy and made her his queen and them the royal family of his land.

"I beg your forgiveness with all my heart. I had no idea she would do anything like this. I'm appalled and deeply contrite." Again, she didn't feel bad saying this in front of his men. It was true and they should all know it.

"Wife, you should never humble yourself to me. You're my queen and my closest companion. I know you'd never do anything to intentionally hurt me or anyone else. This situation is unfortunate, and it'll be resolved one way or the other. We'll pick up the pieces—however they fall—when we return from Kilrymont."

ONCE THEY WERE WELL out of earshot of Mac Duff's settlement, Margaret summoned Grizel to bring her horse up close. Grizel rode astride, in charge of a sturdy pony that was often used as a pack animal.

"Did you sleep near Osgifu last night?"

"We were both in the kitchen, but I was across the room, nearer the fire where it was warm."

"Did you hear her leave?"

"I didn't notice anything. She must have been very quiet."

"Does it seem odd to you that no one awoke when both she and her mother slipped away?"

"I suppose it might if everyone hadn't stayed up so late and drunk so much ale last night. Even the servants were quite fatigued from it. I slept like the dead. If I'd seen her rising I might have been able to stop her. I know that leaving was foolish."

"And stealing that cross was a hundred times more foolish even than that. I can't understand why Aelgith would draw attention and anger upon herself with such a rash and criminal act. I'd never have suspected her capable of such a thing." She spoke the words as much for Malcolm, who rode right next to her, leading her horse, as much as Grizel. "Though I suppose the horrors she's endured in the last few years might have warped her morals. We must pray that they're found with the cross safe and unharmed, that it may be returned to its rightful owner."

THE JOURNEY to Kilrymont went smoothly, with only the lightest sprinkling of rain to dampen their clothes and spirits as they crossed the rugged countryside. Margaret could smell the salty sea air as they drew closer to the coast.

Their first sight of the famous pilgrimage center was a stone tower in the distance, rising above the surrounding trees. "The tower of St. Regulus," she marveled. She was grateful they could arrive in daylight so she might admire it like so many pilgrims before her. "Regulus traveled here from the Mediterranean with St. Andrew's precious bones back when the Romans still ruled most of the world."

"This land has long been considered a safe place for refugees," said Malcolm. "I suppose it seemed like the ends of the earth to them, where no one would follow to claim them."

"You should proclaim yourself to be King of the Ends of the Earth," said Margaret. "It has a certain ring to it."

Malcolm grinned and slapped his thigh. "Except that my stepsons the Earls of Orkney would likely claim that title from me. And they're welcome to it."

As they drew closer they saw the stone-built cathedral, the first that Margaret had laid eyes on since her arrival in Scotland. "It looks to be a worthy home for the precious relics. I'm relieved to see that." The other buildings at the site were of more conventional construction, of turf and weathered timbers, with steep thatched roofs reaching almost to the ground.

One building stood taller than the others, with half-timbered walls. "Is that the bishop's palace?" she asked.

"I believe that's the hospital," said Malcolm. "Where pilgrims stay and where we shall likely rest our heads tonight."

AN EARTHEN DITCH and bank surrounded the enclosure, and they passed over the ditch on a wooden bridge. Bishop Fothad greeted them from the other side. "My monks heralded your arrival, and we're most glad to welcome you, King Malcolm."

Margaret greeted the bishop warmly. He'd performed their wedding ceremony barely a year ago. A tall, tonsured man in the prime of middle age, he had a natural air of authority and nobility, tempered with the kindness and humility one would hope for in a servant of God.

He led the way, walking swiftly over the stone-laid path, past the doors to the Hospital, and to the front of another large building, and waited while they dismounted. "I'm sure you're anxious to see the precious relics," he said to Margaret. "But first take the time to refresh yourselves after your journey. The hospital is packed with pilgrims this Advent, so I'm glad to offer you shelter in my humble home."

Margaret was relieved to see that his humble home was significantly less humble than most of the dwellings round-about. In fact it was built of stone, like the tower, and appeared to be of very ancient construction, possibly even dating back to Roman times.

They entered through an arched doorway and were taken into a labyrinthine suite of rooms. Gnarled and pitted beams over their heads confirmed the ancient origins of the structure. Painted decoration covered the plastered walls, and appeared to have been much patched and touched up over the years.

He showed them their bed and observed that countless kings and queens had slept there, so they were surely following in the footsteps of their forbears, going back to the time of the Picts and beyond.

The bed itself was of blackish oak, carved with images of birds and beasts, with a dark red quilted bed cover that showed almost as many signs of repair as the walls. Margaret hoped that it had been washed—or at least aired—since the time of the Romans, but travel always came with the risk of bed lice or malodorous furnishings. She resolved to bear any such inconveniences without complaint.

Two monks brought them copper bowls filled with fresh water and white linen cloths to dry their faces. Margaret splashed herself with the icy liquid and washed her hands in it gratefully, glad to leave the dirt of the road behind her. Grizel was already shaking out her cloak and airing it in front of the fire so that it could be brushed back to cleanliness once dry.

"Would you like a bite to eat or would you prefer to see our precious relics first?" asked Bishop Fothad.

Malcolm looked at Margaret. "I have my guesses about which my dear wife would prefer, but I'll let her state her preference."

"Please take us to the relics," said Margaret, tingling with excitement. "We ate well on the road."

The bishop led them from the palace, along a cloistered stone path toward the stone church. Made of dressed blocks, the building was very solid. What it lacked in ornamentation, it made up for with a sense of permanence that was reassuring in these changing times.

"The relics have been here for more than seven hundred years," said the bishop, as he led them down the nave of the cathedral, toward the altar. "We've protected them from the Norsemen, the Danes and sometimes it seems from the very devil himself."

"God be praised for their safety," whispered Margaret. Awe overcame her as they approached the precious casket that held St. Andrew's bones. Darkness had fallen since they arrived. Candles now lit the nave, some of them as tall as a man, and others gathered in groups. The flickering light from them reflected off the high, carved arches over their heads. Passing through the tall pillars along the nave felt like walking through the tall trees of a mysterious forest.

Other pilgrims knelt here and there, on wooden priedieus of various sizes. The bishop made the sign of the cross as they approached the altar, and Margaret fell to her knees, overcome with emotion.

God, you've brought me this far, to the ends of the earth, to pay homage to a companion of your very own Son. Grant me the wisdom and courage to do your will on earth.

Tears fell down her cheeks, hot in the cold air.

"Are you ill, my lady?" Concern raised the bishop's voice.

"She's pregnant, Bishop," announced Malcolm proudly.

Bishop Fothad offered his congratulations while Margaret protested that had nothing to do with her sudden weakness. "I was moved by the presence of the relics."

Margaret pulled her own treasured relic, the Black Rood, from the purse hanging on her belt. The tiny cross-shaped reliquary held a precious fragment of the True Cross that Christ had died on. St Andrew was there when that terrible event occurred. Once again the cross and his bones were in the same space, here in this remote corner of the Kingdom of Alba.

Malcolm helped her to her feet, and they continued toward the altar. A small chest with a rounded top held the relics. Decorative tooled metal strapping covered the box, and a large brass key stood in the lock.

They climbed two steps that separated the altar area from the rest of the nave. The bishop approached the box and turned the key. Margaret felt Malcolm's arm grip her elbow —he must be worried that she'd collapse again and possibly tumble down the stairs. She resolved to hold herself steady.

"Come close, and view the remains of our dear Saint Andrew."

CHAPTER 9

The box containing the remains of St. Andrew now stood open. Bright tooled gold covered the interior of the lid. Inside lay pieces of bone—a finger, perhaps, and possibly a tooth—arranged carefully in the rather small space of the box, nestled in purple silk.

Margaret crossed herself and murmured a prayer of thanks and praise. Gazing upon the bones of a man who'd walked with Our Lord somehow collapsed all the time that had passed—a thousand years gone in an instant. The saint's bones, resting safe here in Kilrymont, while his soul rested in Heaven with God, reminded her that all souls on earth walk on a path toward Heaven—or stray from that path at their peril.

Fear gripped her for the immortal fate of her dear husband, who'd saved her from exile and ignominy. As a king —as a man—he'd committed acts that put his soul in peril. He was a good man! Tears blurred her vision and she clasped her hands, begging God to spare her dear husband the fires of hell. She pledged to do her best to help him stay on the path to righteousness.

Sometimes it was enough of a struggle to keep her own stumbling steps on that path—just in the last week she'd been tempted into the use of lies and deceit even if they were employed for good.

Perhaps that's why Aelgith and Osgifu had made their foolish attempt to escape. Aelgith's betrayal of her trust might be a punishment from God. If she'd been more forthright with her husband and he with Mac Duff perhaps Aelgith and Osgifu might be safe beside her here in the cathedral before St. Andrew's precious relics.

She felt her knees buckle and Malcolm caught her. His strong arm around her back somehow snapped her out of her guilty reverie and back to the present, where she dried her tears with the hem of her veil and said another prayer.

"The queen is deeply moved by these holy relics," said Malcolm to the bishop, in a voice so deep it was barely audible. "Perhaps we should rest now."

The bishop nodded. Margaret watched as he closed the box and locked it. She thanked him for the rare opportunity to view the bones up close—most pilgrims were grateful to gaze upon the reliquary itself—and they descended the steps and walked back down the nave.

THE BISHOP DINED with them in a small but comfortable room in his rather humble palace. A fire crackled nearby.

"I know some would say that fish is rather too close to meat for eating during Advent," he said, as a tonsured monk entered with a steaming plate of it. "But here on the salt-drenched and windswept coast we are provided with an abundance of it and very little of anything else, at least during the winter months."

"We must make do with what God provides," said

Margaret, finding this a perfectly reasonable explanation. Barley in a fishy broth accompanied it. The fare was plain in color and flavor and she could find no fault with it and ate it with relish.

"I must apologize for my unseemly behavior at the sight of the relics," said Margaret. "My husband will tell you I am not normally one to be overcome by emotion."

"She's usually as steady as a statue," said Malcolm. "I'd trust her to lead an army into battle."

"God forbid," said Margaret quickly. Though she did appreciate her husband's confidence in her steady nerves. "But I'm not sure I've ever felt such deep emotion."

"You were touched by the Lord, my dear. It's why pilgrims come here from hundreds of miles away. They feel closer to God in the presence of one of his Son's dearest companions."

"We are so blessed to have these relics here in the Kingdom of the Scots," said Malcolm. "And I thank you for taking such care of them."

"Indeed we rely on God's protection from outside forces. At least in recent centuries the invading forces are usually Christian men themselves. They don't wish to destroy their hope for eternal life by picking a fight with God's servants, so they usually leave us alone. A strong king at the head of the nation, who keeps them quiet at home in their own lands, is our best defense."

"And I intend to be that king, God willing," said Malcolm, sipping the monastery's home-brewed ale.

"You must be praised for making this place a peaceful haven for pilgrims from all over the land. Do refugees come here from England?"

"Indeed they do, my lady. Their numbers have rather taxed our resources. We give shelter for as long as we can before we must send them on their way."

"And where do they go after that?"

"I can't be sure."

A silence hovered over the well-provisioned table.

Malcolm broke it. "My wife is much concerned about the fate of refugees. She has arranged for my household to provide weekly meals to the needy. She even has me washing their feet with my own hands."

The bishop's mouth opened and he stared at Malcolm in astonishment for a moment. He recovered himself, blinking. "That is very Christlike of you, my king. Such...humility is surely the road to God's Kingdom."

"That's what my wife says." Malcolm placed his hand on hers where it rested on the table. Margaret drew in a quick breath as the warmth of it sent a mix of emotions to her heart.

"I'm a refugee myself, Bishop," said Margaret, not wanting to depart so quickly from the subject so dear to her heart. "My brother was intended to be king of England but the... invasion upended all his hopes and plans." Never mind that the Witan—a group of foolish old men who claimed to know what was best for everyone—chose another on the death of King Edward.

"Perhaps your brother will sit on the throne of England one day, God willing," said the bishop, clearly hopeful that he was saying the right thing.

Margaret was not very enthusiastic about that idea at this point. It would require more war, for one thing, and the threat of defeat, death and dishonor that came along with it. "If it is God's will, perhaps. But in the meantime I do concern myself with the fate of all those who—like myself—find themselves separated from all their property and prospects and even from their kin."

"Indeed, their suffering is terrible," said the bishop. "We've had people arrive here half-starved or sick almost to death. We nurse them back to health here but we cannot house them forever or we wouldn't have room to take in more desperate souls. And we must always have room for the pilgrims whose presence supports our very existence."

Margaret had noticed a brisk trade in pilgrim badges and other trinkets that the monastery monks manufactured for sale. "I congratulate you on your ability to cater to such a diverse and constant stream of people. Your community and your leadership deserve high praise indeed."

She swallowed before asking a question that always burned at the front of her mind these days. "Do you celebrate the sabbath on Sunday like the Pope?"

Bishop Fothad cleared his throat, shifting awkwardly in his chair. "We celebrate the Sabbath on Saturday like the wise ones in the Holy Land, my lady. We're a very traditional community here. As guardians of the bones of Christ's apostle, we consider it our duty to preserve the ancient traditions."

Margaret drew in a steadying breath. The remote locations of the religious communities here limited communication and oversight from the Church of Rome. And the Scots themselves were a stubborn lot, resistant to outside interference of any kind.

Still, the Pope was the head of the Church and his rules must surely be applied throughout God's Kingdom.

"Has the Archbishop of Canterbury written to you about changing this practice?" Margaret had been conducting a vigorous correspondence with Archbishop Lanfranc, newly appointed to the role. She found him a sympathetic and supportive ear.

Bishop Fothad knotted his hands together. "It's not easy to change the traditions of five hundred years, my lady. Nor am I convinced that we should."

Margaret's spine stiffened. "You disagree with the Archbishop of Canterbury and with the Pope himself?"

The bishop looked down at the linen tablecloth. "Disagree is not a word I would ever wish to use in such a context, my lady."

Malcolm's hand, still resting on hers, squeezed it gently. *Slow down*, was the message she felt from him. "My wife enjoys theological debate, Bishop, and you'll find she's widely read and has considered every argument that can be made from angles that no one else would even think of."

"How unusual," said the bishop, now staring at her as if she might be one of Satan's minions.

"My dear husband praises my erudition too highly," said Margaret quickly. "I've done some reading, to be sure, in my years of quiet study at the convent at Wilton and in the library collected by my dear great uncle Edward the Confessor. But I have no wish to argue with anyone, let alone the custodians of God's precious churches and monasteries."

"I am relieved to hear that, my lady," said the bishop, looking anything but relieved.

Margaret decided to change the subject. "I notice that you have no lay servants here. All the work is done by holy brothers."

"Yes, we have a large community of monks here and prefer to keep the tasks among ourselves."

"They even catch the fish you eat?"

"Yes, my lady. And grow a large garden in the summer and keep a herd of milk cows. We maintain our forests and produce a constant supply of good, dry firewood to survive the cold winters. We have a scriptorium of scribes creating manuscripts for our own use or for purchase by the wealthiest pilgrims. It's no easy feat to provide sustenance for the constant stream of pilgrims here, and we do purchase sacks of grain to supplement our stores."

"And you grow your own wool to make clothing?" Bishop Fothad didn't wear the elaborate gold-trimmed finery of bishops she'd encountered at Westminster, but not the plain habit of a monk either. His dark robe, a color somewhere between red and black, was made from smooth, tightly-woven wool with black and white trim around the cuffs.

"We do indeed, my lady. And card and spin and weave it. If we make surplus to our requirements, it's sold at the local market or traded for grain and wine. We have a large community but each man works to keep it running smoothly."

"It's all the more impressive that you manage to sustain such a bountiful community on this windswept coast. I suppose most of your pilgrims arrive by sea?"

"Indeed not, my lady. The vast majority of our pilgrims arrive on foot from the south. They still have to cross the Firth of Forth, of course. I understand there's a good deal of money being made by unscrupulous boatmen taking advantage of pilgrims desperate to cross that body of water."

"I can imagine. It would take days—weeks even—to walk around it." Margaret looked at her husband. "We cross the Forth regularly, to travel between Dunfermline and Edinburgh. We must look into this. We can't allow pilgrims to be exploited on their journey to see the sacred relics of St. Andrew."

"We must indeed," said Malcolm. "But for now let's take rest. We shall rise early to visit the church again in the morning."

ALONE IN THE comfortable private bedchamber, with a fire burning at one end of the small room, Margaret undressed without Grizel's help. The girl had been banished to wherever they deposited stray single women so they wouldn't distract the monks.

"I'm surprised at you wanting to head to bed early. Are you ill?"

Malcolm laughed. "Sick of making polite conversation, perhaps. I craved some time alone with my wife."

She climbed under the covers and into his warm embrace. "I'm so grateful that you agreed to come with me. I wasn't expecting to be knocked to my knees by the power of the Lord."

"You seem to forget that you're with child," he said, stroking her cheek.

"I've never felt better," she protested. "If anything I have more energy."

"Probably because you're eating well. When you first arrived your eating habits were very worrying. Such constant fasting and abstinence would savage the constitution of the finest warrior."

"Fasting gives me a different kind of strength," She closed her eyes and let out a sigh. "But if even the Archbishop of Canterbury tells me to eat for the sake of my child, I will eat."

Malcolm kissed her cheek softly. "Only you would ask the Archbishop of Canterbury for dietary advice."

"He's the authority of God's will on this whole island. Who else must I ask?"

"Most young ladies would ask their mother."

"She's been nagging me to eat better since the day I was born. As you may have noticed, she barely eats herself. She's terrified of becoming plump."

Malcolm laughed again. "Why?"

"I honestly don't know. She prides herself on having the power to resist temptation. I admire that about her. She likes people to think that she's empty-headed and foolish, and that she can't understand half of what anyone says, but she's guided our family through these tumultuous times like a boatman with a firm hand on the rudder."

"All the women in your family have a will of iron. Especially your sister Christina."

"Poor Christina. She wasn't always so pinched and pious. She used to dream of marriage but now she's scared of her own shadow. I don't blame her. She always seems to be buffeted in everyone else's wake."

"One could say the same for you, my love." His thumb brushed her lip, stirring feelings that no longer felt sinful. "Your fate determined by your royal ancestry rather than your own heart—which craved the cloister."

"I've embraced my fate and consider myself blessed to be your wife," she said honestly.

"And I'll make it my life's work to maintain your enthusiasm for your fate."

"People have no idea who you are," she said. "Archbishop Lanfranc seemed to be under the impression that you couldn't read."

Malcolm laughed so hard that the bed shook. "Did you tell the Archbishop of Canterbury that I know my letters?"

"I told him you'd read the Bible in three different languages."

Malcolm's big chest heaved with a sigh. "Ah, why would you do such a thing? Let them think me a rough-mannered brute without a thought beyond my next meal and my next stag hunt. Then I can run circles around them without them noticing."

"Spoken like a wise man," she said softly. "Your confidence is such that you don't need to brag and show off. I have a lot to learn from you."

"With age comes wisdom, my love, and I do have almost twenty years more wisdom than you." He laid a gentle kiss on her lips. "But with wisdom comes cynicism and I welcome your idealism and optimism to replenish where mine has drained away."

"I shall do my best, though clearly it led me astray in the case of Aelgith." The fate of the mother and daughter had gnawed at her conscience all day. "What do you suppose has happened to them by now?"

"I'd imagine that Mac Duff's hunting hounds have sniffed them out and that they've been brought back to his hall."

Margaret cringed at the thought of the great hairy hounds snatching at the clothing or limbs of the frightened women. "Would they let the hounds hurt them?"

"I doubt it. Mac Duff's not a cruel man. But they won't give them a feather bed and a fine dinner, either."

"Can you preside over their trial when we return?" she asked hopefully.

"You would have me dispense justice that pleases you?" He lifted a brow slightly.

"I would prefer justice that pleases God."

"Is God pleased with a thief who stole a jeweled cross from her hostess?"

Margaret's heart sank. "I forgot about that. Why would she do such a thing?" She let out a sigh. "The poor woman was desperate. She wanted a way to buy bread for herself and her daughter."

"How do you buy bread in rural Fife with a golden cross? Hmm?"

That stopped her thoughts for a moment. Aelgith might have found a merchant to buy or trade for it in London or York...But here amidst these rustic villages of sheep herders, they wouldn't know what to do with it, and might even recognize it.

"I wish she hadn't taken the cross," she said sadly. "But if the mother took it, will the girl be punished for the crime as well?"

"That will be determined by Mac Duff. He's justiciar in his own realm, with the right to dispense justice as he sees fit."

Margaret swallowed. "But as king, you might voice an opinion, surely?"

"I hope to hear what she has to say for herself."

Margaret didn't want to push her luck by prodding and goading him too much. He knew her wishes.

But he also owed justice to the Mac Duffs, who were arguably the most important family in his kingdom and would be dangerous enemies, especially at such close quarters.

CHAPTER 10

The next morning, Margaret rose early, eager to attend Matins service in the church. She left her sleepy husband abed and dressed herself quickly, shaking out her veil and pinning it—she hoped—as expertly as Grizel, who was tucked away sleeping in some dark corner with the other servants.

The fire had burned down to some glowing embers, not even enough to light a candle wick on, so she pushed out into the dark hallway, hoping she could find her way to the outside door without tripping over a cat or stray pair of shoes.

"My lady." Grizel's voice startled her almost to the point of shrieking, but she managed to trap the sound in her throat.

"What are you doing up at this hour?"

"Sitting here waiting for you to rise."

"It's the middle of the night."

"I heard the bells for Matins and knew you'd want to attend."

"Ah Grizel, you are truly a treasure. You'd be even more of one if you had a lit candle."

Grizel giggled. "Don't worry, I know the way. I memorized it yesterday."

They picked their way carefully out of the dark corridors of the ancient bishop's palace, with its floor of trippy and uneven stones, and into the dark, starless night. As she'd expected, they were not alone, since other shadowy figures hurried through the predawn darkness toward the church.

Margaret prayed that she could keep her composure this time in the presence of the sacred relics. She didn't want to embarrass her husband or have the bishop form unfortunate opinions about pregnant women or women in general.

One of the double doors to the chapel stood open, and the warm glow of candlelight welcomed her. Inside, a brazier brought welcome warmth to the predawn hours. She and Grizel found a quiet corner in the back of the church to enjoy the psalms and song without disturbing the holy brothers.

Other pilgrims had risen from their beds to attend and she observed them silently. There were several older couples, husbands and wives whose children had grown and who now enjoyed the good fortune of enough money and leisure to venture on a spiritual journey. Margaret hoped that she and Malcolm would be among them one day, with grizzled hair and the wrinkled but peaceful visages she saw among them.

Except that it wasn't always a king's lot to die peacefully in his bed. Edward the Confessor had managed it, but here in the Kingdom of the Scots, things were different. Her husband had killed his predecessor, and the one before that, too. And then there was William, who'd conquered England and Wales and might yet set his sights on Malcolm's kingdom.

Margaret said fervent prayers for peace and prosperity in the land and pledged to devote her life—however long or short—to being an instrument of the Lord and supporting her husband...hopefully both at the same time.

She also whispered prayers that Aelgith and Osgifu had been captured safely—with the precious cross intact and unharmed—and were being held without undue cruelty. That was about the best she could hope for in the current circumstances.

THE JOURNEY back to Cupar passed swiftly now that she knew the terrain and what to expect. Her hips complained at being torqued to one side in her sidesaddle, while her torso faced forward.

The pain in her hips was compounded by a growing ache of fear in her heart. "What if they've killed Aelgith? Or cut off her hand for thieving?" She spoke as quietly as possible to Malcolm, who led her horse right next to his.

"Since she was our guest, I doubt they'll do anything drastic until we return."

"Until? You mean they might want to do it in front of us?"

"In which case I will prevent it." He looked unbothered. Which was an important kingly quality.

"Will Mac Duff even offer us hospitality again after what happened? We could ride all the way to Dunfermline today if we went a little faster."

"He will. I'm his king. And you're with child so you need to rest."

"I feel no different than usual. I don't know why people make such a fuss about pregnancy. I'm full of energy." She was barely showing at all. If it weren't for her breasts becoming tender and sore, she might not even know she was with child. "Seeing the precious relics in person has lit a fire in me."

Malcolm laughed. "And you had plenty of fire in you already. I worried you were going to take the bishop to task in his own chamber."

"I don't understand why the Culdees celebrate the Sabbath on Saturday. It's been hundreds of years since the Church of Rome declared Sunday as the Christian Sabbath."

"The devotees of St. Columba can be an odd lot, I'll grant you that. But they're faithful Christians and not doing anything against the will of God. They take their teachings from the Bible. Did Jesus insist that the Sabbath be on Sunday?"

Margaret's mouth opened, then closed again. "He rose again on Sunday. The Sunday Sabbath celebrates his resurrection into life eternal."

"Did Jesus himself celebrate the Sabbath on Saturday or Sunday?"

Margaret adjusted her reins in her fingers. This was not the first time they'd had this discussion. "Saturday, but he was Jewish and that was their tradition."

"So who changed the day from Saturday to Sunday, if it wasn't Jesus himself?"

"During the first century after his death the practice gradually—" She broke off, as she heard the sound of thundering hoofbeats in the distance, growing closer. Three horsemen came galloping over the hill in front of them and barely pulled up in time to stop before colliding with their horses. One couldn't stop his horse which reared up and galloped to the side of them.

Grizel screamed. Margaret struggled to keep her composure—and her seat—on her agitated mount.

Malcolm barked at them, then clearly recognized one of

them. "Niall, you almost unseated my entire party. What's the meaning of this?"

"That woman you brought with you has committed a murder."

~

THEY RODE the rest of the way to Cupar at a brisk clip, Margaret clinging to the handle on her saddle to keep herself steady. Her lips moved constantly as she prayed that there was a misunderstanding.

Had Aelgith fought back against her captor and accidentally killed him? The men muttered amongst themselves but the local dialect was still hard for her to understand when people spoke fast. It wasn't her place—at least not right now —to demand more details, so she bit her tongue.

A chaotic atmosphere had descended on Cupar, along with a purplish storm cloud now depositing a steady rain over the settlement. People stood about in groups watching them ride up, despite the rain, staring as if waiting for some pageantry to unfold. Their horses splashed in puddles as they approached the bridge over the defensive ditch.

Guards ran up to them and grabbed the reins of their horses as they entered the inner circle of the settlement. Margaret glanced at her husband, whose stony visage alarmed her. She dismounted her horse and arranged her wet cloak about her, then lifted her chin high.

Mac Duff now strode out of the hall. "Good God, Malcolm, the trouble you've brought upon me and my house."

Alarm—or was it anger?—flashed in Margaret's gut. How dare he speak to his king that way? But Malcolm took it in stride.

"A killing, they said. Who's dead?"

"My daughter, Beitris."

Margaret froze, her feet refusing to move forward under her. Grizel rushed to her and took her elbow. This was far more serious than she'd imagined. There was no way Aelgith could survive killing a mormaer's kin. And even she wouldn't lift her voice to defend Aelgith if she'd done such a terrible thing.

"What dreadful news," exclaimed Malcolm. "How did this come to pass?"

"That woman who left here with my servant and my wife's precious cross has murdered my Beitris in the night."

"Here in your hall?"

"No, in her home at Balbarnie ten miles south of here."

Margaret tried her best to put one foot in front of the other as they walked to the hall door. Her mind was spinning, trying to figure out why the women had traveled south. That would have led them down toward the coast and then where? Perhaps west to Dunfermline. Were Aelgith and Osgifu headed back to her home for shelter that they assumed she'd give them?

No good deed goes unpunished. What had she started?

Inside the hall, Grizel took her cloak and she greeted Mac Duff's pale-eyed wife Enfleda with genuine regret and concern before asking the question foremost in her mind. "Where are they being held?"

"They've not yet been caught. My husband's men are hard after them and we shall find them. They can't escape justice."

Margaret blinked in confusion. "If you haven't caught them, then how do you know they killed your daughter?"

"They were seen running away from Balbarnie."

"By who?"

"By a servant. But by the time her husband mounted his horse and gave chase with his men, they'd disappeared into the landscape."

Margaret wondered why they'd taken the time to mount horses when they could have surely overtaken a half-starved middle-aged woman and her daughter on foot. "Neither of the women knows the landscape well, so they can't stay hidden for long."

"The girl had been to Balbarnie before, since my husband and I travel often visit his daughter Beitris—" She trailed off and pressed a hand to her eyes. "I can't believe she's gone. So young, and with child, like yourself!"

Margaret's hand flew to her belly as if her own growing baby might be under attack somehow. The deep horror of this situation rendered her speechless. And apparently Osgifu did know the countryside well enough to travel it and hide in it.

"Why would the women kill Beitris?"

"Theft, most likely, since they stole from us here. How did I not know I harbored a black-hearted villainess in our household?" Angry spots of color appeared on her cheeks.

This didn't make sense to Margaret. If they'd already stolen the cross, the value of it would give them sustenance for a very long time—provided they could find a way to sell it. Why would they wish to burden themselves with another object to carry on their journey, let alone another crime to suffer punishment for?

"How was Beitris killed?" she asked. Aelgith, though tall, was thin as a reed and her daughter was a diminutive girl even for the age of fourteen. How would they overtake and murder a noblewoman in her own household?

"I don't know. Stop peppering me with questions! We just learned the terrible news. My husband will have revenge!" The anger in her voice chilled Margaret. Would revenge on Aelgith and her daughter be enough, or would they seek revenge on the people who had brought this disaster into their midst?

Enfleda swept away across the hall to where her husband exchanged low words with Malcolm. Both of their faces wore a look of thunderous fury.

We should leave. Margaret had never felt so unwelcome in her life. Would she and Malcolm be safe sleeping here? Unfortunately dusk already drew in due to the short winter days. If they left they'd have to travel in the dark, which was difficult even with good moonlight to ride by. Winter threw a white blanket of clouds across the sky that rarely lifted, and she didn't even remember the last time she'd seen the full face of the sun or the moon.

Left at a loose end by Enfleda's departure, she walked slowly across the hall to her husband and their host.

"Rest assured, we will find them and punishment will be swift and complete. Justice of the Mac Duffs be damned." Malcolm was speaking. "They shall feel the justice of the king. I shall leave no stone unturned until your daughter's murder is avenged."

Margaret swallowed. The poor women were condemned and hanged in everyone's minds. She burned to ask again for more details about how Beitris was killed but knew better than to raise her voice right now. She stood quietly at her husband's side, expressing her sympathies and offering her prayers for the bereaved family.

DINNER WAS A GRIM AFFAIR. Mac Duff shared memories of his daughter's youth. Enfleda sat silent, white lipped and red eyed. She was not Beitris's mother—who had died many years before—but no doubt she'd grown fond of the girl who was likely close to her own age. Beitris's husband now had a party scouring the countryside for his wife's killers and he'd vowed to take them alive or dead.

Margaret was almost ready to turn her prayers to the speedy passage of Aelgith and Osgifu's souls—which were on a dark path to hell—rather than the safety of their mortal bodies.

But details tugged at her. Why would the women go anywhere near a settlement that Osgifu knew to be a close relative of her enslaver?

And she still didn't understand why Aelgith would steal a valuable item from this hall, when it would only intensify any search for her and her daughter. They would have been far more sensible to slip away in possession of only their frail bodies that perhaps no one would care too much about.

The ale tasted bitter on her lips. She could barely eat the barley gruel they served her while everyone else ate meat during Advent as if Christmas had already begun. She wished she could quit the table and tuck herself away in bed with her husband. She'd urge him to keep his sword close to the bed tonight.

Tense and uneasy, she flinched when Grizel surprised her by tapping her shoulder. "The cross has been found," she whispered.

"What?" Margaret turned and held her arms. "Where?"

"It lay lodged in a crack where the wall meets the floor."

Margaret turned to the assembled diners. "My servant just informed me that the missing jeweled cross wasn't stolen and has been found."

Gasps flew around the table.

"Let me see it," said Enfleda, without rising.

One of the servant girls hurried toward them with the precious cross cupped in her hands like an injured bird.

Stunned, Margaret struggled to make sense of this new information. "Aelgith didn't steal it." She spoke the words aloud, in case no one had made the connection. If Aelgith had stolen nothing but her own dear daughter, had she truly committed a worse crime later that day?

"It must have fallen off its hook," said Enfleda. She now held the cross in her hands and examined the chain as if looking for a broken link.

Grizel cupped her hands around Margaret's ear. "It was pushed right down under the wall." Margaret gripped her fingers and squeezed them hard to stop her. She couldn't have Grizel whispering accusations in front of their hosts.

"Who found it?" asked Margaret, of Enfleda's servant, who'd carried the cross over.

"Your girl did. She went into the mistress's chamber and felt around under the bed and in all the cracks and corners and then she pulled it out."

"Who allowed her to go into my chamber?" demanded Enfleda, eyes flashing.

"I did, my lady," said the girl, with a tremor in her voice. "I helped her. I thought it was a good idea to look for it just in case…." Her words disappeared in a gulp.

A halfhearted smile spread across Enfleda's sharp features. "How clever of her."

"This young lady deserves high praise indeed," said Mac Duff. "Perhaps if she searched under the bed earlier she'd have found my missing slave girl before she escaped to murder my dear daughter."

People shifted awkwardly in their seats. Rather than actually praising Grizel or relieving Aelgith of guilt, he'd decided to remind the assembled company that a theft had still occurred—and a murder.

Margaret's initial cheer at the reappearance of the cross had thoroughly faded. Grizel's discovery appeared to have embarrassed their host's wife and by extension their host.

Did Enfleda hide the cross there herself for some reason?

Margaret's already queasy stomach churned and she

wished this mirthless dinner would come to an end. Instead the servants poured another round of ale and Grizel was given a cup of it, too. A toast was made to her cleverness and the poor girl sipped the ale as if it might be poisoned.

Enfleda sat tight-lipped and silent, her jeweled cross hanging around her neck more like a noose than a holy ornament. Margaret reminded herself that her husband's daughter was dead and they were in mourning. They could hardly be expected to be in good spirits.

Malcolm, usually so good at turning even a swords-drawn conflict into cheerful banter and good humor, did not attempt to lift the mood. He uttered more words of commiseration for the loss of Beitris and invited them to share memories of the girl.

Mac Duff recalled putting his little daughter on a horse for the first time and hearing her shriek with a mix of joy and terror. Enfleda said nothing, but fingered the rim of her goblet without drinking.

Where's Beitris's husband? Margaret thought it odd that he wasn't here with his dead wife's family, especially given that her father was the mormaer. Perhaps he was too deeply aggrieved by the loss of his wife to face company right now.

"GRIZEL, why don't you come sleep at the foot of our bed, tonight," she whispered in the girl's ear, as the company finally quit the table. For some reason she felt Grizel had poked a hornets' nest by finding the cross in its odd hiding place. She wanted her safely nearby tonight.

"Yes, my lady. I'll let the girls know and gather my cloak."

Margaret gripped Malcolm's arm firmly, almost as if she needed him to lean on, as they walked to the curtained bed in its nook just off the hall. She didn't want someone to snatch him away from her for a late-night game of dice or a drunken reminiscence about battles gone by.

Grizel undressed her, looking relieved to be away from the hall full of strangers. Margaret climbed into the bed, and asked the girl to come inside the curtains with her and Malcolm for a moment.

Grizel hesitated at the strange request, then climbed up onto the mattress and closed the curtains behind her.

"What made you decide to go look for the cross when it had been given up as stolen?"

"I just didn't think Aelgith or her daughter would do that."

"Do you think it fell off the hook?"

Grizel hesitated. "No. None of the links was broken or even bent, so the chain didn't break. The hook was forged to be very deep, with a narrow opening at the top and a wider area at the bottom, so there's no way the chain could be accidentally knocked out of it, even by someone brushing against it. The only way it could fall is if someone missed the mark when hanging it."

"Which is unlikely given that it's such a precious object and would be treated with great care," said Margaret.

"And it was wedged right underneath the wall," said Grizel. "Between the flags of the floor and the plaster covering the turf or whatever their walls are made of. Almost like someone pushed it in there. I only found it because I felt along inside the small crevice between the wall and floor with my fingers on the off chance that I'd find it there."

"Your instincts guided you well," said Margaret. She turned to Malcolm, who, propped up on one elbow, had listened to this whispered conference in silence. "It seems that our hostess stole her own necklace."

Malcolm lifted a finger to his lips. Margaret hoped that there was enough ambient rustling and crackling of fire logs to obscure their hushed words. "Someone could be listening at the curtains," he mouthed almost silently.

"Thank you, Grizel. You may sleep now," said Margaret quietly. "But stay close."

After Grizel had exited the bed and closed the curtains behind her, Margaret drew so close to Malcolm that her lips almost touched his ear. "Can we pass through Balbarnie on our way home tomorrow, to learn more about what took place there?"

Malcolm hesitated. His big chest rose and fell against hers. "Yes, it's not far out of the way. We can offer our help in finding the perpetrators."

"Who have no good reason to be the perpetrators," reminded Margaret. "Why would they draw attention to themselves with a murder when they wish nothing more than escape?"

"I hope we'll find out tomorrow."

CHAPTER 11

*I*n the morning, Margaret asked Grizel to show her where she'd found the cross, on the pretext that she wanted to admire her clever servant's ingenuity. She seized a moment when Enfleda was busy giving orders to the cook and was as fast and inconspicuous as possible. Grizel was right—nothing could fall off that hook unless it was plucked off first. The crack between wall and floor was narrow and most likely an object of that shape and size would not slide in there by itself but would have to be pushed.

They ate a hasty breakfast of oat porridge with cream and gladly accepted offered provisions in the form of cheese and oatcakes for the road.

Dawn glazed the nearby hills with pale light when they mounted their horses and set off for home. Or at least that's what they told their hosts. No need to inspire the Mac Duffs to offer an escort to Balbarnie or send a party ahead of them.

Margaret hoped to maintain an element of surprise to better catch Beitris's newly widowed husband—a thane called Diarmad Mac Aidh—unawares.

Cold rain misted down on them as they rode across the countryside. Margaret was glad the warm fur lining of her cloak stayed dry and her deep hood provided some shelter for her face. With Aelgith gone they had an extra horse to be led by one of the guards, and the mare carried their food and drink for the journey.

Once they were well away from the Mac Duff's settlement and the surrounding hamlets, she started to relax a little. "That was a very tense night last night."

"As could be expected if they think we brought a murderer into their midst...who has now killed their daughter." Malcolm's serious expression told her he still considered this a possibility.

"I find it odd that Aelgith and Osgifu would choose this route. Why not avoid any settlements if they're trying to escape?" She hoped that the sighting of them was somehow mistaken and that they'd been nowhere near Balbarnie when Beitris was killed.

"Mac Duff's wife said that the slave girl knew the route. She'd accompanied them here on several occasions."

Margaret sighed. It did make some sense that they'd choose a familiar path to avoid getting lost in empty country in the dead of winter. Especially with no visible sun to distinguish one direction from another. "But we do know that Aelgith didn't steal the cross. She's not a thief. She's a well-bred noblewoman, despite her reduced circumstances."

Malcolm laughed. "As if the highborn can't be thieves! They're often the worst. And you only know about her past from what she told you. What if she made it all up and she's the daughter of a pig herder?"

Margaret pursed her lips. "I can tell the difference, as can you, from her speech alone."

"True. She speaks and carries herself like an English lady, I'll give you that."

The scent of pine boughs thickened the air as they passed through a wood. The early morning sun cast long shadows through the trees, which stood like silent sentinels, with tiny creatures hibernating deep inside them.

"I can't imagine Aelgith killing someone. You met her. She's quiet and frail as a dormouse."

"I agree that the prospect of her wielding a knife seems unlikely," said Malcolm.

They'd managed to ascertain that Beitris had been stabbed and bled to death. "Hopefully we can learn more about her demise when we arrive at Balbarnie."

"It will be interesting to see how they respond to the unannounced arrival of their king," said Malcolm. "I rarely turn up at a nobleman's house with no warning unless I'm looking for a fight with him."

"We want information, that's all. And we don't even need to tell them that. Just say we're there to offer our condolences and to help in capturing the suspected criminals."

"They may have caught the fugitives already," mused Malcolm. "We can only hope they haven't dispensed swift justice."

"God forbid," said Margaret, crossing herself. "That's against the law. Especially in a case where a life is at stake. They must allow a justice to decide the punishment."

"In theory, but even the most settled areas of Scotland have a far sparser population than Wessex or Northumbria, and much happens that never even reaches the ears of a justice."

"Well, this is Fife, and well within arm's reach of your seat of Dunfermline. You shouldn't allow men to take the law into their own hands here, even if the Mac Duffs have their own law code."

Malcolm turned to look at her in surprise. "You wish to tell me how to manage my kingdom?"

Margaret swallowed. It seemed like common sense that a king should not allow his subjects to murder each other with impunity—even as a potentially justifiable act of revenge. "No, my king," she said, biting her tongue.

Malcolm let out a roar of laughter. "My dear sweet wife, I welcome your advice as much as I welcome your caresses. Please don't hold your tongue for fear of offending me."

"I am still learning how to be a wife," she said. "And I truly don't know when I've overstepped the boundaries of the role. I'm used to keeping my own counsel and speaking my mind and I know that at times I may be too bold."

"That's the problem with waiting until you're four and twenty years of age before marrying," he said jovially. "If you'd been packed off into my care at age fourteen—when the Confessor first promised you to me—you'd likely have learned to mind your words and your manners like a good little girl."

Margaret wasn't sure how to respond to this. She had her dear great-uncle Edward the Confessor to thank for both her lengthy childhood and the opportunities for education that it had given her. But he had died and along with him her hopes of entering the cloister. "Despite my great uncle's promises, I'd intended to be a bride of Christ, not a mortal man," she said quietly. "I'm afraid I was not properly prepared for the latter."

"Well, thank goodness I rescued you from such a dull fate. You're far too sharp-witted and strong-willed to last long under the stern gaze of an abbess. You're made to ride at the side of a king and help him manage his kingdom."

Margaret's heart filled with a mix of pride—a sin—and trepidation. Did others think this about her as well? "I strive to maintain humility appropriate to my station."

He roared again with laughter. They emerged from the

forest into an open plain. A stag started at their appearance
and bounded away.

"Your station is as my queen. Humility is the realm of
servants and lay brothers. I welcome you to speak your mind
and share advice on all matters."

~

SLIGHTLY DAMPENED BY A DRIZZLING RAIN, they arrived at
Balbarnie in the middle of the day. Used to judging the
passage of time by the sound of church bells tolling the
familiar Hours of Matins, Nones, Vespers, etc., Margaret felt
disoriented by the silence of this vast countryside.

They passed by an ancient stone circle and rode toward
another hunkering mass of thatched roofs. The smoke from
the hearths hung in the air over the settlement like a cloud of
doom. "What's happened to the wind?" asked Margaret,
struck by the eerie sight.

"You're complaining that it's not windy enough for you?"
teased Malcolm. "I'll take such blessings where I find them."

Men on foot emerged to meet them at the point where
frequent foot traffic had beaten a muddy path heading into
the settlement. Their astonishment at seeing the King of the
Scots arriving on horseback soon turned into frantic activity.

There was no ringed ditch or high palisade around the
settlement, just some animal enclosures outside the houses.
Still, Margaret felt a twinge of unease as they rode closer.
Malcolm surveyed the scene calmly. He stayed master of his
emotions in all situations. They approached the tallest and
longest building, clearly the thane's hall. Malcolm asked his
guards to hold the horses, and he dismounted then helped
Margaret down from her horse.

The thane was a youngish man with straggly brown hair

and a pale face with angry blue eyes. He approached Malcolm with a look of confusion and alarm on his face and a noticeable lack of words on his tongue.

"Diarmad Mac Aidh," said Malcolm, in his big gruff voice, "We come to offer our condolences."

"Two vicious escaped slaves have brought tragedy to my door," said Diarmad. His voice had almost the air of a question, like he was testing this as a theory.

"One of the people you've accused was my guest," said Malcolm. Margaret stared at him. This was a far different tack than she'd expected. "So I take these accusations very seriously. Please show me where the crime occurred and tell me exactly what happened."

Diarmad hesitated. "The body's been buried."

"What? So soon? Who performed the services?"

Now he swallowed. "I couldn't bear to have my wife's dear body resting above ground in such a state."

Malcolm took a step toward him. Diarmad Mac Aidh was not a short man, but Malcolm still towered over him by a span. "What state was her body left in?"

"They stabbed her! Like ferocious wild beasts savaging their prey. I could hardly bear to look upon her poor corpse."

Margaret watched him with both doubt and hope swelling in her heart. Not only would the two half-starved women have difficulty committing such a brutal act, they would have no reason to.

"Where did this cruel and vicious murder take place?" asked Malcolm, as if sympathetic. "Show me the very spot."

Diarmad turned and marched into the open door of the hall. It was narrower than Mac Duff's, shaped more like an old-fashioned longhouse. A fire blazed in the hearth in the center of the hall, and Margaret welcomed a brief respite from winter's chill. Grizel asked if she wished to remove her cloak but she whispered that she'd prefer to keep it on. She wanted to stay ready for a rapid departure if needed.

Their damp cloaks steamed as Diarmad took them across the hall and past a partial screen wall that separated the end of the hall from the rest of the space. A bed with crude wood carvings and heavy curtains crouched against the wall on one side.

"This is your bed?" asked Malcolm.

"Yes." He walked past the bed to a dark wool curtain on the far wall. He lifted the curtain to reveal a door with a low lintel. "She was killed in this doorway."

"Where does it lead to?" asked Margaret.

Diarmad stared at her as if she had three eyes. Then he looked at Malcolm as if wondering if he should answer this strange female creature who had dared to utter words in their presence.

"Answer my wife," said Malcolm gruffly.

Diarmad answered by lifting a heavy iron latch and opening the door to reveal a misty view of a meadow with a sheep enclosure occupying part of it.

Margaret's heart sank slightly. If his wife had died in her own bed it would be almost certain that he'd done it himself. But if she'd surprised someone breaking in...

Malcolm walked over to the doorway, and Margaret followed him closely. Signs of recent scrubbing had not entirely removed the dark stain of blood on either the flagstone threshold or the earthen floor inside.

"How did she come to be surprised here?" asked Malcolm.

"I hardly know," said Diarmad. "I was fast asleep in my bed." He indicated the curtained bed.

"That's very close," said Margaret. He'd have been less than the length of a good horse away from where his wife was being killed in the doorway. "Did her screams wake you?"

Diarmad raised his hands to his head and pressed them to either side of his brow in a theatrical gesture. "To my shame and regret, they didn't. As anyone will tell you I drank a great deal that night and slept like the dead. I didn't discover her death until I woke in the morning and found her bleeding in the doorway."

"Then how do you know who did it?" she asked.

"Because two strange women were seen hurrying away from the settlement in the early hours of that morning, both soaked in her blood! Then a shepherd saw them just over the hill."

Margaret frowned. Bloody clothes would be damning indeed.

"Did they not stop the pair?" asked Malcolm.

"No, because no one knew at that time that anything had gone amiss."

"I'd say two women with blood-soaked clothes is something amiss," said Malcolm, his voice deeper than usual. "Would it not be hospitable to at least ask if they're injured and need assistance?"

"I suppose they thought their clothing was just wet. It wasn't until after the murder was discovered that they realized it was blood that darkened their cloaks."

Doubt—and its companion hope—rose again in Margaret's chest. Whether or not the women had blood on their clothes would surely tell much of this story.

"Who discovered the body? Did you find her on awakening?"

"To my eternal mortification she was found by another." The thane rubbed his face. "The girl feeding the fowl before dawn stumbled across her as she lay there."

Malcolm frowned. "So she lay dead there for some time?"

"It seems she did." Diarmad wouldn't look at them.

"Was the door open or closed?" asked Margaret. There

was blood on both sides of it. Surely if the door had stood open in the night, a cold wind off the lake would have rattled the bed curtains and disturbed his sleep.

"The door was closed."

"Then how is there blood on the threshold and inside the room?" asked Margaret.

"Blood flows like water," he said, looking at her as if she might be daft.

"So, was she killed inside the room or outside it?"

"Outside of course. I'm sure I would have wakened if she'd been stabbed to death so close to me."

Margaret looked at her husband to see if he believed any of this unlikely account. While blood did flow, would it flow up over a stone threshold? And in these almost-freezing temperatures she struggled to believe it would flow much at all.

"I must see her body," said Malcolm.

"As I told you, she's been buried. I could not bear to look upon her desecrated corpse."

"Take me to where she's buried," said Malcolm.

Diarmad frowned but led them out the door. They walked along a slippery path and around a small turf building with a carved wooden cross in front of it. "She's buried in the graveyard next to the chapel."

"She died unshriven, and has had no funeral services, yet she's been buried in hallowed ground?" Margaret couldn't make sense of this. The rushed burial only deepened her suspicions that Diarmad was involved in his wife's murder.

"Where else should she be buried? She was a good Christian woman." Diarmad's nose reddened, though Margaret suspected it was either the cold or growing anger, rather than grief. Even when a man didn't shed tears—having learned to bite them down lest he reveal weakness to an enemy—he showed other signs of emotion that she'd learned to read.

A pile of freshly disturbed earth the length and breadth of a woman's body revealed her hiding place in the small churchyard. "How many people saw her before she was buried?" asked Margaret.

"Probably everyone in the settlement," said Diarmad. "She lay stretched out on the ground, wrapped in her cloak, while they dug the hole."

"How were you notified of her death?"

"I heard the goose girl scream at the door and that roused me. She screamed and screamed and I jumped out of bed." He paused and did the hand-to-head gesture that he apparently thought signified great grief—"and there was my dear wife crumpled in a heap on the ground."

"Did you call for help or pick her up yourself?"

"I picked her up."

"And put her on the bed?" asked Margaret. The bed was mere feet away from the door.

"On the bed? She was drenched in blood. It would have stained the curtains which were woven by my mother." They were a russet-colored base with a green stripe running through it both ways, in a typical pattern of the Scots.

"So where did you lay her?"

"I took the padded coverlet off the bed and wrapped her in it, then laid her outside the door."

Margaret glanced at Malcolm. "I hope that if you found me stabbed to death you'd place me on the bed and not in the cold mud."

"Perish the thought, my dear," Malcolm crossed himself, and Margaret did, too. Diarmad followed suit.

"And who examined the body, after you had wrapped her up? Did jurors come, or a justice?" Margaret knew that the thanes and mormaers served as justices over their realms, but were they accountable to anyone at all?

"Why would I allow any eyes to gaze upon the desecrated body of my dear wife? Mac Duff himself is justiciar for all our kin and clan and he knows the truth of what happened." His growing anger showed in the increasingly tense lines of his body. His shoulders seemed to be rising toward his ears.

"My men will dig up her body to examine it."

"What? You can't!"

"I am King of the Scots and you'll find that I can," said Malcolm, looking him dead in the eye.

"But why?"

"You've accused my guest, who I brought into your father-in-law's home, of murdering her. I must determine for myself if I believe this to be true."

Diarmad seemed to relax a little. Perhaps he thought he was under suspicion and now remembered that another stood accused. "Surely, since the two women were seen in blood-drenched clothing not a mile from here, that proves what happened."

"Who saw them? I wish to speak to these witnesses."

Margaret felt a sense of panic. Every person in this settlement lived their lives in service to or with the forbearance of their thane, so if he told them to say one thing they'd hardly say another. "You must stay here and not speak to anyone."

Diarmad opened his mouth as if to make a haughty reply, then glanced at Malcolm and mastered his tongue. Two guards hovered in the doorway and Malcolm asked one to watch Diarmad while he sat in his hall, and another to find tools and helpers to exhume the body of Beitris from her freshly dug grave.

~

A CHILLY FOG descended as two servants started digging with primitive farm tools. Margaret pulled her cloak tighter around her. She'd sent Grizel into the hall to make sure the guards didn't slack in their duty of watching Diarmad or get tricked by him into being distracted.

She and Malcolm stood watch, offering prayers, while poor Beitris's body was extracted from its earthy tomb.

"Where is the priest who performs the services in your chapel?" asked Margaret of one of the servants doing the digging. You could hardly have a chapel without a priest.

"He left some months ago."

"What do you mean, he left?"

"I don't know my lady. He was gone before All Saints' Day." A young man with greasy blond curls spoke. "Maybe he went on a pilgrimage."

"So he's expected to return?"

"We haven't been told, my lady," said the other servant, a grizzled man of two score years or more, with a weathered face and thick muscled arms beneath his tunic.

"So you've been two months with no priest to say mass here?"

"Yes, my lady."

Margaret looked at Malcolm. She could barely imagine the privation of going without holy services for two weeks, let alone two months. Malcolm shrugged. Perhaps such a thing was more common than it should be here, where priests ready to serve a congregation might be thin on the ground.

Holy men in Scotland seemed to prefer a hermit-like existence or small communities of their own kind instead of living among ordinary men. She resolved to discuss the matter with the bishop when she returned to Dunfermline.

Their shovels revealed woven fabric barely two feet

below the soil. Margaret gasped at the sight. "Such a shallow grave would surely be dug up by dogs or pigs."

"Indeed it is not anywhere close to deep enough," said Malcolm. "But that may be because the soil is frozen further down. "Perhaps they planned to rebury her after the spring thaw. Such a thing is not uncommon here."

Now carefully scooping the soil away, they revealed the wrapped corpse. The servants grew visibly uncomfortable the closer they came to pulling Beitris's lifeless body from the ground.

"What are they saying?" asked Margaret of Malcolm, as the servants muttered to each other. She couldn't understand their rustic speech.

"They're worried that her spirit might haunt them for disturbing her rest."

Margaret inhaled slowly. Was such a thing possible? She'd had odd experiences that sometimes made her wonder if the spirits of her ancestors hovered nearby. She crossed herself. "Beitris can surely only rest when the circumstances of her murder are discovered and the killer brought to justice. Tell them that."

Malcolm repeated her words to the servants. She could understand him because he didn't speak with their thick accent and odd regional words. She'd have to ask Grizel to help her become more familiar with the speech of the common people so she could understand and speak it better herself.

The two servants bent over the body, one at her feet and one at her head, and lifted her gingerly out of her shallow grave. They struggled under the weight of her corpse, though it looked insubstantial enough to Margaret, then laid it on the ground nearby.

Margaret hated the idea of unwrapping the dead woman

outside in the cold, under the unforgiving iron sky. "Is there a room we can bring her into?"

Malcolm shook his head. "They won't want to bring a dead person inside after burial. It would be bad luck." He asked them to unwrap her so they could see the body.

Crossing themselves and uttering fervent prayers, the servants unwrapped the damp and soil-stained fabric and pulled its corners away from the body.

CHAPTER 12

argaret flinched at the sight of Beitris's white face with its dead eyes open and staring blankly toward Heaven. Her face was unmarked, though a loose strand of hair crossed in front of her nose. Margaret felt an urge to push the dead girl's hair behind her ears, but she crossed herself again instead.

The woman's wool gown was so totally soaked in blood that only the sleeves and hem revealed the original moss-green color of the garment. Her pregnancy was quite advanced, and clearly visible through her clothes.

"She was killed at night but she's wearing her gown as if it was daytime."

"That's not so unusual in the cold of winter," said Malcolm. "She may even be wearing another one under it. People often sleep fully dressed." Margaret knew that servants generally did this, due to sleeping exposed to the chilly night air rather than in curtained beds, but it surprised her that a noblewoman would sleep in her clothes.

As her eyes adjusted to the shock of seeing all the blood, Margaret started to notice tears in the fabric where a blade had plunged through it and pierced her body. She counted three holes.

"Please turn her over," asked Malcolm. The servants hesitated, clearly appalled by the awful bloody sight of their mistress and reluctant to touch her poor murdered body again. "She won't haunt you."

Their king's promise seemed to give them courage, and they went to each end of her and attempted to turn her. The effort was halting and made Margaret shudder as Beitris's poor body flopped and flailed while they struggled. A gasp behind her made her realize that others had come out of nearby buildings and were watching at a distance.

Should she shoo them away? Or was it better to have witnesses to their mistress's fate? If they believed Aelgith and her daughter had done this then the pair were doomed. But if someone else had...perhaps even their own master? Better for them all to know the truth.

Beitris's back, though soaked with blood, bore only one tear, a longish one where perhaps a knife thrust had bounced off the bones of her ribs.

"I wonder if her attacker surprised her from behind with this blow," said Margaret softly. "Then when she turned he followed with the rest of them."

"He, or she," said Malcolm.

"You really think a woman rained all these violent blows upon her?" Did Malcolm still think poor, frail Aelgith had done this?

"I've seen some things in my time that would make the Devil gasp."

"Surely a degree of strength would be required to pierce the sturdy wool of her fabric, let alone flesh and bone."

"That is true." Malcolm approached the body and leaned over it, inspecting the single slash in her back.

We should undress her to better examine the wounds. The

prospect made Margaret's stomach turn and she worried that she might not be able to maintain her composure at the sight of a woman's dead, naked body exposed to the cruel sky under the gaze of her people.

No. Better not to. They could see enough already.

"Can you tell what kind of weapon was used?" she asked.

"A knife," said Malcolm with certainty. "Not a long one. The kind of knife any man might have in his belt."

She moved toward him and leaned close to his ear. "Can you ask to see Diarmad's knife?"

Malcolm seemed to consider this. "I shall ask to see the knives of each man in the settlement, starting with him."

Margaret admired this rather diplomatic solution. They'd be able to examine his without pointing the finger of accusation. "Can we wrap her back up again?" She hated the sight of poor Beitris face-down on the ground.

"Turn her over and wrap her back up, but don't rebury her yet," he told the servants. "One of you must stay with her to keep animals and curious people at bay."

"We could put her in the hay shed," said the younger man who had helped to dig her up. He spoke nervously. "She could rest on the hay."

Moved by his concern for the dead woman, Margaret touched Malcolm's sleeve. "I think that's a good idea, do you?"

"I do indeed. Well suggested, young man. Please place her there and stay with her body."

THEY LEFT poor dead Beitris to the servants and headed back into the hall through the same back door that led directly into the thane's chamber. Diarmad paced across the far end of the small chamber, clearly itching to leave it. He looked up when they entered.

"May I see your knife?" asked Malcolm.

Diarmad froze. "Why?"

"I wish to examine the knife of every man in the settlement, starting with yours."

Diarmad frowned and heaved a sigh as if this was a great inconvenience, but he pulled his dagger from the sheath at his waist and handed it to Malcolm. Malcolm took it and walked from the chamber into the hall.

Margaret stood back waiting for Diarmad to follow him. The surly thane looked almost apoplectic with fury that another man—even his king—had casually taken command of his hall.

"Summon your men to come and present their daggers," said Malcolm without even looking back at him. Instead, he surveyed the hall, taking in the various men and women hovering around the fire and in the shadowy corners. Would any of these have a reason to murder their thane's wife?

Margaret itched to examine Diarmad's dagger. She watched closely as Malcolm walked to the table nearest the fire—where the light was best—and placed it on the scarred wood surface. The blade had an incised design like a curling vine, and the wood handle had a different design of cross hatching.

Once Diarmad had moved away and busied himself with commanding his men to surrender their knives, Margaret leaned in close to Malcolm's ear again. "That design would hold blood unless carefully washed. The blade as well as the handle."

"The light in here isn't good enough to see it, though. We must take it outside, but we'll wait until more of them are gathered so our suspicion isn't too evident."

Margaret wondered at his hesitation. "Are you worried

he'll attack you?" She glanced around and was reassured to see two of Malcolm's armed men standing close by.

"I don't know the man well enough to know what he'll do," said Malcolm under his breath. "He's young and they do say he's foolish. I've never relied on him as an ally other than as one of a large party under Mac Duff's command."

The men surrounded the table, brandishing their knives and slapping them down on the wood surface. The sight of so many unsheathed blades—and so close to her husband—discomfited Margaret greatly. The flickering firelight from the hearth illuminated the polished edges of the blades—and the flashing eyes of their owners. The men were not happy to part with their knives and viewed both Malcolm and Margaret with deep suspicion. She attempted to maintain an expression of quiet composure.

More men swept into the hall, bringing a chill that dissipated the warmth of the fire, and laid their knives before them until there were at least three dozen. Most were of rustic construction with little to no ornamentation, but each had a sharp and shiny blade that could slit the throat of a ewe —or pierce the gown and chest of a slim woman—as quickly as they could slice a carrot or cut a switch from a bush.

Margaret asked Grizel to find a basket to carry the knives out into daylight, and she hurried away to ask a servant for one. Grizel returned with a good-sized one and gathered the knives into it. "How will everyone know whose knife is whose?" she asked, since many of them had the same plain handle and blade.

"A man's knife is as individual as his thumbprint," said Malcolm.

"I'm not sure I'd know my own thumbprint in a big pile of them," said Grizel.

"Trust me, each man will know his own knife as intimately as he knows his wife," said Malcolm with a grin.

Grizel carried the basket out of the hall through the main door, and Malcolm took Margaret's arm and they followed her.

The bright daylight and grit from the smoky atmosphere of the hall stung Margaret's eyes and made her blink. Once her vision adjusted, her gaze honed in on the distinctive ornamentation of Diarmad Mac Aidh's knife, where it sat at the edge of the low, wide basket probably more accustomed to carrying laundry to the river.

"May I?" she asked Malcolm.

He nodded and she pulled out the thane's knife and held it up to the light. Malcolm pulled another, and asked one of his men to look at a third, perhaps to distract from Margaret's singular focus on their host's blade.

As she'd suspected, the curved incisions in the blade held brownish debris. Dried blood. The blade had been wiped, but not washed, which would have likely removed the residue. She peered at the handle, where the cross-hatched design similarly held onto grime. "There's blood on this knife," she said quietly to Malcolm. "Have a look."

She handed him the blade and he held it up at eye level so the light from the sky fell directly on it. "I see it." He frowned at her. "But if he stabbed his wife," he said softly, "surely he'd have blood on his clothes."

"He might have removed them," she suggested quietly. "We should search his chamber, his chests, dig in and around his bed."

Malcolm nodded. He instructed the guards to examine the knives and put aside any that showed traces of blood. Then—to Margaret's horror—he approached Diarmad Mac Aidh and showed him the blade.

"What of it?" said the thane. "I skinned a hare yesterday."

"Why?" asked Malcolm. While it would be quite normal

for a peasant to prepare such a creature for his stewpot, the thane had servants to do the work.

"Am I supposed to sit at my table twiddling my thumbs?"

"Who saw you do it?" asked Margaret.

Once again he stared at her as if a cat had suddenly started to talk. "I don't know. Anyone might have, I suppose."

"Where did you skin the hare?" she persisted. "Inside the hall?"

"I'd hardly want hare guts on my dining table," he said quietly. "I did it outside."

"Where?" asked Malcolm, probably growing irritated at Diarmad's dismissive treatment of his wife and queen.

"I don't know. Under a tree somewhere. I was just passing the time."

He's lying. She knew it as sure as she knew her own name.

"And what did you do with the skin of the hare?" asked Margaret. The flesh may have already been eaten but the skin would surely be saved to line a hood or mittens.

"I gave it to one of the lads."

"Which one?" asked Malcolm. Diarmad had the decency to squirm under the penetrating stare of his king.

"I forget. You can ask them."

Perhaps he trusted his men to lie for him. If he was the brute and bully she suspected they'd probably do it without even being asked, for fear of repercussions if they didn't.

"Come with me," said Malcolm. He headed back to the hall. Margaret hung back, waiting for Diarmad to follow him. The thane hesitated, then appeared to realize he had no choice, and stumped after him. Margaret followed at a distance, with Grizel close behind her. Malcolm still held the bloody knife in his hands.

They walked through the hall—where both men and women stood about silently, watching them, in an atmosphere of growing unease. Margaret's skin prickled under the gaze of so many eyes. Did they love their master and resent her and Malcolm for accusing him of a crime? Or did they love his wife and wish justice for her?

Back in the bedchamber, Malcolm yanked back the curtains and asked Grizel to pull the bedding off the bed. She jerked the heavy, quilted coverlet and pulled it onto the stone floor.

The dark fabric showed no signs of staining beyond normal wear, nor did the pale linen mattress cover. A feather-stuffed pillow similarly showed nothing beyond the stains of Diarmad's greasy head on it night after night.

Grizel flapped each curtain, sending a flurry of dust motes into the air that made Margaret want to sneeze, but she managed to stop herself by pinching her nose quickly. She was forced to admit that the bed itself showed no trace of blood. A chest was opened to reveal folded garments and an empty knife sheath but nothing else.

What rag did he wipe his bloody knife on? And what of his clothes? She approached Malcolm and whispered in his ear. "You must ask him to undress."

Malcolm hesitated. Such a thing was a lot for even a king to ask of one of his nobles—especially these testy Scots who'd carry a blood feud for generations over the suggestion of an insult, if the rumors were true.

Malcolm asked Margaret and Grizel to leave them alone in the room, and they hurried outside and hovered by the closed door. She could hear Diarmad's protests, but also the sound of him removing his belt and lifting his tunic over his head to reveal his undergarments. She couldn't make out their mumbled speech, but after what seemed a very long time, the door creaked open and Malcolm said that his clothes were clean.

Diarmad's lips pressed together in barely contained rage. "My honor is gravely assaulted by these accusations," he said to Malcolm. "That you ask me to undress and show my nakedness is bad enough but that you accuse me of killing my own dear wife?"

"Please show your wrists to my wife."

Diarmad Mac Aidh looked like he'd rather punch his king in the gut than turn back the sleeves of his tunic. With a great inhalation of breath, he rolled them back, which revealed that he had brown staining like dried liquid, almost like slim bracelets, around his wrists just below the sleeves of his tunic. "It's from when I skinned the hare," he hissed.

If he had blood on him, his clothes would be stained. "Why is there no blood on your sleeves?" she asked.

"Because I changed my clothes." He leveled her with a withering stare.

"Where are the clothes you took off?" she asked.

"The servants took them away to wash them."

"Please summon the servant who you gave them to."

"I don't remember such petty details."

Margaret asked Grizel to go among the servants and ask them if he'd removed clothes with small amounts of blood on the sleeves for washing. If they hadn't been washed yet, she wanted to see them.

A knifing took place at close quarters and there would be no way for him to avoid getting blood on the chest of this tunic, and maybe the skirt, as well as the arms. If someone were stabbed while their heart was still beating, the force of the heart pumping the blood would cause it to shoot out of the wound. She'd observed as much on the monastery farm of the convent at Wilton Abbey, where the farmhand's sometimes inexpert management of the butchering process was cause for a scolding.

There was no way he'd handed such blood-soaked clothes to a servant and casually told them to take them away for washing. Not without an elaborate story about killing a wild boar or some other large creature—which would also require him to produce the dead body of the animal.

Margaret's eyes lit on the brazier in a corner of the room. The fire had gone out and the coals didn't even glow hot, but it would have been lit overnight. She approached it and peered in. There was a great deal of ash—more than there should have been if servants emptied it daily.

Grizel returned quickly, having spoken to the servants who hovered anxiously nearby. None of the three responsible for attending to Diarmad's personal needs remembered taking any clothes for washing.

I thought as much. "Grizel, please sift through the ash and charcoal of this brazier, looking for scraps of burned fabric."

"Yes, my lady." Grizel glanced nervously at Diarmad Mac Aidh.

"When was the last time you saw your wife?" asked Margaret. Malcolm seemed quite content for her to ask the questions.

"In the hall after the evening meal, I suppose."

"She went to bed before you?"

"I don't recall, I was in my cups," he said gruffly. "You can ask the servants since they seem to know more about my business than I do."

"I shall take your advice," said Margaret calmly. She realized that the servants were unlikely to speak plainly in front of their master. His glowering looks already promised a fierce beating to anyone who might be in arm's reach after the king left.

"I'll be right back," she said to Malcolm, hoping that he understood the assignment—to keep Diarmad in one place and not allow him to coerce another into backing up his lies.

Outside the bedchamber, the servants hovered anxiously. A middle-aged woman with crinkled skin said she couldn't remember when her mistress had gone to bed because she'd been helping the cook clean the kitchen.

Nor could a dark-haired boy of about fifteen who'd stocked the brazier with charcoal while the master was still drinking in the hall. He couldn't remember how much ash was in it already. He said he didn't know if his mistress was in the bed or not at the time because the curtains were closed.

The third was a plump, red-haired woman of five and twenty or so—around Margaret's age—who hesitated and prevaricated, unsure of what she remembered.

"This was only two nights ago. Surely you can dredge the details from your memory. Did you hear the couple argue at all?"

"Oh no. Never," she said quickly.

"They had a loving relationship?" She looked at all three of them.

The silence told a story. Finally, the middle-aged woman spoke. "They got along fine."

"What do you mean by that?"

The servant glanced toward the door. "The master's wife knew the master had a temper and she knew best how to manage him." She spoke quietly, obviously not wanting him to hear. The screen between the hall and the bedchamber was not even a full-height wall.

"How long have you known him?"

"My whole life. He sat on my knee when he was a babe." An odd look flickered over her face at the memory. "I was a maid to his dear mother, God rest her soul."

"Has he always been quick-tempered?" asked Margaret softly. She wanted to know more about his character.

"Quick to anger and quick to recover. He's not a bad lad," she said hurriedly. "As long as you stayed out of his way when he was—" She trailed off.

"When he was what?"

"Drinking," whispered the older servant, whose tight grayish kerchief hid every scrap of her hair. "Strong drink added fire to his temper. Sometimes he'd wake up in the morning with no memory of the things he'd done. One time he almost came to blows with his own father, then the next morning he was prostrate with apologies." She crossed herself, perhaps at the memory of her dead master. "But I'm saying too much and speaking of things that are none of my business."

"Your mistress is dead and I seek to discover who killed her," said Margaret quickly. "Surely you don't wish her murderer to go free."

"I heard she was killed by two escaped slaves," said the boy who'd stocked the brazier. His gray eyes widened. "That's what everyone's saying."

Margaret felt a surge of irritation that this ridiculous accusation had reared its head again when the true killer seemed so obvious. She was also surprised that a servant would speak out of turn and to his queen. But she didn't want to dampen their will to share information that might be helpful. "Did anyone see them here, near the hall?"

"They were seen running up the hill over yonder," said the boy. "Away from the houses."

"Who saw them?"

The door to the bedchamber opened and Grizel's anxious face appeared. "Come back in, my lady. I found something."

CHAPTER 13

*O*n the brink of hearing some story—which would need refuting—about the missing women, Margaret was reluctant to stop her questioning. But had Grizel found evidence that Diarmad Mac Aidh burned his bloody clothes? This would be solid evidence of his guilt and would absolve the escaped women of Beitris's murder.

She told the servants to wait where they stood and followed Grizel back into the bedchamber. Grizel led her to the brazier and bent over it. Margaret peered into the pile of white ashes and the burned remains of charred wood. Grizel reached into the ashes and plucked out something with her thumb and finger. "Charred fabric."

Margaret took the tiny fragment between her own thumb and finger. "I must look at this in daylight." Malcolm and Diarmad were in a discussion about the boar population in a nearby forest—no doubt her husband was wisely keeping him calm and occupied while they looked for evidence. Grizel opened the back door, with its still blood-stained threshold, and she stepped outside.

Blinking in the light, she tried to make out the outlines of the tiny blackened item in her fingers. She could see the crisscross pattern of woven fibers. That pattern did not occur in nature and was clearly man-made.

Margaret held the burned fabric up to the light. The morsel was tiny, barely the size of a thumbprint. The fibers were so fully charred that no color remained. "Is there more? It would be helpful to see the color of the cloth."

Grizel went back inside, and Margaret took a moment to look around the doorway again. The area had been churned by recent footfalls—including her own—so there was no way to discern more about where Beitris had been killed or how she'd fallen. Even Beitris's blood had been trampled into the dark mud and was gone almost everywhere except the threshold and the stone floor just inside it.

Grizel came back with another two morsels, one larger and one even smaller. Both were singed to the point of almost total destruction. Despite holding each of them up to the light and peering at them closely, she could make out no traces of color.

Margaret sighed. "Without any color it'll be hard to prove that it's from Diarmad's tunic," she said quietly. "He could easily claim that he'd tossed a dirty rag in there, or that a servant had." Burning rags and other rubbish in the nearest fire was unremarkable. "But save them. They may yet come in useful."

Margaret walked back through the bedchamber. Malcolm and Diarmad's conversation had moved on to the construction of his new tower, with its second-floor hall that enjoyed the heat from the fires below and comfortable distance from the damp ground. She passed quickly back into the hall and was relieved to find the three servants still nervously standing there.

Unfortunately, they'd now been granted time to consult

among themselves and perhaps even agree on a story that might—or might not—reflect what happened.

"Remember that God sees all and he knows the truth of what happened to Beitris. Our duty is to discover what he saw." She hoped her words would put the fear of God into them and steer their tongues toward the truth. "Who saw the two women running toward the hill?"

"I did," said the red-haired girl, who'd been so unsure of when Beitris went to bed. Her name was Mary. "I was out at first light to look for eggs and I noticed movement on the horizon. I looked up and saw two figures running over the crest of the hill."

"Take me to where you were standing."

The dimpled girl, whose gown fit a little too tightly over her full chest, took them through the hall and out the front door. They walked to the right and passed a low shed for animals, to where there was a wide view of a nearby hill. As she'd described, the lower areas were treed, which gave the round top of the hill the look of the bald pate of a tonsured monk.

"How could you tell they were women?"

"They both wore long gowns, which they held up with their hands."

"Could you see their faces?"

She shook her head. Red curls escaped from her wool kerchief whipped against her face in the wind. "I didn't. One even turned to look back, perhaps to see if they were being followed, but there wasn't enough light to make out a face. And they were too far away by then anyway."

"So you would swear before a judge that you saw two women running away."

"I would," said Mary, with conviction.

"But you could not say who they were?"

"That's true," she admitted.

"Which makes me wonder if they were perhaps people from this very settlement, perhaps chasing a stray ewe or pursuing a fat hare in the early hours of the morning?"

Mary hesitated. "I suppose that's possible. But I don't know who would do that. They didn't look familiar. And the shepherd boy saw them running down the other side of the hill. He was close enough to see the blood on their clothes."

Margaret's heart sank. Tiny black fragments of cloth versus two trusted servants who said they'd seen two strange women running away from the scene of a bloody murder would not likely buy Aelgith and Osgifu's freedom before any justice.

Her only hope was to find the two women and extract the truth of what happened from them. If Diarmad's people found them first they'd likely be killed before sunrise so they couldn't testify to their own innocence.

Margaret frowned and looked at Mary. "If you were running away from this place, hoping to hide yourself from pursuit, where would you go?"

The young woman seemed confused and alarmed by the question. "Why would I run away from my home where I've lived my whole life?"

"I'm not saying you would, I'm trying to determine where the escaped women might have run to." If they'd run up to the top of the hill, it might have been to better see the terrain and choose their route.

Margaret knew that Aelgith and Osgifu had likely left the local area by now and crossed water somewhere. The dogs would have found them otherwise.

Mary hesitated. "There are some natural caves by the coast at Wemyss. They say people live there for months at a time if they've nowhere else to go. And there's the forest west of there, which is dark and dense enough for a person to hide. It has hares and doves to eat if a person could catch them."

"Thank you." She glanced toward the door of the bedchamber, which stood closed. "Did your master and your mistress ever argue?"

Panic flashed over the servant's face. "I wouldn't say so," she said in a high thin voice. Margaret hoped she might continue, but her lips clamped shut.

"Did he ever get angry at her? Perhaps after he'd been drinking?" She saw the red-haired girl struggling, wondering how much trouble any statement might get her into. "Remember that the Lord is our final judge," she said quietly but firmly. "Untruths are boulders on the path to Heaven."

Mary blinked rapidly and her chest rose as she drew in a harsh breath. "I don't want to speak ill of the dead."

"We're trying to learn who killed your mistress, who can no longer speak for herself. Did she argue with her husband?"

"Sometimes, my lady. She'd find fault with him and he didn't like that."

"He'd become violent?"

"He does sometimes get...disturbed when he's drunk too much. He'll lash out at anything and anyone. Even the dogs."

"Could he have killed your mistress, perhaps without even realizing what he was doing?"

Mary's whole face was taut, and her brow furrowed beneath her rustic wool head covering. "I couldn't say, my lady. I didn't see or hear anything."

Margaret nodded. "I believe you're telling the truth." She looked at the next servant, an older woman. "Did you hear—or see—anything unusual on the night of your mistress's death?"

She shook her head rapidly. "We went to sleep in the

kitchen by the fire." The kitchen building sat near the hall, but both had thick walls and heavy thatch.

"You don't sleep in the hall in case your master or mistress needed a servant in the middle of the night?"

The older woman and young Mary looked at each other. "No, my lady," said Mary. "The master doesn't like to be disturbed in the night. If they needed anything they'd come looking for us."

Margaret looked around the hall. The bedchamber was up one end. The kitchen and pantries were connected by a covered passage at the opposite end. "Who sleeps closest to the bedchamber?"

"Del here sleeps near the fire to keep it from going out overnight." She gestured to the dark-haired boy, who'd been very quiet. He didn't look to be more than about seven years old. "He can sleep through anything. That's why the master chose him to do it."

"What about guards?" Margaret couldn't imagine a noble sleeping without armed guards nearby in case of a surprise attack.

"They're in the settlement only a shout away," said the older woman.

"So there's no one in the hall overnight except the dogs and one small boy?" asked Margaret, incredulous. It wasn't a huge hall but this seemed like a waste of heated space in such a harsh climate.

"That's right, my lady. The master sometimes gets up and walks around in the night, and it doesn't do to disturb him."

Now it was Margaret's turn to blink in confusion. "He walks around outside, or in the hall?"

"In the hall."

"Don't the dogs wake up and bark?"

"I suppose they're used to it. And he might beat them if they did. So they know to be quiet."

Margaret liked this man less every moment. What kind of villain would beat a dog trying to guard its household? An odd thought occurred to her. "When he walks at night, is he awake or asleep?" She looked at the boy, who'd have been most likely to see him do it.

Again the servants looked at each other. "I don't know," said Del. His gray eyes widened again. "If I hear his footsteps at night I lie still and hope he doesn't notice me."

"We know better than to go near him when he's like that," said the younger woman.

"Why?" said Margaret.

There was a long pause, then Mary spoke. "Just what we've always been told, my lady."

She crouched down to be closer to eye level with the young boy, who shrank away from her. "Did you hear or see anything out of the usual on the night your mistress was killed?"

Wide eyed and white lipped, the boy backed right into Mary, who put her hands on his shoulders. "No, my lady." His voice trembled. Was he telling the truth or not? Would the evidence of such a young boy even be taken seriously in a trial for the murder of a nobleman?

Margaret glanced at the door to the bedchamber and wondered what Malcolm had found to talk about with Diarmad Mac Aidh to keep him engaged and out of their hair for so long. Whatever it was, she praised his cunning.

She was curious to learn how long Diarmad had been the Thane of Balbarnie. "When did your master's father die?"

"Three years ago," said the middle-aged woman, brow furrowed. "God rest his blessed soul. He was a good and kind man."

"And his wife? Diarmad's mother?"

"She died right along with him. A broken heart, they said."

Margaret crossed herself along with the rest of them. "Where did Diarmad sleep when his father was alive?"

The older woman licked her lips. "As a lad he slept in the hall, along with his sisters and a brother. But when his midnight wanderings started they built him a house on the edge of the settlement so he wouldn't disturb everyone in the night."

"How long ago was that?"

"Five years at least," said the older woman. "He went to fight for the king with his father and brother, but he was never the same after he came back. He turned jumpy and short-tempered and the nighttime wanderings started."

"Diarmad is the oldest son, I take it?" she asked. "So he became thane when his father died?"

"His brother Oengus was the eldest but he died in a hunting accident a few months before his father fell sick."

"So Diarmad never expected to be Thane of Balbarnie, and found himself thrust into the role with little warning?"

"Yes, my lady. It all happened in such a hurry."

"Do people respect him?"

The servant hesitated. "When he married Mac Duff's daughter, that was a big boost to his standing. Mac Duff is a great man in these parts."

"Is Mac Duff feared, or respected, by the common people?"

This time, she responded with no hesitation. "Both, my lady."

Margaret noted with alarm that darkness had fallen outside even though it was only a few hours past midday. This meant they'd have to stay here for the night, as guests of Diarmad Mac Aidh.

~

DURING THE EVENING meal and what passed for entertainments—a sad old man with a shock of white hair and his flute—Margaret ate her food cautiously and sparingly. She was uncomfortable breaking bread and drinking ale with a man who might well have the blood of his wife on his hands. She expected Diarmad to offer his king his bed for the night, and to find somewhere else to sleep, but instead he arranged for the servants to make accommodations for her and Malcolm to sleep in a different building, perhaps the one he had been exiled to before his father died.

Instead of being offended and discomfited by this, Margaret felt relieved. She didn't want to sleep under the same roof as a man who might have stabbed his wife to death —possibly in a drunken stupor or even while sleep-walking. She relished the opportunity to have walls, lined with her husband's loyal armed guards, between herself, her husband, and their unpleasant host. She kept Grizel with them again, sleeping near the fire, for her own safety.

She'd longed for the chance to be alone with Malcolm, so she could discuss the discoveries of the day. But once they lay in bed together, she was surprised that he didn't share her convictions about how to proceed. "Don't you think we should arrest him?" she asked.

"He's subject to the laws of Clan Mac Duff. If Mac Duff decides he should be arrested, he will be."

"You'll tell him what we learned today. You'll send a messenger?"

"I will indeed."

"So the thane will be arrested and tried?"

"If Mac Duff wants it."

"Surely he'll want his daughter's killer to be hanged?"

"It's customary among the Mac Duffs to pay a fine instead of a death penalty."

"What? Even if it means letting a murderer walk free?" Margaret couldn't believe this.

"They decided it didn't make sense for members of the clan to kill each other," said Malcolm. "And since I need as many men as possible available for muster in times of war, I can't argue with the logic. Especially if I'm in need of a good fighter."

Her heart sank. The logic of needing access to a practiced company of ruthless murderers appalled her. And it wasn't like he'd killed a stranger! "What kind of fine would you get for killing the mormaer's daughter?"

"Something substantial. Eighty cows, perhaps."

"Does Diarmad Mac Aidh have eighty cows?"

"If he doesn't, he'll have to steal them."

"You're joking. Aren't you?" Was he? She had a terrible feeling that he wasn't.

Malcolm nuzzled her cheek gently. "As of right now, we have no particular proof that Diarmad Mac Aidh has killed anyone. The servants swear up and down that the two women did it. They were seen running away and at least one person—a shepherd who saw them at close quarters—swears that they were soaked in blood."

Margaret frowned. "That can't be true. You know how stories get twisted."

"I do, but if every man, woman and child in the country-side stands up to swear that Diarmad Mac Aidh is innocent, I can hardly hang him for murder. You do see that?"

"The servants mentioned that he has drunken rages."

"He and half the men in my kingdom. I don't wish to interfere in clan business when it's not my problem to solve."

Margaret pressed her hand into his chest. She could feel his strong heart beating under his linen shirt. "You're the king. You're the ultimate authority to dispense justice as you see fit."

"It's my duty as king to keep my subjects content so they don't scheme amongst each other and gather forces to rise up against me."

"Would they do that?"

"The men of this country are not shy about taking power away from someone they consider unworthy to wield it."

"So you must tiptoe around your own countrymen? I can't imagine Edward the Confessor thinking like this."

"Edward the Confessor was never king of the Scots. You need to get some sleep. If Diarmad Mac Aidh is a murderer, he will be punished."

"I'm surprised his wife's family aren't baying for his blood."

"As far as they know, their daughter was killed by our guest Aelgith and their escaped slave Osgifu. Their fury is directed at the two women."

"The only way we can prove their innocence is to find them and discover the truth of where they were when the murder happened."

Malcolm's silence did not offer the encouragement she sought. Margaret spent a fitful night of sleep. She worried that a killer might go unpunished—except by the duty of an onerous amount of cattle thieving, that he would surely outsource to underlings. And she worried more that the two exiles would either spend the rest of their lives with a charge of murder hanging over their heads—or would meet a swift and cruel fate at the hands of their captors.

In the morning they were woken by a sharp knock on the door and a shouted message from one of Malcolm's men. "They've found the missing women, my king! Arrested in the woods near Dunfermline. And both of them soaked in blood!"

CHAPTER 14

*M*argaret was grateful for the excuse to leave the unpleasant thane's settlement at the break of dawn and without many niceties. They broke yesterday's bread—quite literally—while waiting for their horses to be tacked up, rather than sitting at the table.

Malcolm promised Diarmad that if the two women were found to have killed his wife, he'd have the opportunity to seek justice against them. Margaret bit her tongue and prayed for the humility to support her husband—her king—even when she bitterly disagreed with him.

And the morning's news brought fresh questions. How could she argue for their innocence if they'd been found with blood on their clothes? As they rode across the hard-edged and unforgiving winter landscape, she prayed for the grace to admit that she'd been wrong about the women—if she was wrong.

They arrived back in Dunfermline in the afternoon. Margaret wanted to rush immediately to the fortified building where prisoners were kept under armed guard, but Malcolm insisted that they eat a good meal first. When she

149

protested, he observed that she owed it to the child in her belly, even if she had little appetite.

Thoroughly chastened—it was his child as well—she did her best to choke down a steaming pottage of barley and root vegetables. Before she had the chance to quit the table and hurry off to the stone-walled prison, Malcolm announced that the two prisoners would be brought into the hall for questioning before him and four of his most trusted advisors.

Margaret braced herself for the arrival of the women. The last time she'd seen Aelgith, she'd pleaded with her not to do anything foolish. Aelgith had ignored her warnings and kept her own counsel, apparently to disastrous effect.

She wasn't the only person to gasp when the women were brought in. In addition to looking bedraggled, they did both have dark, spreading stains across the front of their gowns. Margaret crossed herself at the grim sight.

Aelgith's eyes met hers for a brief instant before falling to the floorboards. Was Aelgith afraid to meet her gaze because she'd committed a murder? Or because she'd failed to trust her?

"Is that blood on your clothes?" asked Malcolm, in about as gruff a voice as Margaret had ever heard.

The two women nodded, lips pressed together.

"Whose blood?"

Aelgith's lips fluttered, but words didn't rise to them.

"Beitris, wife of Diarmad Mac Aidh," uttered Osgifu, in a tiny, thin voice. "But we didn't kill her—"

"Silence!" barked Malcolm. "I'll ask the questions and you answer them."

Margaret almost jumped out of her chair. Why would he stop the girl from pleading her innocence?

She reminded herself that the appearance of things sometimes mattered as much as the substance. Malcolm needed to be seen to uphold the law—and the rights and grievances of his thanes who claimed these women had wronged them.

And Osgifu knew the dead woman by name. She'd visited their hall. Did she have a reason of her own for wanting Beitris dead?

"Why did you creep away from Mac Duff's house in the middle of the night, stealing his property?" he asked of Aelgith.

Her lips trembled again. "I took only my daughter. I wanted to save her."

"Had my wife not promised you that we would try to secure her freedom?"

Aelgith swallowed. Margaret wasn't sure she had promised any such thing, though that was certainly her intent. "Yes, my lord."

"And you didn't trust her to manage your affairs?" Malcolm's harsh voice rang with accusation.

Aelgith hung her head. "I regret my decision to leave, my lord."

Margaret tried to keep her breathing steady. She'd risked her reputation to bring Aelgith with her on their journey and Aelgith had betrayed her trust.

"How did you come to be at Diarmad Mac Aidh's house in Balbarnie?"

"My daughter knew the way there, my lord, because she'd been there with her captors, who went there often to visit their daughter."

Malcolm looked doubtful. "Would it not have seemed more sensible to stay away from settlements if you're trying to hide and escape?"

"I was afraid we'd get lost and freeze to death. I know how dangerous this country is in the winter and we have no fuel or fire or way to warm ourselves."

"So you went into the settlement to beg for food or a

place by the fire?" Malcolm clearly didn't accept any of this as reasonable.

"No!" protested Aelgith, speaking over her daughter. "We were passing by the outside of it in the hour before dawn, when there was just enough light to make out the outlines of the buildings. We were stopped in our tracks by the sound of a creature whimpering."

"What kind of creature?"

"We thought it might be a wounded animal," said Osgifu. "That we might eat." Her gaze fell to the floor. "But it was a gravely injured woman, bleeding out on the moor in the dark."

"It was Beitris?"

"We didn't know that at the time," said Osgifu. The girl had found her voice. "It was too dark and she could no longer speak. She could only draw tiny breaths."

The stab wounds in her chest likely injured her lungs, though Margaret.

The furrows in Malcolm's brow grew deep. "Surely if you were trying to escape capture you should have left her there."

"Perhaps a more sensible person would have done that," said Aelgith. "But I was raised by my mother and father to tend to my fellow man in time of need. I couldn't leave her there to die in the dark and cold."

Aelgith spoke with the dignity of a Saxon noblewoman, in stark contrast with her bloodstained and filthy appearance.

Osgifu had lifted a hand to her face and now sobbed into it silently. Perhaps remembering how much they'd lost before they even stumbled across the half-dead body of a Fife noblewoman.

"So what did you do?" Malcolm asked the question more gently.

"Between us we managed to pick her up and carry her. It wasn't easy. She's not a large or heavy woman, but we're both of us weak from years of privation, and we struggled to lift her, which I suppose is why we have so much of her blood on our clothing. I managed to get under her and enclose my arms around her chest from behind, and my daughter held her legs."

"She was still alive at this time?"

"She was alive when we heard her whimpering out on the moor. We first realized she was dead when we placed her gently on the ground outside the hall."

Margaret swallowed. Could someone argue that they did kill her? If she'd been alive when found and died in their care?

"Why did you put her at the back door to the hall?"

"If we took her to the front we might have been seen by someone coming or going from the kitchen. Osgifu wanted to leave her further away so we could get away without being seen, but there were no guards awake or anyone to find her and we thought she was still alive. We wanted her to get help."

So you set her down by the back door to her own bedchamber, from which she'd recently escaped, fleeing death at the hands of her husband.

Margaret hated the irony of it. And that she couldn't say the words aloud without being seen to usurp her husband's authority in the proceedings.

"So you left her there, dead," said Malcolm. "Did you try to rouse anyone?"

"No. There was no reason to risk discovery and capture since she no longer drew breath. We hurried away from the settlement as fast as we could. Dawn rose in the east so we could find our bearings and head for the coast."

Margaret dug her nails into her palm. Had they really intended to flee back to Dunfermline and ask her—or Grizel's mother Beathag—for help again after ignoring her warnings and pleas? She wanted to be angry with the women, but their plight was so desperate that she couldn't summon any fury.

"That's when the servants must have seen them fleeing to the south," said Margaret quietly. "What reason did they have to kill or injure Beitris?"

She was killed by her husband.

She didn't dare say the words aloud, though she burned to utter them in front of everyone present. Malcolm knew her thoughts. She'd shared them with him last night and pleaded for Beitris's murder to be avenged. Surely he didn't believe these two frail women had murdered a noblewoman they barely knew—and for what?

"So you maintain that she was already injured almost to death when you came upon her."

"Yes. And there was so much blood that her gown was drenched, front and back. She must have been bleeding for some time."

Margaret looked at Malcolm, silently pleading with him to say something about their suspicions regarding Diarmad Mac Aidh. "Who do you think killed Beitris?" she asked, after a long silence.

Malcolm shot her a rather stern look. "We shall have to determine that. Beitris wasn't murdered in Diarmad Mac Aidh's hall, or in the bedchamber, or we'd have found a great deal of blood there."

"There was blood on the threshold of the bedchamber," said Margaret, not yet chastened enough to stay silent.

"That's where she lay dead," said Malcolm.

"But once a body is dead, it doesn't bleed much," said Margaret. Anyone who'd witnessed the slaying and butchery of animal flesh knew that. "So she'd have bled heavily when she was first stabbed, and while they were carrying her still-living body, but the bleeding would have slowed or even stopped by the time they placed her outside the door."

Diarmad must have murdered his wife right outside the doorway. Perhaps Beitris was trying to escape through it when he struck the first knife blow on her back.

She turned to the women. "Did you see blood on the ground outside the hall as you carried the body?"

They both shook their head. "It was before dawn. We could barely make out the buildings."

"Where were you trying to escape to when you happened across the dying woman?" asked Malcolm, cutting in.

"We were hoping to get back to England," said Aelgith. "Back to Hampshire where our accents and manners don't mark us as strangers."

"That's a long walk," he said with a frown.

"Better a long walk than a life in captivity," said Aelgith with a surprising amount of defiance.

Margaret wondered what kind of life she expected to have, as a landless, friendless, penniless widow in middle age. Or maybe she hoped to find friends still alive there. And if a husband could be found for her daughter—a farmer or tradesman perhaps—that could provide both of them with a means to survive.

She hugged herself as a shudder crept through her. The fate of war widows and orphans had clawed at her even before she met Aelgith. Poor Osgifu still wept into her hands, a tender girl of fourteen with far too much experience with the horrors of the world.

Margaret leaned toward her husband and touched his arm. "I think they've answered enough questions for now," she said softly, hoping no one could hear. "We must let them rest."

The muscles of his arm tensed under his wool robe. "Take them back to the jail."

Margaret opened her mouth to protest, but the look on her husband's face silenced her. Still sobbing, Osgifu followed her mother as they were led away with more than necessary roughness by her husband's guards.

"Shall we go for a walk, husband?" she said after she'd taken a moment to gather her thoughts. "I find myself in need of air."

"I think you'll find that the air outside will freeze your breath into a cloud in front of your face," said Malcolm. He spoke the truth. An unusual frigidity had settled over Dunfermline on their return. It came in the form of an icy mist that rolled in from the Forth. The ground in the woods around the tower had turned rock-hard and slippery.

I suppose that's a no. Margaret still struggled with knowing when to push her husband and when to stop—at least when they were in public view in the hall.

"But if you wish a breath of fresh air, I shall not deprive you of it, my love." He called for their cloaks. Margaret's heart lifted at his kind gesture. Soon they were cloaked and gloved, heading out into the wintry woods around the tower.

As soon as they were out of earshot of the tower guards and servants, Malcolm took her hand. "What secrets do you wish to whisper in my ear, my love?"

Margaret wanted to protest that she simply craved some exercise and his company, but he knew her too well for that. "You don't think the women are guilty, do you?"

Malcolm sighed. "They were found running away from the settlement, drenched in the fresh blood of the murder victim."

"But they told you in detail how that happened. Surely you don't think they were lying?"

"As king of Scotland, whose word am I to believe? That of an escaped slave who betrayed my wife's trust, or a thane of the realm whose father was a good friend to my father?"

Margaret considered this. "So tradition trumps the truth."

"The truth is yet to be discovered. You must admit that Diarmad Mac Aidh had no blood on his person, or in his hall or bedchamber."

"There were traces of it on his wrists. And there were stains of blood on the threshold."

"Where his wife lay dying after the two strangers claim to have deposited her there. What reason would he have to kill his wife, who is also the daughter of his overlord and his most powerful neighbor after myself?"

Killing the daughter of the Mormaer of Fife did seem to be an unusually ill-starred move on the part of Diarmad. "How long have they been married?"

"Not so long. Perhaps three years. And she was pregnant, soon to give him an heir, so it's not as if he'd found her barren. He has no conceivable reason for wanting his wife dead."

"Perhaps he killed her without knowing what he was doing."

Malcolm stopped walking and stared at her. "How?"

"If he was drunk to the point of insensibility, he might have lashed out at her without realizing that he could kill her."

"With a knife in his hand? I've heard of people being killed accidentally by a blow from a fist or from being shoved and hitting their head on a stone or a doorpost, but I've never heard of an accidental knifing." He looked almost entertained by the idea.

"They say he rambles about in his sleep. What if he was asleep—his mind fully elsewhere—when he took the knife and stabbed his wife in the dark? If he did it while insensible, he's surely still guilty of the crime."

"That's an interesting question," said Malcolm, after a pause. "I can't say I've ever come across a case like that, in all the years I've been pronouncing judgment. And I've seen more than a few murders in my decade as king."

"At the very least, the blame can't be made to rest on an entirely different person who just happened to be in the vicinity at the time."

"Except perhaps when they happen to be drenched from head to toe in the victim's blood."

"That is an unfortunate circumstance of their charitable deed of trying to help the injured woman!" How could he not see that?

He sighed, and they started walking again. "It may well be, but it is damning in the eyes of most people around here."

"What motive would they have to kill her? Mac Duff said it might have been for theft, when they first told us about it, since at the time they were thought to have stolen the cross. But the cross was found, so that was a lie. Diarmad Mac Aidh never even claimed that anything was stolen." Margaret could hear the desperation in her voice.

"Beitris might have surprised Aelgith and Osgifu and threatened to take them prisoner," said Malcolm.

"Why would Beitris have been outside, alone, in the night?" As a noblewoman she'd have a chamber pot to relieve herself, especially in these frigid temperatures.

"You of all people ask that, who loves to creep out of the house to attend service by herself in the dead of night?"

Margaret swallowed. Malcolm questioned the practice, but she explained that she was used to attending Matins and Lauds from her years at Wilton and felt closer to God in the silence of the night when the world slept.

"We know she couldn't have been attending services," said Margaret. "There'd been no priest at the settlement for two months. Her husband is known by all to have a temper, to the point where servants and even his trusted men will no longer sleep in the hall! What more proof do you need of his volatile and abusive nature?"

"That is strange indeed." He squeezed her hand. "And I do trust your instincts. But I have to not only do the right thing but be seen to do the right thing. As of this moment that is to defend the interests of my friends and allies, the Mormaer of Fife and the Thane of Balbarnie."

"Even at the expense of the lives of two desperate and friendless women?"

"They're not friendless. They have the greatest friend in all the land."

"Me?" Was he giving her permission to tend to their needs and protect them?

"Of course."

Hope swelled in her heart. "So can I remove them from the jail and make them comfortable while they wait for justice to run its course?"

"I think it would look better if you made them comfortable in the jail, in as inconspicuous a way as possible."

"I think I see what you mean. You must wage a campaign to change hearts before any verdict in their favor can be pronounced."

"I knew you would understand."

"But what of Diarmad Mac Aidh? You don't intend that he be punished for murdering his wife? What kind of message does that send to the men of your realm? Can they murder their wives with impunity if they simply grow tired of them?"

Malcolm stopped and turned to face her, grasping both of her fists—now clenched in frustration—in his. "Give me time, my love. I must get Mac Duff on my side. His family is powerful and I must always treat them with respect and keep them as my ally—lest they become mortal enemies."

"I understand." Margaret now wrapped her hands around

his. "I really do. You're more subtle and cunning than people think."

"And I don't need anyone to know it," said Malcolm.

"Thank Heaven for all the winding, wooded paths around the tower. They allow for private conversation." Dusk was descending on the land. The days in winter seemed so short in this part of the world that there was barely time to catch your breath between dawn and nightfall. "I shall take your counsel and provide some comforts—and some hope—for Aelgith and Osgifu, but not so much as to draw gossip and conjecture."

"I trust you to manage it well."

Margaret drew in a steadying breath. She'd betrayed her husband's trust by bringing Aelgith along on their journey without warning him of her ulterior motive. She'd not do it again.

Or at least she hoped she wouldn't.

CHAPTER 15

*B*ack in the hall, preparations were underway for the evening meal. Grizel hurried up to Margaret and removed her coat and gloves and her leather overshoes. After she returned from hanging them, Margaret summoned her to a quiet corner.

"My husband agrees that the two prisoners should be treated with kindness. We must find fresh clothes for them and water to wash them and food to nourish them, though they'll stay in the jail for now. They must have a brazier with fuel and blankets to keep them warm overnight and pillows so they can rest their heads."

Grizel looked flustered. "Where am I to find clothes for them, my lady?"

"I shall find some and leave them on the bed for you to retrieve. We must be subtle about this since they're still officially under suspicion."

"I understand, my lady." Grizel looked relieved, possibly grateful that her mistress didn't insist on washing their feet herself. Margaret regretted the missed opportunity to offer humility and charity but she'd promised her husband that her care for them would be clandestine and she intended to stand by her word.

Margaret approached her mother and sister Christina where they sat near the fire. Her mother's fingers were busy embroidering a strip of ribbon with rather jagged-looking leaves and flowers. Christina was reading a leather-bound book of psalms with tiny, neat writing, tracing each line with a finger.

They looked up as she approached. "You must tell us more about the shrine to blessed Saint Andrew," said her mother. "Did you experience any miracles in the presence of the relics?"

I'm still hoping for a miracle.

"I'll tell you all about it later, but now I have an urgent need for some clothing for two women in desperate circumstances."

"The prisoners?" asked Christina. "They're accused of murder."

"Accused wrongly, in my opinion," said Margaret, keeping her voice down. "And even if they were murderers, Christ called upon us to show mercy."

"You've already made us give away most of our clothes, darling," said her mother, needle still moving through her ribbon.

"I know, but you need new clothes anyway. Your current garments are too plain for the royal court. I've already sent out orders for new fabrics and trimmings."

Christina glared at her. "Preening ourselves in fancy raiment is not Christlike."

"Supporting the king brings peace and prosperity to the kingdom. We're simply doing our part to increase confidence in my husband's reign."

"Well said, darling," said her mother. "I shall endure the punishment of a gorgeous new wardrobe of imported silk hemmed with golden thread."

"I'd rather wear sackcloth," muttered Christina.

"If you'll part with another sturdy wool gown right now I shall have Beathag spin and weave some sackcloth especially for you," said Margaret blithely.

"And have it studded with jewels, I suppose," said Christina glumly.

"Look upon our blessings. We're safe and comfortable here in Dunfermline this winter thanks to the shelter and protection my husband granted us. We must do our best to offer the same helping hand to others in desperate circumstances. The two prisoners are Anglo-Saxon noblewomen driven from their homes and turned into slaves!"

She glanced around realizing she'd become impassioned and raised her voice.

"Are you serious?" asked Agatha. Margaret had told Christina about the women but asked her not to tell their mother, who had more of a tendency to gossip.

"Serious as old Sister Wilfreda who used to smack our knuckles with a switch. They're a mother and daughter from Hampshire in England. Their menfolk were killed by the Normans and they've been driven from pillar to post ever since."

"I can see how that might provoke someone to murder," said Christina, fingering her prayerbook. "But it's still a mortal sin."

"I'm telling you, they didn't murder anyone." Margaret tried to convey her passion while keeping her voice low. "They got blood on their clothes while trying to help an injured woman. I'm sure the woman's husband killed her and I'm trying to prove it. He, of course, is trying to blame two desperate foreigners. They're victims of circumstance who were in the wrong place at the wrong time and made the mistake of attempting an act of Christian charity."

"Poor things," said Agatha. Her watery eyes showed that Margaret's speech had affected her. "And they're in that freezing hovel with the leaking roof?"

"Yes. I've asked for a brazier and fuel but they must have warm, dry clothes or they won't survive. They're thin and exhausted from years of privation."

"Come girls," Agatha stood. "Let us go to our clothing chests and find some good items for them."

"They can have all my clothes," said Christina. "I can stay in our room and pray and not come out."

"That won't be necessary," said Margaret quickly. She knew Christina might actually be happy to do just that and didn't want to give her the excuse. "But we can put together an outfit for each of them without leaving us naked."

They each went to root through their chests of clothing. Margaret's dresses had been made for her trousseau and were all rather elaborate, woven in multiple colors, with long trailing sleeves and thread of gold in the patterns. They would draw unwelcome attention to Aelgith and Osgifu if they wore them. She needed something plainer like Christina's clothes.

She did have an extra linen shift, though. It was brand new, freshly sewn by a village woman, clean and folded at the bottom of her trunk. It had been made extra large to accommodate the later stages of her pregnancy. Glancing down at her belly, she reflected that she would soon need its extra capacity.

Securing the door, she had Grizel help her out of her dress and shift, and she donned the new, larger shift. The new linen felt stiff and crispy against her skin, but the discomfort was a welcome mortification of her flesh that experienced too much luxury while others were suffering. Grizel folded the shift, still warm from her body but cleaner than what Aelgith and Osgifu wore.

"Here, take these stockings as well." Margaret pulled out some rather itchy wool stockings that lay rolled up at the bottom of the trunk.

Sadly Margaret found that her mother and sister's wardrobes were already much depleted by acts of charity she'd forced upon them over the last year. Christina was persuaded to part with her last two dresses. She protested vigorously when Margaret presented her with one of her own to wear, with a gorgeous pattern of blue and silver threads woven in a diamond pattern with tiny red accents. "Think of it as a penance," said Margaret.

"I'd rather be dead than wear this. Quite literally," said Christina, eyeing the sparkling fabric with deep suspicion. Margaret compromised by giving that one to her mother, in exchange for a wool gown of deep forest green, with burgundy trimmed cuffs, that Christina reluctantly agreed to wear.

Her mother's girlish figure, which she was quietly proud of, fit neatly into the silver and blue dress. "You'll be fighting off the widowed thanes and mormaers," said Margaret, admiring her in it.

"God forbid," said Agatha with a smile, while obviously enjoying the compliment. "I can't understand a word they utter with that silly accent of theirs." Agatha spoke good English but had never lost her strong continental accent and said she found the prospect of learning another language too exhausting to even attempt more than the occasional word of Gaelic.

Grizel headed off to the jail with Christina's dresses and

with shifts and stockings pillaged from all of them. She summoned a boy to bring a copper tub of steaming water and some soft rags.

"We look like peacocks," said Christina, obviously embarrassed to walk into the hall in her new finery.

"Peacocks are God's creatures," said Margaret. "He created them for us to enjoy and why should we not celebrate the gift of life on earth by arraying ourselves in finery like them?" She knew it was a stretch.

Christina shot her a withering look. "I wish to secure a plain gray dress first thing tomorrow morning if I have to borrow a worn nun's habit."

"That would be a dream come true for you," said Margaret. Why had her sister so totally given up on the world of men? She still hoped to find her a good husband, but it would take time.

"It would," said Christina with a sigh. "I still don't know why Mother and I can't go back to Wilton now that you're safely settled here. Even the Normans would never disturb us there."

"Because I need you!" said Margaret. "I love you, for one thing. And I cherish your companionship and support. How can I bring my first baby into the world without your help and encouragement?"

"You can't, darling," said Agatha. "Which is why we'll be right here with you. I can't wait to squeeze those chubby baby cheeks! And of course you need us to help manage your brother."

Margaret sighed. Her brother—the Aetheling—was a whole other project, which would require careful long-term management of his ego and prospects. She couldn't think about that for now. She had too many other things to worry about.

Back in the hall, Malcolm looked up at the three of them

entering and for a horrible moment Margaret thought he would let out some kind of whistle or whoop of appreciation. Instead, he just stared at them all.

"Have we each grown an extra head?" asked Margaret.

"No, but I have just realized the incredible riches in female beauty that surround me."

"I was wearing this dress when I left the room not long ago."

Christina pouted beneath her white veil. "Earthly life is suffering," she said, coming to sit at the table near him. Malcolm laughed heartily. Christina almost smiled. Margaret knew that Christina appreciated her husband for his good heart and for the mercy and generosity he'd shown their whole family.

Her brother Edgar had been away hunting with a local thane and joined the table in good spirits. Tall and handsome as well as young and unmarried, he turned heads everywhere with his golden looks. Margaret could feel even the servant girls' eyes swivel toward him as he entered the hall. "Did you witness miracles at the shrine to St Andrew, my sister?"

"I prayed for continued peace for our kingdom, a miracle that I hope will unfold over time."

"I hope you prayed for me to be restored as the rightful king of all England," he said, raising his cup. He was only half joking. And it wasn't entirely impossible. William the Bastard was a force to be reckoned with—or rather avoided —but if he were to drop dead tomorrow....

"Of course she did, darling," said Agatha. "We all pray for it daily."

"I hear there are two murderesses holed up in the jail," said Edgar to Malcolm. "Will they be hanged or burned at the stake?"

Margaret was about to protest but Malcolm beat her to it. "Don't gather a crowd for the execution so quickly. They insist they're innocent and I'm still trying to discover the truth of what happened."

"I heard they were drenched in blood," said Edgar. "Which seems rather damning."

"They claim that they carried the injured woman to safety and she died in their arms."

Edgar laughed and slapped the table. "That's a good one. I'll have to claim that next time I kill someone in battle."

Agatha crossed herself. "Don't talk of such things, darling. It ruins my appetite. How was your hunting party?"

"We killed three big boars and they put up quite a fight. It was good sport. I've invited Fearghas here to hunt in our forests, if that's all right with you, Malcolm."

"It is indeed," said Malcolm evenly. "Our boar grow fat on acorns over the winter in our woods and will make his look like puny piglets by comparison."

The conversation continued in a trivial direction, with no further mention of the two imprisoned women. After the meal was over, Margaret excused herself and summoned Grizel to attend her. They headed downstairs and to the kitchens as if to discuss the next day's meals. Once there, Margaret requested bread and cheese and a jug of ale. The cook asked no questions of her queen but provided the items wrapped and ready for her to take to her bedchamber for a midnight repast.

Once they'd left the kitchen she asked Grizel to fetch her cloak. Grizel returned with her cloak and overshoes. "Would you like your prayer book?"

Margaret stopped in the middle of fastening her cloak pin. Usually, when she went out at night, she was headed to the chapel to pray. "Yes, please fetch it."

With her prayer book in hand, as if it was an ordinary night, Margaret nodded to the guards as they left the tower.

But instead of turning toward the chapel, she beckoned Grizel to follow her toward the jail.

THE SMALL, high-walled jail sat at the edge of the village at the bottom of the hill. The walls were of cut stone, possibly pillaged from an ancient Roman structure since hewn stone was rarely used in this part of the world. Above them, a mossy and poorly maintained thatched roof barely kept out the rain.

A guard stood outside the building and startled as they approached in the dark. "We are here to visit the prisoners," said Margaret. She saw no need to offer further explanation.

The guard unlocked the door and lifted two giant latches that would have contained a herd of wild horses, let alone two small, half-starved women.

Margaret saw the glow of coals in the brazier she'd ordered. Beyond that, the interior was so dark that even with her lantern, Margaret could barely make out the two women. They huddled together in a corner, their faces hidden under their cloaks. When they realized who'd entered they both sprang to their feet.

"Thank you for the clothes, my lady. I don't deserve more of your kindness," said Aelgith grimly. "I should never have run away from Mac Duff's hall in Cupar. It was a foolish mistake that my daughter and I will likely pay for with our lives."

Margaret asked Grizel to unwrap and offer the food and drink, and told Aelgith to sit down, before she asked, "Why did you run away?"

"I saw a chance in the dead of night. I rose to relieve myself and everyone was asleep. I saw my daughter sleeping in a corner of the hall and thought—I could wake her and we could run out into the night right now and be free!" She sighed. "It was a foolish whim."

It was indeed, thought Margaret. But she saw no reason to pile misery on the head of one so clearly despondent. This was her first opportunity to address Osgifu. "Did the Mac Duffs treat you ill?"

"They treated me as a slave, doing menial work, but they fed me and I slept near a fire." The girl's flat voice revealed a lack of hope and joy in life. "I tried to attend to my duties from one day to the next without drawing censure."

"Your mother was worried that the men there might try to...take advantage of you."

"I know, but at least so far no one has tried." The girl was thin and slight and looked younger than her fourteen years. That at least had hopefully protected her to some extent. "I almost died of shock when I saw my mother arrive with your party."

"We had no way to warn you," said Margaret. "We didn't even know if you'd be there. All your mother remembered was that the man who took you from Northumbria had dark red hair and one of his men called him *Beithir*, which means dragon."

"I wish I'd left you there," said her mother. "You'd be far safer there than on trial for murder here in Dunfermline."

"My husband believes your story." *At least I think he does.* "But there must be a process of investigation. We need to learn who really killed Beitris so the weight of guilt can rest on them." She looked at Osgifu. "You visited Beitris with your master and mistress?"

"Yes. We went there several times, so I knew the way even in the dark."

"But your mistress, Enfleda, was not her mother?"

"No, Enfleda was her stepmother." Margaret's eyes had

adjusted to the dim glow of light from the brazier and her lantern. She could see hesitation written in the girl's mouth.

"Was Enfleda cruel to you?"

Osgifu hesitated. "She was always quick to find fault with things and scold. Not just with me but with everyone." Margaret remembered the "missing" cross and wondered if Enfleda herself had tucked it into the crack.

"Did she get along well with her husband's daughter?"

"Not really. I got the impression that Beitris didn't like her very much. They were almost the same age which I suppose was a bit awkward. Enfleda would act imperious and give her motherly advice, and Beitris would laugh at it."

"Did you get an impression of Beitris's husband Diarmad, and what he was like?"

"Not really. He didn't seem to be much of a talker. Enfleda would try to start conversations with him, but they never really went anywhere."

"Could you tell how he felt about his wife?"

"No, but I could tell Beitris didn't think much of her husband. She criticized his every move." Osgifu glanced about. "I feel awkward just speaking of it. Enfleda would try to take his side and then Beitris would roll her eyes at Enfleda."

"Beitris sounds like quite a character," said Margaret.

"She had strong opinions, to be sure. I suspect that as the daughter of Mac Duff, who's a powerful man in the region, she was raised to think of herself as a sort of princess."

"I can't imaging Mac Duff had an easy time with two such strong willed women in his hall."

"Oh, he wasn't bothered. He could hush either of them with a look." Osgifu glanced around. "I feel odd speaking of such things. Like I could be whipped for insolence."

"Do you have any idea why Enfleda might try to steal her own cross?"

"What?" Osgifu looked confused.

"The heavy gold cross she wore when I was there. It disappeared and you and your mother were accused of stealing it. Then Grizel found it tucked away under the wall like someone had pushed it there."

"I have no idea why she would do that."

"Did Enfleda seem happy with her husband?"

Osgifu hesitated. "He's a difficult man." Again, she glanced about as if she might be beaten for saying such things. "And old enough to be her father. He'd taken to asking her when she was ever going to get pregnant."

"Enfleda's never had a child?"

"No. And once Beitris grew big with child, the two women bickered more often. Enfleda would say to Beitris that she wasn't a good wife to her husband, and she would argue back that Enfleda was barren. It was very awkward to be nearby when this happened."

"They did this in front of Mac Duff?"

"Oh, no. We sometimes went to visit Balbarnie without him."

"Why? If Enfleda disliked Beitris so much, I wonder why she would visit?"

Osgifu hesitated and frowned. "I think Enfleda got bored staying in Mac Duff's hall and Balbarnie was one of the few places she could travel to without drawing censure. And she seemed to like talking to Diarmad, Beitris's husband. I think she liked that it annoyed Beitris."

"Was she jealous that Beitris had a handsome young husband?" For all his lack of charm, Diarmad was not ugly to look upon.

"I dare say she was. And I suspect she envied Beitris for being mistress of her hall, when she was barely more than a servant in her own."

"Did Diarmad and Enfleda ever spend time alone?"

"I really couldn't say," she said quietly, avoiding Margaret's gaze. Clearly the girl was afraid to bring more trouble on her own head.

"But Enfleda would engage him in conversation?"

"Yes." Osgifu's hazel eyes met hers, and the look of desperation in them chilled her.

What did it mean if Diarmad Mac Aidh had a relationship —of any kind—with Mac Duff's wife? Enfleda couldn't have killed Beitris herself as she was at Cupar the whole time. But could Diarmad have killed his wife the better to continue an affair with his neighbor's wife?

None of it made sense. Many men carried on adulterous affairs during their marriage and felt no need to send their wives away, let alone kill them. Margaret had witnessed many such affairs in the English royal court, albeit carried on in the shadows, away from the pious gaze of their king.

If Mac Duff heard rumors that his wife was cheating on him, and that this somehow caused his daughter's death, he'd likely be even more furious than he was now and would seek to save face. Two stray refugees would be a better scapegoat than the man he'd chosen as his daughter's husband, especially if that man was also tupping his wife. He'd want the whole affair hushed up and swept away as quickly as possible.

Osgifu was right to be wary. This news likely wouldn't help her cause or her mother's. "The one thing we must hold onto is that neither of you had any reason to kill Beitris."

"They think she surprised us and threatened to betray us."

"Did either of you have a knife on you at any point?" Many women carried a knife for practical purposes such as harvesting wild mushrooms or prying open a door.

"No, neither of us," said Aelgith quickly. "You dressed me for the journey so you know every scrap of clothing that I had on."

"Slaves don't sleep with knives," said Osgifu. "Even the cook's knives are locked in the pantry overnight while she sleeps."

That made sense. Margaret couldn't imagine sleeping with unwilling captives taking fitful rest from their forced labor under her own roof.

A thought occurred to her. "Could Beitris still speak when you found her? Did she say who'd stabbed her?"

The two women looked at each other. "She was struggling to catch her breath, but she did utter a sound," said Aelgith slowly. "I don't know if it's a word, but she said it again and again."

What did she say?" asked Margaret, heart now pounding. This could be the evidence she needed to finally get Diarmad Mac Aidh arrested.

Osgifu frowned and knotted her hands together. "I've learned some of the language since I've been here, but it wasn't a word I've heard before."

"Just make a similar sound so I can hear it."

"*Tas*," said Osgifu. "At least that's what it sounded like. *Tas*. It came out on a gasp each time."

"Das?" asked Margaret. She looked at Aelgith. "Does that mean anything to you?"

The two women looked at each other again. "I don't know," said Osgifu. "I don't remember hearing it before. She could hardly breathe. It may have been the only sound she could make."

Margaret wanted to go ask Malcolm if the word had any meaning. If it was a word from anywhere in his lands, or in nearby Cumbria or Northumbria, he'd know it. He took pains to learn obscure points of dialect so he could converse with any of his subjects and neighbors as one of them.

Grizel had unwrapped the bread and cheese she'd brought with her, but so far neither of the women had touched it. "You must eat," urged Margaret. "Keep your strength up."

Neither of them said anything. The cold night air seeped into the stone cottage from every direction, and the burning brazier barely made a dent.

"Keep hope alive," she urged. "I shall ask my husband what this means. It may help save you."

CHAPTER 16

*B*ack in the hall, a rowdy singing match had erupted amongst some of the young men, with her brother Edgar leading the charge and singing a bawdy French song that rattled her nerves. The salacious words were bad enough, but to sing in the language of the enemy who'd overthrown your intended kingdom? Sometimes she felt mortified for her brother. But he was thin-skinned and attempts to correct him could make things worse.

Margaret knew better than to argue with men who were into their cups so she simply whispered her excuses in her husband's ear and headed to their bedchamber with Grizel.

Grizel unpinned her veil, shook it out and draped it over the back of a chair. She untied the ribbon wrapped around her braids and carefully unwound each braid until Margaret could feel the weight of her hair all the way down her back.

Margaret would have preferred to keep the braids in overnight, the better to prevent tangles while she slept, but her life and her hair were no longer fully her own. Her husband had told her, time and time again, how much he enjoyed her long silky tresses trailing over their pillow, or his chest, at night until she no longer felt she could deprive him of this pleasure.

Grizel worked the comb through the ends of the hair, freeing any tangles. She wet a soft cloth with water and Margaret rubbed her face with it. She felt at least a morsel of satisfaction that Aelgith and Osgifu had been restored to cleanliness and no longer looked like the blood-thirsty savages they'd become in so many people's minds.

Tas? Or *Daz*? What could have been on Beitris's mind as she drew her last breath in the aching arms of foreign strangers?

Margaret awoke when the mattress tilted under Malcolm's weight. He smelled of smoke and spiced wine. She extended her arms to welcome him into their bed.

Under the covers, he kissed her. She knew she should calm her thoughts and go back to sleep quickly, or she might lie awake with thoughts running through her head like red squirrels.

But that was not her nature. "Husband, I have a strange question. Do you know the meaning of the word *Tas*?"

"It's an old word for father."

Margaret felt her heart quicken. "I thought *athir* meant father?"

"In Gaelic it does. But the ancient Picts, whose blood still flows in all our veins, spoke a different language. Many words remain in daily use. *Tas* is one of them."

"It was Beitris's last word as she died. She said it several times while the women tried to carry her to safety."

"How are you able to wake from the depths of sleep and instantly function as a justiciar of the realm?"

"I have royal blood." She enjoyed ascribing any eccentricities and unusual proclivities to her ancestry. It was a good distraction at least.

"Ah, so you do." He kissed her cheek softly.

"Was she trying to tell them something? If I was dying I'd want to tell anyone nearby who had killed me."

"It's not unusual for someone to call out for their mother or father as they lay dying. I've heard it on the battlefield. The mind goes to a strange place between life and death. It almost seems like people see the souls of their ancestors calling to them."

Margaret felt a tiny shudder rock her husband's strong body. Would the spirit of his father Duncan—murdered by Macbeth—call to him one day? Or would Macbeth—whom Malcolm killed to seize the crown—be there waiting for him on the other side with a drawn sword?

She drew in a breath and tried to wrestle her thoughts back from this grim and alarming thought.

"But her father's not dead. Mac Duff is alive and well and served us ale in his house not two days ago."

"This is true. But I hardly think he rode to Balbarnie and murdered his own daughter while we were kneeling before the relics of St. Andrew."

"It does seem unlikely." And Margaret was so sure that Beitris's husband had killed her. "But I suppose we must find out where he was during the time of her death."

Malcolm propped himself up on his elbow. "You want me to summon the Mormaer of Fife so I can accuse him of murdering his daughter?"

She hesitated. "I suppose I do, yes."

"Just hours ago you were convinced that Beitris's husband had killed her and anxious to have him clapped in chains and thrown in the jail."

"And you hesitated because you don't want to disturb the peace in your kingdom." Margaret appreciated the wisdom of her husband's caution. "Which sometimes means tiptoeing around a dragon so as not to waken him and get consumed by his fiery breath." Margaret mused that she needed to study diplomacy more closely.

"I consider myself entirely capable of slaying any dragon should the need arise, but I must be sure to slay the right dragon."

"How can we find out more about Mac Duff's movements while we were in Kilrymont?"

"The girl who escaped captivity in his household might know which servants can be trusted to tell us about his whereabouts."

"Osgifu. You're right. But if she suggests someone, another slave girl, perhaps, then how do we inquire of them without alerting Mac Duff and his wife?"

"Perhaps you could send a servant to look for something we lost there?"

Margaret frowned. "Grizel could go. It should be something sentimental, not valuable. We don't want to accuse them of theft. Not after all the drama about the stolen cross that wasn't stolen. Why would Enfleda do such a thing?"

"It was odd, to be sure, but has nothing to do with the murder of her daughter-in-law."

"It speaks to her character. Which may be relevant in a way that we don't yet understand." She pressed her hand into her husband's chest while trying to gather her tangled thoughts. "Osgifu accompanied Enfleda on visits to Beitris's house on more than one occasion. She said that she seemed unusually intimate with Beitris's husband."

"With Diarmad Mac Aidh?" The disbelief in his voice surprised her. "Unless Enfleda is a damned fool, she'd hardly carry on an affair with her stepdaughter's husband."

"I agree. That does seem a good way to get murdered. But then why would Beitris end up dead in this scenario?" There were many links in this chain but none of them fit together. "And the two English women escaped at the perfect time to be unwitting scapegoats for this strange crime."

"Don't agitate yourself, my love. I can tell this matter has upset you greatly."

"I feel a kinship with Aelgith and Osgifu almost as if I were a blood relative—which I may well be if you go back far enough into the history of our people. Where would my family be without our resources and connections? Without you offering us a safe haven?"

"Your compassion for them is admirable, but there are hundreds—thousands—of people in their situation. Are you going to rescue them all?"

He obviously hadn't intended for her to take the question seriously. But God had put this matter into her hands. Did He intend for her to take on this urgent task?

"It makes me nervous when you're silent like this," said Malcolm softly. She could hear the attempt at humor in his voice.

"I just want to see God's will done here on earth. But what is God's will?" God had allowed William's horsemen to run roughshod over the land of the Anglo-Saxons, driving them into exile, poverty and humiliation at the hands of strangers.

Malcolm watched her in silence for a moment. "I shall invite Mac Aidh and Mac Duff to Dunfermline to celebrate Christmas in my hall."

"A killer under our roof?" And which one was the killer?

"Keep your friends close, and your enemies closer. I shall send invitations first thing this morning," said Malcolm. "They won't dare refuse.

~

180

MARGARET SPENT the day bustling about the tower, giving orders to prepare for the imminent arrival of their visitors. "We shall all enjoy the blessings of Christmas so much the better if no meat or fish is tasted in the days before it."

The cook, an older woman who'd cooked for the family since the time of Malcolm's father, tut tutted. "A bit of game never hurt a man," she said in her strong accent. "It gives them strength for war."

"We're not in a war," said Margaret, trying to maintain a peaceful expression. The longtime servants were used to being treated as family members and had no qualms about speaking their minds. Maybe it was a Scots thing. She'd certainly never seen such cheerful insolence at King Edward's court. "And I encourage you to plan a feast of game and all manner of rich fare for us to enjoy on Christmas day. We must use the fine silver dishes," she insisted. "And jeweled goblets."

She'd been surprised by the plainness of tableware in Malcolm's hall on her arrival. Some of the men still drank out of hollow animal horns that they carried on their person. Malcolm insisted that Scots cared more about the strength of their ale than the number of gemstones encrusting its container. "And all the linens must be sparkling clean."

She ordered beds to be carried from the former royal residence and the bishop's palace for use by their guests. Unfortunately, once placed in the new tower with its bright plaster walls and pale wood floors they looked tired and grubby, especially the curtains.

"Do we have time to wash and dry the curtains?" The ones from the bishop's palace were especially dingy and reeked of incense. They didn't appear to have been washed in a century.

"These windows do let in an awful lot of light," said Grizel, peering up at the pale sky through the new openings.

The windows weren't large, but on the second floor and right at the tree tops they admitted a harsh and critical view of the elderly furnishings.

"It is a shame that Mac Duff and Mac Aidh are both relatively young and well-sighted," said Margaret, trying to make light of a situation that would be hard to remedy. "But even if they weren't, they'd smell these curtains from downstairs. We must replace them. What can we use?"

Margaret summoned her mother, who had a keen eye for decor as well as fashion. Agatha coughed as soon as she entered the room. "Goodness. They'll suspect us of trying to poison them."

"I know, The bed can be pushed into a corner but we still need curtains for at least two sides."

"It's not that large a bed. What about those big plaids that the men wear?" Will two of those do? Your husband must have a few lying around."

"That's not a bad idea. Grizel, can you please look through his chests and see what you can find?"

Grizel looked doubtful. "Should I ask him first, my lady?"

"He won't mind." She looked at her mother. "Will he?"

Agatha shrugged. "I suppose it depends on what he has in there tucked amongst them."

"What do you mean?"

"I wouldn't go through a man's chests without asking his permission," said Agatha.

"I shall ask his permission first, then."

But she couldn't find him. He'd gone out hunting with Edgar, and they were often—nearly always—gone until after dark when that happened. Since the guests had been summoned to arrive tomorrow she didn't want to wait until the morning.

In addition to a whole storeroom full of crates and boxes, Malcolm had three large wooden chests that lined one wall of the chamber. He often sat on one of them while donning his stockings. All three were made of dark oak ringed with iron bands, with a large lock on the front.

Malcolm's steward was summoned to unlock them but seemed skittish about doing it in his master's absence. "Does he keep the skulls of his enemies in these chests?" asked Margaret, growing exasperated over his hesitation. "What might we find within that has you so concerned about my seeing it?"

It occurred to her that his trunks might contain mementos from his first marriage to Ingibiorg, but she wasn't afraid of being confronted by tokens of his affection for his former wife. "Open it, please. I'm sure my husband won't mind."

The steward, an ancient man with a thick accent from some distant part of the kingdom, reluctantly opened the central chest with a large iron key. Margaret prayed that there would be a large enough expanse of plaid within to cover at least one side of the bed.

The Scots men wore this item slung about their body in several ways—sometimes as a cape, sometimes as a sort of toga like the ancient Romans—and Malcolm had told her they would fashion it into a makeshift tent when sleeping outdoors. He reckoned his people had been wearing something similar for a thousand years or more. Surely he'd have a few of them, perhaps even from earlier generations if they were of such ancient usage.

But the heavy lid opened—with the help of both Grizel and Margaret—to reveal a tangle of shimmering gold and silver treasures. Margaret froze at the sight. A golden cup—like a priest's chalice—sat on top and caught a sudden ray of sunlight coming through the window.

"What is all this?" she asked the steward in a rather breathless voice.

"Treasure, my lady."

"I can see that." Her family had no shortage of treasure that they'd hauled across Europe from Hungary to London and now to Scotland, but it was neatly organized and sorted and each item carefully wrapped in soft cloths. "Why is it all jumbled in here."

"I suppose because no one but the king has access to these chests."

"You have the key. Is it not your duty to sort and arrange these treasures?"

The steward swallowed and rocked slightly. Another item caught her eye. A large, engraved gold cross. "What a beautiful cross!" She picked it up with both hands. It was three spans high and surprisingly heavy, worked with gorgeous intricacy. "This is almost like something you'd see over the altar in a grand cathed—" Suddenly the cross seemed to burn her hands. She put it down quickly on top of the pile. She peered at the steward. "Where did these items come from?"

"I couldn't say, my lady," he mumbled.

Margaret felt her breaths quicken. "Open the other two chests, please."

Again, the steward hesitated. "I really think that the king should be consulted."

"Very well then. I shall speak to him myself. She turned and marched from the room, still shocked and confused by what she'd seen. And still in need of curtains.

BY THE END of the day, Margaret had secured several large woven plaids, each in good condition and with no offensive odors, from the steward himself and from various men about the court. She'd promised to return them without damage and thus they'd been secured to the beds with pins like a veil pinned around a woman's head.

Wooden partitions were erected to give each guest a measure of privacy. An artist was hastily painting rural scenes and patterned friezes on the newly plastered walls in an attempt to create an atmosphere of lived-in elegance that the new tower—still smelling of freshly-hewn timber and damp plaster—sorely lacked.

Her brother and husband returned from hunting after dark, along with Malcolm's sons Duncan and Donald. They were all in good spirits, the oldest boy, only ten, having shot his first hind. Margaret congratulated the lads and Malcolm gave them each a celebratory sip of strong drink.

Such was the festive atmosphere and loud revelry in the hall—with pipes and drums and all manner of loud singing—that she retreated to her chamber at the earliest opportunity and put her hands over her ears while she knelt at her prie-dieu.

Dear God, please give me the forbearance and humility necessary to be a good wife to my husband. As you know, I had hoped to serve only you, and to devote my life to praising you. But you chose to deliver me into the world as a daughter of the ancient royal house of Wessex and to assign me duties that are different from my own selfish desires. I accept my duty to represent my family—and to protect their future—by taking my husband's hand in marriage. He is a good man in many ways and I am grateful for that. But—

She halted her prayer as it was heading in a direction of ingratitude. She retreated into well-worn prayers invoking divine assistance and lost herself in her reassuring faith that all was part of God's plan and she had but to do his will here on earth and all would be well.

As usual, she was fast asleep with the covers pulled over her head when her husband climbed into bed. He kissed her cheek and apologized for the noisy festivities and she reassured him—truthfully—that their joy brought her happiness.

"The little lads are growing into men," he said proudly. "You should have seen how brave young Donald was today."

"I'm glad to see him so happy." The boys were rather quiet and subdued and Margaret often forgot they were there. They'd lost their mother at an early age and had suffered somewhat from the lack of a mother's affection. She tried her best to be a mother to them, but their relationship was rather undercut by the knowledge—keen in all of them—that she would naturally want her son to become the next king of Scotland in their stead.

The treasure, jumbled into the locked trunk, had dominated her thoughts since the moment she'd laid eyes on it. She burned to ask her husband about it. But he'd had a good deal of drink and now perhaps might not be the best time.

Or was it?

In vino veritas. "Husband…" She found herself suddenly nervous. Would he be upset that she'd had his steward open his chest without asking him?

"Wife?" He rolled onto his elbow. "What is it you mean to ask me?"

She had a feeling he already knew. "I asked your steward to unlock your chests for me. I was surprised to find them filled with a great jumble of treasure."

"I'm not sure why you'd be surprised, my love," he said softly. "I am King of the Scots. Did you think I'd be a pauper?"

"Well, no, but—" She steeled herself to ask the most burning question. "There was a great cross on top of the chest. Gold and very large, like something from a church or a bishop's palace…." She let her question trail off. She hoped he would jump in with an explanation about the cross. Perhaps a reassuring one.

"Yes," he said cheerfully. "My treasure is your treasure. You may use it as you wish. Would you like to hang the cross up in our hall?"

This was not the direction she'd anticipated. "I think it would more appropriately hang in the new cathedral you are building. But where did it come from?"

"I don't recall," he said lazily. "Somewhere in Northumbria."

Margaret tried not to stiffen under his resting arm as she prepared to ask her next question. "When you raid Northumbria with your men...do you steal from churches and monasteries?"

"Stealing? The fruits of conquest aren't theft. They're the spoils of war."

"If someone came here and stole your crown, or even your saddle, I'm almost certain you'd consider it stealing. But stealing aside, do you attack religious establishments?"

"If they come out to fight against us, we have no choice. I'm sure you understand."

"And you maintain that these regular forays into Northumbria—to attack and pillage for treasure—are essential to keeping your men trained for war and happy to serve you?"

"How else am I to reward them for their service?" He squeezed her.

She steeled herself to speak her mind. "I think you should give the holy items back to the places they came from."

"I'm afraid I don't know where they came from. I didn't seize them with my own hands. Perhaps you could take those items and distribute them to churches here in our kingdom, or sell them and use the funds to feed and clothe the poor?"

"I like that idea." Her mind started working. "Perhaps they could do more good than they ever did sitting on an altar."

Her husband fell asleep almost as soon as his head hit the

pillow. He wasn't one to ruminate on doubts to disturb his peace. She, however, had a tendency to lie awake worrying in the dark.

Were Aelgith and Osgifu suffering from the cold tonight? How many endured worse privations? English women and men who'd grown up in peace and comfort, now driven into slavery and starvation by William's invasion.

What could she do to help them?

To help Aelgith and Osgifu she'd now invited a murderer into their home—into the king's own fortress. The one who killed Beitris would be sleeping under their roof tomorrow night.

CHAPTER 17

*T*heir guests arrived the following day. Diarmad Mac Aidh came first, living nearer, with an entourage of men—no women at all—and a sour expression. He wore his plaid swathed around him, but under the woven wool she could make out the outlines of a great sword at one hip and a long knife at the other; likely the same knife she'd examined and found to have dried blood in the carved design of the blade.

Diarmad was welcomed into the hall, and Margaret sent Grizel to offer to remove his plaid and hang it to dry. He refused—which wasn't surprising—it wasn't easy to get a Scot to part with his plaid. Near the heat of the fire they gathered it over one shoulder, but always kept it about them and even slept wrapped in it. Sometimes the smell of a plaid entered a room before its owner.

Malcolm was out somewhere, so Margaret greeted him as warmly as she could manage and offered him ale and oatcakes. She was waxing on about the blessings of the season and celebrating the birth of our Lord—watching his

189

expression all the while—when he raised a hand to silence her.

"I'm mourning the death of my wife," he said with a surly expression. "I see little to celebrate."

Margaret felt like she'd been slapped across the face. *I am your queen.* The words quivered on her tongue but she smothered her indignation. "My condolences on your loss."

"I hope that while I am here I'll see those cursed English witches hang for their evil crime."

Anger now prickled inside her. "Justice will be done in due course. As is God's will."

Diarmad's brow lowered and she saw fury flash in his eyes. This is a man who holds his temper barely controlled, she thought. The temptation to poke the bear was strong, but it would serve her purpose better if she did it in front of an audience. Let Diarmad Mac Aidh show them who he was: a volatile man more than capable of killing his wife, especially in a drunken rage or a somnolent trance.

Margaret sat him at the high table with three of her husband's men. They'd been told to drink with him and learn anything they could about him and his wife. Margaret found her husband's men rather inscrutable and difficult to talk to. She wasn't sure if they were intimidated by her or wary of her, but either way their conversations hushed and their movements stiffened when she came near. Still, at least she could trust them to keep Diarmad from using his sword to express himself.

THANKFULLY MALCOLM HAD RETURNED by the time Mac Duff and his wife Enfleda arrived. Darkness had descended over Dunfermline but beeswax candles and braziers illuminated and heated every part of the hall and instruments filled the air with soothing music.

Mac Duff's grim expression cast a shadow over the bright atmosphere she'd created. "We look forward to seeing justice done," he said, as he took a cup of ale. Margaret noted the outlines of his weapons under his plaid. Surely it would be prudent to remove everyone's weapons for safekeeping? She resolved to ask her husband about this at the earliest opportunity.

"This is only my second Advent here in Fife," she said, as she led him to the high table. "Is the weather typical for the season?" The weather was usually a safe topic of conversation anywhere on these islands, it being so changeable.

"My daughter is dead. I am not inclined to notice the weather," said Mac Duff with a flat expression. Shocked by his rudeness, Margaret glanced at Malcolm, whose face revealed nothing of his emotions.

Enfleda pressed her hand to her husband's. "Calm yourself, my dear. Our king has the murderesses in custody and they will soon pay for their evil crime." Margaret bit her tongue. Her urge to defend the women was strong but must wait for the right time.

"Indeed justice shall be done but let's save that for the morrow," said Malcolm. "Tonight we shall enjoy good food and drink and music." He gestured to the musicians who hovered nearby. The blast of a pipe pierced Margaret's ears. She did not love loud music nearly as much as her husband. At least now it might warm the frosty atmosphere that had swept in with their guests.

Diarmad sat at the high table, nursing his cup of ale with a sour expression. He'd risen to his feet when Mac Duff entered and now the two exchanged words that Margaret could barely understand.

"My daughter must be given a proper Christian burial," growled Mac Duff.

"Indeed, sir," said Diarmad nervously. "In the absence of the priest, I did not want my dear wife's body to lie uncovered and unburied and I…." He trailed off.

"Where is the damned priest?"

"He disappeared. No one's seen him for two months."

"We have sent men looking for him," said Malcolm. "They're inquiring of the Culdees throughout Fife. Perhaps your daughter could be buried at Cupar by the priest in your settlement?"

"She should be buried in her marital home at Balbarnie," said Mac Duff. "When I send a girl away to be married I do not expect her to be sent back to my hall like a stray dog."

Margaret looked from Mac Duff to Mac Aidh. Had Diarmad attempted to send Beitris back to her father?

Though she normally sat at the high table with her husband when there were guests, today she'd resolved to follow Enfleda's lead. "Let's go sit away from the men and their difficult business." She wanted to disarm and relax Enfleda—if that was even possible—and try to get under her chilly exterior.

She led Enfleda to a seating area she'd arranged around the second fireplace. Sturdy carved chairs with well-stuffed cushions allowed them to warm themselves in comfort. The dogs had already decided on this as their favorite spot in the hall, and three hounds stretched out luxuriously on the warm hearth.

Enfleda seated herself stiffly into the cushions, adjusting her gown under her. As planned, Grizel hurried over with a plate of rich pastries, juicy with imported delicacies like dates and raisins and rich spices.

Normally Margaret would refuse such indulgences, but today she took a tiny tart and encouraged Enfleda to do the same. "It's good to fortify yourself against the cold of the season, and what could be better than fruits from warmer climes?" she said brightly.

"Rich food upsets my stomach," said Enfleda, looking at the tarts as if they were roasted insects. The gold cross that had caused so much consternation hung against her bony chest. Smooth polished stones of various colors—an emerald, a sapphire and a ruby among them—shone in the firelight.

"You're very thin," said Margaret. She absolutely hated it when people said this to her.

Enfleda stiffened. "Is that a crime? Should I be stuffed and fat like a suckling pig?"

Margaret felt a pang of sympathy. "I've been subject to the same accusations. I find fasting clears my mind and I crave the absence of food more than I crave the taste of it in my mouth or the weight of it in my stomach."

Enfleda looked intrigued. "I've heard you're very pious."

"If that's what people are saying about me, I suppose I'm glad of it," she said. But she wanted to get back to the subject of Enfleda's weight, or the lack of it. "But I've succumbed to the urgings of all around me to eat well to make my body a good vessel to carry a baby."

Enfleda's gaze dropped to the floor. Then returned to Margaret. "Ah yes, a wife is mostly useful as a baby-maker."

Margaret hesitated before sinking the next sharp blade into her guest. "Do you have any children?"

"I do not."

Margaret leaned close enough to speak low. "You've been married some years, have you not? Do you worry that your husband is too old to give them to you?" She cringed even as she said the words. Luckily no one at the high table could hear them over the cacophony of the pipes and the harp.

"My husband has four children from his first marriage," said Enfleda coldly. "I'm sure we'll have children in time if the Lord wills it." Her voice shook slightly at the end. As expected Margaret knew she'd touched on a sensitive topic.

"It might help if you gain some weight," said Margaret. "That's what they told me." Grizel had set the plate of pastries on a folding table within easy reach of them. She now returned with a jug of a drink made with cream and spices. Margaret found the drink utterly nauseating in its richness but she took the offered tiny silver cup of it and urged Enfleda to do the same.

"It seems to have worked for you." Enfleda glanced at Margaret's belly, which was now visibly rounded, at least when she sat down. "When is your baby due?"

"In the spring, God willing."

"I'm surprised you're riding around the countryside in such a condition. Surely it would be safer for you to stay at home in your own hall."

Margaret was already well-armed against such criticisms. "I feel sure that a pilgrimage to visit the blessed bones of St. Andrew will only draw blessings from the Lord that will ensure the safe arrival of my baby." She pushed a smile to her lips and steeled herself for her next question. "Is your husband upset that you've not yet given him a child?"

"Why would he care?" asked Enfleda quickly. "When he has children already."

"My husband has children from his first marriage but could hardly wait to have more. I found his urging and cajoling quite provoking." Of course, her mother's urgings had been even louder. *You must give him sons that will be future kings of Scotland. Only that will secure your future and ours.*

"He must be happy that you're expecting," said Enfleda flatly. The chilling look she gave Margaret might have buckled her knees if she'd been standing.

"Oh yes, he's thrilled." She took another bite of her sweet

and sticky pastry. "I admit I'm somewhat anxious about being a mother."

"Why? Surely servants will do the work of motherhood for you. You can pick and choose how much or how little you do."

"I shall be grateful for uninterrupted time to pray, to be sure." She would have to make confession to the priest for asking her next questions. "Your husband's daughter Beitris, was expecting, was she not?"

"She was." Enfleda's lips settled into a thin line.

"When was she due?"

"How would I know?" Her voice rose a little. Enfleda glanced over her shoulder to where her husband was drinking with Malcolm and his men. And Diarmad. Diarmad looked up and caught her gaze.

Margaret froze. Was it possible that there was some kind of illicit relationship between them?

Enfleda had snatched her head back around so quickly that it almost spun on her neck. Clearly she'd not intended to attract Diarmad's attention—or the scrutiny toward herself that it might garner.

"Did you know Beitris and her husband well?" asked Margaret, now very curious, but wary of having Enfleda clam up altogether.

"How would I not?" she snapped. "She's my husband's daughter."

"They came to your hall regularly? Or you went to theirs?"

"Both. You've made the journey. It's a short one."

"Did you ever go to Balbarnie without your husband?" She tried to sound light and breezy.

"I suppose I might have, once or twice."

"Did Osgifu, the slave girl, ever go with you?" Again, she tried to sound curious, rather than like an inquisitor.

"I have no idea." Enfleda's face tightened. "How would I remember what servant did or didn't attend me?"

She knows Osgifu was there. She's hiding something.

"You immediately assumed that Osgifu and her mother stole your gold cross." She looked at the rather gaudy necklace for a moment. "I take it that you didn't like the girl."

"I have no thoughts about her one way or the other. I barely noticed her."

Margaret summoned Grizel to bring them fresh drinks. She'd arranged for Grizel to make each of Enfleda's drinks a strong concoction that might loosen her tongue and chisel away at her flinty exterior. Hers would be made separately to keep her mind clear. While the drinks took effect she intended to enlighten herself about some ideas that perplexed her.

"I'm disappointed to find slavery still practiced here," she said, as if musing aloud. "When it seems to run counter to the teachings of Christianity."

"I think you'll find that slavery is in the Bible."

"Achieving freedom from it is a constant theme in the Bible, to be sure. And Jesus exhorted us to help the poor and needy, not to hold them in bondage and extract labor by force. I never saw such practices before I came here."

"You lived in the king's court, not among the common people. There were slaves in my father's house in Northumbria. It's not my business to pass judgment on the world around me," said Enfleda, sipping her drink. Margaret had tasted it herself to assure that it was delicious—fruity and sweet—with no strong or bitter aftertaste. "As a woman, my duty is to support my husband."

And bear him children.

Margaret was curious about something. "You're English yourself. Does it not pain you to see your countrywomen in such reduced circumstances as these poor refugees, taken prisoner against their will or forced to beg in the settlements?"

"They're a nuisance. We don't have room or food for all these strangers. The land is harsh and unyielding and we need its few resources to support the people already here."

Margaret had heard this sentiment repeated ad nauseam during her time in Scotland, especially by Donald Ban. "Where should they go?"

"Back to their home country, naturally. Let William deal with them as he sees fit."

"King William has certainly made haste to distribute the kingdom amongst his nobles, though I'm sure many farmers and peasants are valued for staying put to work the land. But what of the dispossessed? Noblewomen like yourself whose homes have been burned and their husbands killed? You've heard what William did to Northumbria only last winter? They say he torched nearly every village and town and destroyed their grain stores and cut down fruit trees and even soured the land so that life cannot be sustained there now. Surely such ruin touched even your noble family?"

"My father was killed and both my brothers. A Norman knight now inhabits our ancient home." Enfleda's thin mouth quivered as she spoke.

Margaret crossed herself. "My heart breaks for you, truly."

She watched Enfleda sip her drink again. Was she cruel to attempt to disarm Enfleda when perhaps she was just holding herself together by a few worn threads? She reminded herself that Aelgith and Osgifu's lives were in her hands. They could hang for a crime they didn't commit unless she could learn more about who really killed Beitris.

"So you have no home to return to, then?"

"My home is with my husband," said Enfleda sharply.

"Where else would it be?" She fingered the gold cross that hung at her breast.

"Do you have wealth of your own? Treasure that you brought with you into the marriage?" Such riches could give a woman a measure of protection if she suddenly found herself cast out or widowed. It was common for noble-women to take some cushion of wealth with them into a marriage, but in these last turbulent years, such luxuries were harder to hold onto.

Enfleda's eyes narrowed. "What business is it of yours?"

"I'm your queen," said Margaret sweetly. "I care deeply about every person in this kingdom. Did you bring that lovely cross with you from Northumbria?"

"No. It belonged to my husband's family." She sipped her drink again.

"It came down from his mother?"

"I think it was from his first wife's family."

So Enfleda likely couldn't take it with her if she were to be sent away. With no family left to defend her interests, she had little to no bargaining power. If she felt that her time in Mac Duff's hall was growing short, would she be motivated to steal it to secure her future?

Margaret could tell that Enfleda had drunk about half of the strong cordial. It was time to dig deep before she became too inebriated to think. The music and hum of conversation provided the cover of privacy she needed to ask questions that would vibrate in the ears of anyone who heard them.

"Ah. So if your husband were to put you out—because you couldn't bear him children or he decides he wants a newer, younger wife—you'd have nowhere to go and no resources to support yourself."

Fury flashed in Enfleda's pale eyes and her drink sloshed in the silver goblet in her hand. "My husband already has children from his first marriage. As does yours, who has two strong sons to sit on his throne after him. Neither of them has need of further brats to disturb the peace in their hall."

Margaret felt Enfleda's barbed response like a dagger to the gut. The baby in her belly would indeed be a rival for the throne of Scotland. Especially since Scots did not necessarily follow the English custom of granting lands and privileges to the eldest son, but rather chose the one they found most capable. "My husband would be deeply disappointed if I could give him no children. He eagerly anticipates the birth of this baby."

"You may find that others will think of little but ensuring that your babe will fall from his horse or eat a poisoned mushroom." Enfleda's chilly gaze ate into her. She wasn't wrong. She knew in her heart that Donald Ban would seize the throne himself if he could find a way onto it. Malcolm's two sons were still young but in a few short years they'd be men with ambitions and jealousies that could make them dangerous to her children.

"The Lord will protect those who honor him and do his work." She spoke with hope as much as conviction.

"He didn't protect my husband's daughter from being slaughtered by your English friends," said Enfleda coldly. She took another sip of the sweet cordial.

Clearly, her mind was still sharp enough to point blame where she wanted it. But why would she protect Diarmad? "Did Diarmad and his wife have difficulties in their marriage?"

"How would I know?" She spoke too quickly and shifted in her chair.

"Because she's your husband's daughter. What was she like?"

"It seemed to me she was always dissatisfied and complaining."

"Complaining about what?"

"The usual. She wanted her husband to build her a newer hall, buy prettier horses, make more profits with his sheep and cattle. She reminded him that she was a mormaer's daughter and used to a certain lifestyle."

Margaret didn't see a tremendous difference between the dark, smoky, drafty hall at Cupar and that at Balbarnie. It was larger but not more pleasant. A glance up at the bright plaster walls and new wood beams in their sturdy stone tower reminded her that she'd been that complaining wife who insisted on a better hall—for her husband as well as herself. She felt a sudden pang of grief for poor, unhappy Beitris.

"Was Diarmad unwilling or unable to fulfill her requests?"

Enfleda shrugged. "I don't know. It's not my business."

"Did your husband not discuss his daughter's marriage and happiness with you? I'd think it is your business—as her stepmother."

Enfleda recoiled visibly at this, which struck Margaret as odd. "Beitris was the same age as me. You make me sound like an old crone."

"How old are you?"

"Two and twenty years," Enfleda straightened her back and took another sip. She swayed slightly in her chair.

"You were married very young. How did you feel about marrying a much older man?" asked Margaret.

"Probably the same as you did, my dear," said Enfleda with an eerie smile.

Margaret stiffened. "My husband is youthful and energetic as a man half his age." To a fault, sometimes. "I'm grateful for his wisdom and experience in the ways of the world."

"Same," said Enfleda, regarding her coolly through narrowed eyes.

She's drunk.

Margaret leaned in, as though wanting more intimacy. "I've heard that some men in middle age have trouble...you know...?" She couldn't bring herself to say the words. But she knew it could be the reason why Enfleda was unable to get pregnant.

"What?" Enfleda tilted her head. Margaret suspected she was playing with her.

"Performing their duties in the bedchamber."

"Their duties?!" Enfleda burst out in laughter that drew attention from the main table. She was beginning to forget herself. "You must be such great fun for your husband. Did you let him do his duty only once a week in between your prayers?"

Alarm pricked Margaret's fingers. Enfleda was becoming too unguarded. They still had the evening meal to get through and she'd arranged to eat it at the high table with the men, to better watch how Enfleda interacted with Diarmad.

"You speak of your king and queen," she said, quietly. "Be more cautious with your words."

Enfleda didn't look much chastened by this, but stared directly at Margaret's small, rounded belly. "Your duty has been done, one way or another." Enfleda's pale skin had turned shiny, and her eyes glassy.

"Is it possible that duty was not done in your case?" asked Margaret quietly. "And that the reason for your barrenness lies not in yourself but in your husband."

"And what should I do about that? Recruit a cowherd to assist me?" Enfleda laughed again.

Margaret suspected such efforts were far from rare. A woman's safety and security depended on producing an heir. It was her business to produce one by any means necessary. She leaned close again. "I'd think that a local noble would serve far better than a cowherd. He'd be more likely to keep your secret, for one thing, especially if he were married to another and had his own secrets to keep."

Enfleda froze, her goblet tilting in her hand. Then she lifted the cup and knocked back the last of the drink.

"Diarmad is a handsome man," continued Margaret, boldly. "Young and virile. And his wife was with child, so he was clearly able to sow his seed." She could hardly believe she was talking like this. But Osgifu's words had planted a seed in her mind and it had taken root.

"Perhaps your husband would not like you casting glances at other men and calling them comely," said Enfleda, turning to look at Malcolm. Malcolm was now leading the men in a Gaelic song and luckily didn't notice.

"My husband is secure in my devotion to him," said Margaret quietly. She hated the way Enfleda kept turning her accusations back against her. In truth their situations in life were not so different: except that Enfleda had no child, no personal wealth, no family, and—without her husband—no future.

Unless she could get pregnant by another man.

Margaret stood. "Let us join our men at the high table."

CHAPTER 18

*M*argaret watched Enfleda closely as she sat in the chair next to her husband. Mac Duff didn't even glance at her but instead watched Margaret as she sat down opposite him. Malcolm, by comparison, greeted her warmly and kissed her on the cheek.

Mac Duff seemed to find his affection amusing. "Ah, the newlyweds. Such a sweet time in a marriage."

Margaret seized this opportunity. "Your wife is even younger and lovelier than myself, my lord." She smiled warmly at Enfleda. "Surely you still feel like a newlywed yourself."

Enfleda glowed for a second, basking in the praise. With her striking pale eyes, almost translucent skin and her long, pale-gold braids, she did look beautiful.

"My wife is like the mountaintops," said Mac Duff. His voice had a teasing tone. "Magnificent to behold but capped with snow and ice. A man risks frostbite trying to climb her."

Enfleda's smile stiffened into a grimace. Margaret could tell she was trying to maintain her composure despite her intoxication. For a moment she felt guilty for disarming another woman—an English one no less—at the king's table.

"Surely it is your work to melt the ice," said Malcolm, beckoning the lad to refill their cups. They drank out of engraved silver goblets, each with different color jewels embedded in the cup.

"Do you bring a furnace to the bedroom?" asked Mac Duff, grinning.

"And an anvil, if required," retorted Malcolm. The two men guffawed. Margaret cringed. Clearly, there'd been no shortage of strong drink among the men, either. She gestured to Grizel to bring her a plain herbal tisane instead of whatever the lad was pouring.

She glanced at Diarmad. He stared morosely toward the fire as if he sat all alone in the room. She saw another opportunity. "Husband, you make bawdy jests when one of our guests has lost his wife to tragedy only days ago."

"I lost my dear daughter," said Mac Duff. "And now I only have three of them left." He seemed to be making a joke, but no one laughed. Margaret wondered what kind of a brute Mac Duff must be to make a joke like this when his daughter lay brutally murdered. She felt a pang of sympathy for poor Enfleda who had to share her bed—and her life—with such a man.

Diarmad picked up his cup and drank. "My wife was expecting our first child. Two were lost that day." His comments were directed toward the fire, since he didn't look at anyone in particular while he spoke.

Malcolm and Margaret both murmured condolences. She said a silent prayer for the poor lost babe. Was she wrong about Diarmad? If he were guilty, then why would he remind them that in his crime of killing his wife he'd taken another innocent life as well?

She took her tisane from Grizel and sipped it, trying to

hide her confusion. "Your grief must be immense," she said softly, to Diarmad.

"I'm glad you think so," he said, looking at her for the first time since she'd sat down. His face was flushed with drink, but she noted reddening around his eyes as well. Sadness over his wife's death? Or for his own uncertain fate? He likely remembered her examining his knife and his blood-ringed wrists and her disbelief while hearing his story about the slain hare.

"How long had you been married to Beitris?" she asked.

"Two years," he said. "We were only just starting to get used to each other."

Margaret found this an odd thing to say. "What did you find difficult to get used to?"

"Sharing my bed," said Diarmad. His apparent honesty disarmed Margaret.

"The servants said you're prone to wandering at night."

"Yes. I recall nothing of it in the morning."

"Do you wake up in your bed, or do you sometimes wake up somewhere else altogether?" asked Malcolm, clearly curious.

"Usually in my bed, but sometimes in the morning I find things disturbed from my nighttime activities."

"I'd imagine Beitris found that...perplexing," said Margaret.

Diarmad stared into the fire again. "She did. She'd try to wake me up and bring me back to bed but she'd say I argued with her and had the strength of ten men while I was in this state."

"I had no idea he suffered from such an odd affliction before the marriage," said Mac Duff, to Malcolm. "It was never spoken of."

"Did your daughter tell you she was distressed by it?" asked Margaret.

"She did, aye. I think anyone would be distressed by their husband roaming the hall at night."

"Your servants said that no one else sleeps in the hall, just you and your wife."

Diarmad didn't say anything.

"Where in hell does everyone else sleep?" asked Malcolm. The hall of any nobleman usually contained a number of people, sleeping around the fire or tucked away in the corners.

"In the nearby buildings. They're within calling distance."

Malcolm peered at Diarmad as if finding him a very odd fish. The sleepwalking was an affliction indeed, but not one he could be entirely blamed for. Was it possible that he'd murdered his wife while in a deep sleep and had no awareness of doing the deed?

He'd certainly have realized what happened after he awoke and found his clothes and his knife soaked in her blood. At the very least he must have lied and covered for himself after the fact.

But if the door was bolted from the outside, how did his wife try to escape through it?

She forced herself not to stare at him and instead focused on the dishes now arriving at the table. Eggs and fish and all manner of things that she'd prefer not to eat during Advent. She bit her tongue. Compromise was part of marriage and at least the table wasn't laden with roasted pheasant and seared venison.

Margaret steered the conversation away from Beitris's death and Diarmad's strange sleeping habits, by asking which animals were best to hunt during the winter. As expected, the men enthusiastically discussed the topic in great detail and regaled the company with their most exciting adventures. After dinner, they listened to a bard recite a long and barely comprehensible Gaelic tale of how Malcolm's ancestors had defeated their ancient enemies, the Picts.

So much war. So much blood. So many lives lost or ruined. Where does it lead us? Was it part of God's plan to have men fight each other? Or was the true challenge in the effort to prevent war and promote peace amidst the constant warlike rumblings that seemed to fire men's souls?

Her own dear brother—a kind and gentle man by nature, with an interest in philosophy and even in art—talked of little but his plans to take his ancestral homeland back from King William.

He'd already tried and failed twice. Was there no lesson to be learned from his failures and the blood shed in his futile efforts?

Margaret struggled to keep her eyes open as the night stretched on. The bells for Compline sounded and the bard sang on, accompanied by the strumming of his harp. But she didn't dare go to bed and risk them discussing the murder or somehow pinning it all on Aelgith and Osgifu in her absence. She felt in her heart that her purpose on earth—at least right at this moment—was to defend their innocence when they had no one else to stand up for them.

HEADS WERE NODDING and eyes sagging with sleep when the company finally parted. Margaret had been pinching herself and tapping her feet on the floor for some time in her efforts to stay awake. She took her husband's arm gratefully and steered him to their bedchamber.

Sleepy-eyed Grizel led Mac Duff and Enfleda to the bed prepared for them. Margaret had asked her to sleep near their guests to listen for anything that might prove useful in discovering more about them and their relationship with Beitris or her husband.

Diarmad was bedded near enough that Grizel could keep half an ear on him as well. Margaret wondered if he'd rise during the night and make mischief in the king's hall. She'd arranged for two trusted guards to intervene if he even tried to part the bed curtains.

Margaret undressed Malcolm herself, enjoying the affectionate gesture of removing his shoes and untying his hose and even helping to lift his tunic over his head. It always got stuck on his big broad shoulders, where his muscle was so thick that it impeded him from raising his arms high enough.

She felt blessed to have this strong man to protect her. Even if he weren't the king, Malcolm was a man who'd guard his wife and family with his life. She'd never felt safer than in his arms.

They climbed under the covers together. Although sleep crept over her like strong drink, she wanted to put some thoughts in her husband's head before tomorrow's "trial." She might not have a chance in the morning.

"I'm almost certain there's something going on between Enfleda and Diarmad."

"Mmmm." Malcolm murmured sleepily and pulled her closer. His heavy arm on her rib cage pulled her toward sleep.

"Did you hear what I said?" She whispered in his ear as loud as she dared. "I really think Enfleda might have been trying to convince Diarmad to make her pregnant."

Now Malcolm stiffened. It was too dark to see if his eyes snapped open but she could feel his gaze on her. "Enfleda doesn't seem that stupid." His voice was gruff with tiredness. "Did she admit it?"

"Not yet. I need to press Osgifu for more details. Enfleda's been married to Mac Duff for many years with no sign of a baby. She fears to be cast out when she has nowhere to go and no resources to fall back on. Such worries will make a woman take risks that otherwise might seem foolish. I think that's why she stole her own cross. Such a valuable object could secure her future, but it's not truly hers so she'd lose it if she was turned out. I think she saw Aelgith's disappearance as an opportunity. But I suspect her foremost aim was to become pregnant, by any means necessary, because then surely Mac Duff would value her and keep her."

Malcolm hugged her closer. "Truly? You've heard of women doing this?"

"No one I know personally, but I'm sure it happens."

"Should I be worried that my brother Donald Ban is the father of the baby in your belly?" He rocked her gently and she felt his chest shake with silent laughter.

"God forbid. I was blessed to become pregnant easily, but many women are not so lucky."

"Then they spend their lives childless. Like Queen Edith. That's why King Edward had no children and started this whole succession mess which destroyed your entire nation."

"See? If she'd found someone to provide an heir, that might have been prevented."

"Yes, and a pot-boy's son would sit on the throne of England!" Malcolm's broad chest shook with laughter. "I'm telling you, it's preposterous and doesn't happen."

Margaret felt a big sigh rise in her chest. "If you think about it, it makes far more sense for a desperate woman to do...the deed...with someone who has as much to lose as she does. A pot boy might tell everyone he'd tupped the queen."

"And have his head cut off for his troubles."

"True. But a noble, already married and with a reputation —and a head—to keep, would never tell anyone."

"You do make some sense."

"And Diarmad is their nearest noble neighbor. He's a handsome man. Strikingly so, in fact."

"Oh, he is, is he?" Malcolm rocked her in his arms. "Does my wife have eyes for this comely golden youth with his shaven chin, when her husband is a hoary old boar with a full beard with silver hairs in it?"

"Husband, you provoke me! Be serious. You saw how Enfleda's husband treats her, calling her a frost-capped mountain and mocking her. Surely such cruelty would only push her into the arms of a foolish swain her own age. From what Osgifu told me, his marriage to Beitris was unhappy as well. Did you catch the hint that Beitris tried to go back home to Mac Duff but he'd refused?"

"I most certainly did not catch that. I think your mind is muddled by mead."

"I drank nothing but herbal infusions, I assure you." She sighed again. She could see she was knocking on a door that stood firmly shut and bolted. "I shall talk to Osgifu in the morning and see if I can learn more. I just wanted to share my thoughts."

Malcolm's arm had grown limp on her chest. He's asleep! She reminded herself that it was late, he was tired. He'd ignored her ideas. She had to admit they were far fetched. But so was the suggestion that two total strangers—running for their very lives—had taken the time to slay a noble-woman outside her home in the dead of night.

In the morning she'd visit Osgifu and Aelgith and see if she could glean more details that might help prove their innocence.

CHAPTER 19

$\mathcal{M}$argaret rose early as usual. She roused Grizel to accompany her—not to the chapel for prayer, but to the jail. She wanted to go there in secret before the household awoke. She couldn't be seen to side with the captives—not in front of their guests who all hoped to see them swinging from a gibbet or put to the sword before sundown.

Bitter cold made her clutch her fur-lined cloak about her as they navigated the slippery, frosty path to the jail in the dark morning hours. She could wish for stars or even a cold moon above them, but the clouds blotted them out. Grizel's lantern threw enough light for them to pick their way down the hill through the leaf litter on a less-used path where they'd be unlikely to encounter anyone.

The jailer, leaning against the stone wall of the crude building, snapped his head up when Margaret greeted him. Did he sleep standing up? She couldn't imagine how anyone could sleep with this icy wind tugging at their clothes.

He opened the door and let them in. The two women lay curled up like creatures in a burrow. The brazier she'd installed for them had gone out and a cruel chill descended in the cramped space. Margaret asked Grizel to tell the guard to build a fire at once.

Rubbing their eyes, their fingers and toes stiff with the cold, Aelgith and Osgifu tried to rouse themselves. Margaret offered them leftover morsels from last night's feast and a hunk of not-quite-stale bread, along with some small ale to wash it down.

Before long, Grizel had kindled a fire in the brazier, and welcome warmth stirred the cold, damp air. Aelgith and Osgifu ate the food with obvious hunger, but still with the neat manners of gentlewomen, offering each item to the other first, and taking small bites in between thanking Margaret for her kindness.

After they'd had time to awaken and nourish themselves, Margaret readied herself to ask some hard questions. "I don't wish to frighten you, but today you will be on trial for your lives. To better direct the questions, and to make sure the full truth is aired before all, I'd like to see if we can unearth some more details about the events of that fateful night and the time leading up to it."

Aelgith nodded. "We'll tell you everything you want to know. Again, I'm so sorry I was foolish enough to escape in the night. Mac Duff's wife put such fear in me with her tales of beatings and selling girls to Norway."

"Believe me, I understand your fear. She seems a strange and cruel woman. And my most important questions are about her." She sat on the crude bench where Osgifu had been sleeping, close enough to the girl that their knees almost touched. "Osgifu, you said that Enfleda seemed to have an interest in Diarmad, more than his wife. Did they spend time alone together?"

Osgifu hesitated. "I didn't see them do it."

"You didn't see them do what?"

Osgifu wound her hands together. "Anything, really."

"But they did go off together, perhaps while you were in the hall with Beitris?"

Osgifu's mouth worked. "I'm afraid."

"Afraid of what?"

"She said she'd cut my tongue out if I told." The words rushed out of Osgifu's mouth.

Margaret startled. "Enfleda said that?"

The girl nodded.

"What was she afraid of you telling?"

She watched Osgifu's throat move as she swallowed.

Margaret reached out a hand and laid it over the girl's cold, bony fingers. "Telling me now might save your life as well as your tongue."

Osgifu drew in a deep breath. "Enfleda invited Beitris to come visit with her that very day. She asked her to bring a strange assortment of things—wool, linen, needles and thread, all kinds of items for them to make something together. While Beitris was busy gathering these things, and supervising the packing for the journey, she asked Diarmad to show her their new sheep that she'd heard so much about." Osgifu frowned. "Beitris then said that they had no new sheep and she must be confused."

"What did Enfleda say?"

"She ignored her and summoned Beitris's husband outside with her."

"What did Beitris do?"

"She tried to protest, but they were gone before she could form the words."

"Did you get the impression they'd done this before?"

"Yes. He didn't hesitate or seem confused, but hurried out like a cow running to be milked."

"Did you go with her?"

"I started to, but she told me to stay and help Beitris."

"How long were they gone?"

"Not long at all. Just long enough to walk out and see some sheep and admire them and walk back."

"Then what made you think they did more than that?"

"The way they both looked when they returned." She swallowed again. "Diarmad glowed pink like a newborn pup and his eyes sparkled. Also, his dagger was now on the other side of his waist and his hair looked tousled as if someone had run their fingers through it."

"And Enfleda?"

"She looked like the cat that got the cream. Her lips were red as if she'd been eating raspberries. And there were shreds of bark on the back of her dress like she'd been leaning against a tree." Osgifu shuddered suddenly. "But I didn't see them do anything! I don't even know why she said she'd cut my tongue out. I suppose she might have guessed that I'd suspect something and didn't want me gossiping with the servants."

Margaret was disappointed by this lack of solid evidence that something untoward happened between Diarmad and Enfleda. "Did Beitris seem to suspect anything?"

"She seemed angry the whole time we were there. She scolded her husband. She treated him more like a child than a grown man."

Margaret frowned. "I suppose that would help drive him into another woman's arms. Did you see anything between Diarmad and Enfleda—some flirtation perhaps—either on the journey back to Mac Duff's or while they were there?

"Diarmad didn't come on the journey. He stayed at Balbarnie. If anything I'd say Beitris was glad to leave him behind."

"What gave you that impression?"

"Back at Cupar, she complained about him to her father.

Said he was a fool and a wastrel and that his nighttime wanderings unsettled her."

"How did her father react?"

"He told her not to speak ill of her husband. He didn't want to hear any of it. She didn't say anything after that."

"How did Enfleda and Beitris get along with each other?"

"They were cordial, in a stiff, polite way. They certainly didn't confide in one another. I found it odd that Enfleda didn't say anything about Beitris's coming baby or even her pregnancy. Not even once that I heard. Like she was pretending it didn't exist."

Margaret shivered inwardly, remembering that poor Beitris must have been only weeks from delivering her baby when she was cruelly murdered. But she still didn't understand why anyone would want her dead.

Jealous Enfleda couldn't have killed her since she was at Cupar when Beitris died. Servants had confirmed that neither Mac Duff or Enfleda left the hall on the night Betris was killed. And with Beitris dead Enfleda would have no pretext to visit her lover at Balbarnie. If he even was her lover. Right now there was nothing but supposition to suggest that anything really happened between her and Diarmad.

"Did you ever see Diarmad act cruelly toward Beitris?" She hoped Osgifu could give her at least a seed of motive to plant in the minds of those still sleeping in the tower, who would decide her fate today.

"Not that I can think of. Diarmad was always on his best behavior in front of her father when they came to visit."

"How did Mac Duff's family treat you during your captivity there?"

"I was treated like any other servant. They have servants who are kin to local families and slaves captured in England

and they're not treated that differently, except that some-times the slaves are sold or traded."

"Who do they sell them to?"

"I don't know. One young man was just told to dress himself in his cloak and boots and he left with a party of Mac Duff's men. We never saw him again." Osgifu's lip quivered. "I think we all lived in fear of that."

"Why did Enfleda not try to sell you if she thought you suspected something between her and Diarmad?"

"She did suggest it to Mac Duff. One of the girls told me she heard her telling him I was lazy. But he wouldn't hear of it. He said I might mature into something worth keeping about the place."

Margaret swallowed and Aelgith's hand flew to her mouth.

"How did Enfleda react to that?"

"She stormed off, from what I heard."

"Did Mac Duff ever...take advantage of the female servants or slaves?"

"Yes."

Margaret's felt her chest constrict. This was why Aelgith journeyed to this northern kingdom by herself, desperate to rescue her daughter. But disgraceful and ungodly though it was, such treatment of powerless young girls was hardly rare, even among English nobles. Would Aelgith have been able to keep her daughter safe even if they did escape?

"Can you tell us anything else you know about Beitris? Is there any reason someone might want her dead?"

Osgifu shook her head.

Margaret looked at Aelgith. "It puzzles me...why would Diarmad kill his wife when she's about to give him an heir? Such a thing makes no sense to me. Even if his wife was an unbearable shrew he'd surely at least wait until the babe was born and suckled before ridding himself of her."

"It does seem that Beitris was unhappy with her husband," said Aelgith. "And complaining to her father about him."

"But her complaints fell on deaf ears," replied Margaret. "All women probably complain about their husbands to some extent. Especially during the early years of marriage when they're getting used to each other. In many ways her father is right, it's her duty to make the marriage work."

She turned to Grizel. "Have you managed to find out any more from Diarmad's servants?" She'd asked the girl to listen to their conversations where possible, and to ask any questions she might without giving away her purpose.

"Nothing damning. Diarmad is a difficult man, to be sure, with his nighttime wanderings and a short temper. But he didn't beat her or berate her from what I could gather."

Margaret sighed. "I do so wish you hadn't fled on that night. That you'd given me time to bargain for Osgifu's freedom."

Aelgith lowered her gaze. "I panicked. I wanted to take her home."

"Home? Where is freedom and safety to you, in these troubled times? You do realize the Normans rule Hampshire now, as they do all of England? Any speech that isn't French may mark you as their enemy."

"I'd hoped to disappear, perhaps into the great woodlands there, and live quietly, away from men, as outlaws do." She looked up and Margaret saw tears filling her eyes. "What more could I even dare to hope for?"

Margaret couldn't see how two women living in the woods could hope for much in the way of peace and safety without at least a male companion with swordsmanship skills, but she held her tongue.

"I suppose true safety lies only in Heaven," said Aelgith grimly. "And I surely don't wish to risk my passage there by murdering a stranger."

"Indeed, the peace of Heaven is our one true place of rest," said Margaret. These two women might find themselves standing at the gates of Heaven before dusk. Would that not be a blessed release of sorts from the horrors and hardships they'd endured here on earth?

Her flesh recoiled from the idea that they should die—sacrificed to save the true killer—to somehow maintain the natural order of things here in this strange northern kingdom of fierce warlords.

She did not intend to let that happen if she could help it.

"Pray with all the energy you can muster," she pleaded. "Pray for your lives and pray for your souls and above all pray that God's justice be done here in Dunfermline."

CHAPTER 20

$\mathcal{B}$arely stirring when they left, the household bustled with activity when they returned to the tower. Men and women from the village brought baskets of eggs and buckets of milk and sacks of oats and flour for the kitchen. Three young boys arrived, each carrying a live chicken squawking under each arm, which gave Margaret a moment of alarm.

She headed into the kitchen in a separate building directly next to the tower. "They're not going to kill chickens for the table during Advent, are they?" she asked the cook.

"No, my lady. But Christmas is in three days. We're storing up the plumpest and juiciest fowl to celebrate the birth of our Lord. Rest assured they shall not meet their end until the time is right."

She climbed the stairs to the hall, where servants were setting up the trestle tables and benches for the morning meal. The dogs sleeping near the fire moved reluctantly away from the brooms and took themselves downstairs and outside to do their business. The two story hall had initially confused the poor creatures, and their habits had required some retraining, but thankfully all but the oldest, a white-muzzled retired hunting dog, had now warmed to this new routine.

Margaret would have loved to slip away to the chapel—or just a quiet corner—to spend time in prayer but with their guests about to make an appearance from behind their bed curtains, and their attendants already stirring in their various sleeping locations, she reluctantly devoted herself to hostess duties.

She told Grizel to listen in on their guests as they awakened. She was busy criticizing the crumpled tablecloth and the haphazard placement of bowls and cups, when heavy footsteps clumped up the stairs, causing the old dog to stir and bark.

"My lady, a messenger has arrived," said the young page she'd been training to announce visitors.

"You should tread more lightly on the stairs," said Margaret, as gently as possible. The boy was only twelve or thirteen but already taller than her. "Where is he?"

"I'll get him." He thundered downstairs again and returned with a tired and cold-looking man wrapped in a cloak with frost still dusting the hem, his nose and cheeks reddened by the wind.

"I'm from Bishop Elwerde's," he said, somewhat breathless.

Bishop Elwerde? She'd never even heard of such a person. "What is your message?"

"Your husband requested information on the whereabouts of Father Torcall, and the word spread to Bishop Elwerde. He would like to inform you that Father Torcall has been living among the Culdees in a cave only three miles from his seat in Perth."

Margaret's heart beat faster. Father Torcall was the priest who'd lived at Balbarnie and attended to the Mac Aidh family there. He'd have heard confessions from Diarmad and Beitris and everyone else in the family and would surely be able to share at least some insight into them.

"Is he here?" She looked behind him.

"Nay, my lady. He was in rather a state when we found him."

"A state? What do you mean?"

The messenger swallowed. "Addled with drink, my lady. We managed to get him onto a horse but were unable to keep him up there."

Margaret stared at him in disbelief. "So where is he?"

"We sent a cart to carry him here. It's on its way by now, I'd imagine, but it will be some hours before he arrives since a cart travels slowly over the countryside."

Margaret wasn't convinced that a cart would make much headway at all, given the lack of roads. On the plus side, the ground was frozen so it was less likely to sink into a bog and the journey would give him time to sober up.

"Please bring him to the hall at once when he arrives, and thank Bishop Elwerde for helping us find him." She would have to visit Bishop Elwerde and give him a donation or other reward in the new year.

A runaway priest living in a cave and drinking himself into a stupor? Whatever would she hear of next in this wild land?

Enfleda emerged from behind the screen set up to give her and her husband privacy while they dressed. A fresh white veil covered her head and her two plaits hung freshly braided and wrapped with criss-crossed blue ribbon beneath it.

Her face looked pale as a ghost, with almost no color in her lips or cheeks, only a little redness around her eyes, perhaps from the late night. Or fear of what might be uttered about her during today's proceedings.

Enfleda's entire bearing seemed rigid with tension, shoulders hunched and fingers crooked around her bejeweled cross as if it was flotsam in the sea that might keep her afloat in a tempest.

"God's blessings upon you this fine morning," said Margaret, with feigned cheer. She did wish God's blessings upon all his creatures, even the more unpleasant ones. "Can I tempt you with fresh apple pastries, hot out of the oven?"

Enfleda looked as if she'd been offered a plate of broken glass.

"Wife, bring me the hot pastries in bed!" Margaret jumped at the sound of Mac Duff's voice booming out from behind the bed curtains.

"Yes, husband." The look on Enfleda's face made Margaret feel an unexpected pang of sympathy for the woman. She looked embarrassed at being treated like a servant, especially in front of her queen. She wondered if Mac Duff had done that on purpose, since he must have heard them talking.

"Let me have Grizel fetch those for you," said Margaret, since Enfleda had already moved toward the table to do her husband's bidding. "You and I shall take up seats by the fire and sup some hot milk. The servants have banked the hearth high and soon it will feel like a June morning in here."

"I'd better get them myself," said Enfleda quietly. "My husband is particular."

Margaret nodded her assent and watched as Enfleda took a plate and piled three pastries upon it. She also had a servant pour a cup of small ale and then carried the plate and cup to the edge of the bed curtains, in full view of all the servants in the hall—many of whom were now staring at her.

Is this such a strange sight? Why do I never carry my husband breakfast in our bed? She couldn't think of a time when she had. It was second nature to ask someone else to do it. Which perhaps was the most appropriate behavior for a queen, though it did suggest a lack of Christian humility.

"What a wonderful idea," said Margaret aloud. She walked toward the table, a beatific expression on her face, as if serving one's husband breakfast in bed was the most natural and normal behavior in the world. Grizel beat her to the table and had anticipated her needs and put three pastries on a plate before she even reached it. "Small ale as well, my lady?" asked Grizel, with a rather bemused expression.

"A lovely idea," said Margaret. It was! First, it would surprise and possibly delight her husband. Second, it was a mortification to her own pride, which was in constant need of mortification, especially now she was queen. And third it would perhaps make her guest feel less awkward, and she always strove to provide comfort to her guests.

Margaret allowed Grizel to carry the plate and cup out of the hall and into the bedchamber, since her dress was too long to allow her to walk without holding up the front at least a few inches. As she approached the bed she took the plate and cup and announced her intention so as not to surprise Malcolm in the middle of itching himself or worse. He snatched back the curtain and stared at her in confusion.

"What's the meaning of this, woman?"

Margaret wobbled, almost spilling the ale. "Enfleda is serving her husband pastries in bed and I thought you might enjoy the same."

"Ah." He looked at her as if she might have lost her mind. "Well, these pastries do look tasty. Why don't you come join me to enjoy them?" He patted the bed covers next to him.

"I think I'd better entertain our guests," she replied quickly. She wished she had learned something truly damning from Enfleda that she might whisper in his ear to point the finger of blame firmly at Diarmad or…well, anyone except Aelgith and Osgifu, but she couldn't.

Still… She leaned in and lowered her voice. "Enfleda told Osgifu she'd cut her tongue out if she said anything about what she'd seen her do with Diarmad."

"What did she see her do?" asked Malcolm, with a bite of pastry in his mouth.

"She saw them disappear off outside and come back disheveled and flushed, as if they'd been—" She swallowed, unsure of a polite word for what they'd likely been doing. "Up against a tree. Enfleda had bark on the back of her dress."

Malcolm's eyebrows rose. "I struggle to believe that even Diarmad is stupid enough to tup his father-in-law's wife."

"They're both young. I hear the temptations of lust can compel men to take dangerous liberties. And she may have been motivated by a need to become pregnant to keep her marriage and status. Her husband is older and perhaps no longer capable of…"

Now he frowned. "Her husband is barely older than me!"

His raised voice alarmed her and she raised a finger to her lips. "He's at least ten years older than you. Look at the age of his children! Yours are still youths and his are all married."

He huffed. "That does make me feel a bit better."

"Be serious, husband! Today Aelgith and Osgifu are on trial for their lives."

"And who is to be the judge that determines their future?" His placid expression was intended to be a provocation. But his words soothed her. Did he intend to protect them using his authority as king?

"Our Father in Heaven?" she said, afraid to be too hopeful.

"The King of the Scots, that's who. On the other hand,

given Mac Duff's freedom to dispense law in his own realm, he will need to be thoroughly convinced of their innocence—as will everyone else in attendance."

"Including your brother, Donald Ban."

"Especially him."

Margaret's heart sank. Donald Ban loved to sow unease and discord wherever he could. He also hated the English. He only tolerated her and her family because his brother forced him to. Even then he could be surprisingly rude.

She drew in a shaky breath. If she were Malcolm she'd banish Donald Ban. "You're the king, not him."

"Aye, but he's the king's brother." He took another bite of pastry, followed by a swig of ale. "And with any luck he won't turn up." His expression told her that the discussion was over.

"Enjoy your breakfast, husband." She closed the curtain to leave him in peace.

Unsettled, she wished she could hide away and pray. She'd pray fiercely for the salvation of Aelgith and Osgifu. Or, if the worst must happen, for the safe passage of their souls to heaven.

But raised voices suggested that her guests had now all risen and were gathering around the table to break their fast.

Margaret sent Aelgith and Osgifu a comb and water to make themselves presentable for the trial. Every new arrival on the stairs made her stomach clench. Would Donald Ban arrive to interfere with the proceedings? How would he even know that Mac Duff and Mac Aidh were here to determine who had killed Beitris?

Did he have spies in the court? She hadn't thought about it before, but it made sense that he would. Or perhaps

Malcolm had told him? She didn't understand her husband's affection for his brother, but then her own brother irked her greatly on many occasions—some of them involving bloodshed and danger to the whole family—and she couldn't imagine turning away from him. So she understood.

More people arrived, suggesting that Malcolm must have sent word to some nearby manors. As they were announced, she deduced that these men weren't mormaers or thanes, but were knights of a sort—some Scots, at least one Norse and two possibly Irish—who must have been invited here to watch or even participate in the proceedings. Each of them came and bowed to her, and she nodded and said polite greetings in her best Gaelic.

Benches, chairs and stools had been gathered from every corner and even then there were not enough to seat the gathered company. Burly men stood along the walls and hunkered down in corners, murmuring to each other in heavily accented Gaelic.

Margaret sat off to one side in a throne-like chair, slightly elevated on a dais, which gave her a commanding view of the proceedings. Her husband's chair sat empty next to her. He'd chosen, at least for now, to sit at the table among the other men.

The English queen. She knew that's how they referred to her. Perhaps they'd hoped for one of their own daughters to marry the king and resented the interloper. Or maybe they thought that Edgar, denied the throne of England, might set his sights on Malcolm's throne.

She struggled not to flinch each time one of them cast a curious glance in her direction. She'd tried to encourage Christina and Agatha to take up seats next to her so they might present a united flank, but they both begged off and had now disappeared into the crowd.

Margaret tried to keep her eye on Enfleda, who also

seemed intent on invisibility. Mac Duff's wife had spent the early morning hours bent over some needlework—an attempt at Opus Anglicanum from the look of it—with one of her women, though they didn't seem to be making much progress. She suspected they were unpicking more stitches than they sewed.

All heads swiveled to the staircase as the young herald announced Aelgith and Osgifu's arrival. She saw them shrink even further into their frail bodies under the punishing stares that greeted them as they topped the stairs. Likely every man here already assumed they'd murdered a young pregnant woman—the flower of Scots nobility—on her own manor.

Dressed in the clothing she'd scavenged for them, with Aelgith in Christina's blue gown, they looked like respectable Englishwomen, not escaped slaves. Aelgith wore her braids bundled up under her veil, but Osgifu's long light-brown braids hung down over her shoulders, neatly wrapped with ribbon, and her head was bare, revealing her youth and her frightened expression.

Aelgith held her head high, which must have taken considerable effort given the wave of disapproval washing toward her from all directions. Osgifu made the same effort but soon faltered and dropped her gaze to the floor.

The two women were brought to stand before the high table, where Malcolm sat with Edgar, Mac Duff and Diarmad and several other prominent nobles. No sign yet of Donald Ban, thank goodness.

"Murderers!" Diarmad rose to his feet, chair scraping then falling to the floor behind him with a loud clatter. "They killed my wife and baby!"

The outburst startled Margaret to the edge of her seat and generated a rumble of agreement and surprise among the crowd.

Margaret cursed inwardly. Diarmad's calculated and aggressive effort to pin blame on the two women surprised her. Perhaps he was less stupid than she'd bargained for. She wished her husband was here beside her so she could whisper about the injustice of this outburst in his ear.

But perhaps that was why he'd chosen not to sit with her. She'd promised herself that she'd try to sit quietly and let her husband lead the proceedings. She knew his standing among his men and their respect for him held up his kingdom like the pillars in a cathedral. An English queen was bad enough but one with a mouth full of strident opinions was surely even worse.

The two men next to Diarmad had grabbed him. She couldn't tell if they meant to offer him a hug of solace or to restrain him from climbing over the table to wring Aelgith and Osgifu's necks. The two women now clutched each other, and Margaret could hear Osgifu sobbing gently.

Malcolm said something to Diarmad. He spoke fast and in the Gaelic tongue but she suspected it was something about getting a grip on himself.

Malcolm now banged a heavy silver goblet on the table to command attention. "Silence! Any further outbursts by either the accused or the accusers will be punished. In agreement with my dear friend and ally Mac Duff, Earl and Mormaer of Fife and chief of the Clan Mac Duff, I, Malcolm, King of the Scots and high justiciar for this realm will be the final arbiter of guilt and punishment."

Margaret attempted to relax enough to draw some air into her lungs. It wouldn't do to faint and fall off her dais.

"I shall conduct these proceedings in English as it is the only language spoken at least in part by all relevant parties, including the accused." Margaret silently thanked God for this, as Aelgith and Osgifu could hardly defend themselves if they couldn't understand a word being uttered around them.

Though she reasoned that Osgifu must surely have picked up some of the Gaelic tongue during her months in captivity in Mac Duff's household.

She already knew that Mac Duff and Diarmad spoke English, like most of the nobles she'd met in the southern reaches of her husband's kingdom. She'd been told that the further north one ventured the less likely one was to understand a word anyone said—regardless of what language they spoke in.

"These two women"—Malcolm gestured toward Aelgith and Osgifu—"Stand here today accused of murdering Beitris, the daughter of Mac Duff and the wife of Diarmad Mac Aidh, as they passed by his settlement at Balbarnie. I will ask the older of you first, what have you to say for yourself?"

CHAPTER 21

$\mathcal{A}$elgith, who already looked pale and frail as a stray feather, swayed as if buffeted by a breeze. Then she stiffened. "My Lord, I must first apologize for abusing your wife's hospitality by quitting her company without warning."

Margaret stiffened. She rather wished Aelgith hadn't reminded them of this first betrayal.

"But when I laid eyes on my dear daughter, only fourteen years of age, held captive in slavery, my only instinct was to set her free." Her voice wobbled. Osgifu stared down at the floor, head bowed. "My hope was to escape back to our home in England. We did pass by the settlement at Balbarnie in the hours before dawn but we did not kill anyone."

Aelgith paused to take a breath. Margaret watched her bony chest rise under her gown.

"Then how did you come to be drenched in the blood of the lady of Balbarnie?" asked Malcolm. His gruff voice held an accusatory tone that caused Aelgith to shrink back slightly.

"As we hurried past, keeping our distance from the settlement, we heard a cry in the dark. At first, we thought it was a wounded animal and—"

Margaret clenched with horror. Would Aelgith now say that she'd thought of roasting and eating the creature now known to be Mac Duff's wife? She prayed with all fury that Aelgith had the common sense not to introduce that image into the heads of these Scotsmen.

"And it caused us to pause. We decided to see what kind of animal it was and when we drew closer we discovered it was a woman, lying on her side, hunched in pain." Aelgith paused, perhaps wondering how to describe what happened next. The silence stretched out until Margaret forced herself not to squirm in her chair. Perhaps Aelgith was lost in a dark world of the mind, reliving the horrors of that night.

"Did you speak to her?" asked Malcolm.

"Yes." His words seemed to startle Aelgith back to the present. "We were scared, to be sure, but even in the darkness of the pre-dawn hours we could tell she was hurt and fallen to the cold ground. On a winter's night a body could freeze and perish quickly. I asked her if she needed help getting up."

"What did she say?" asked Malcolm, apparently impatient of another pause.

"She couldn't really talk anymore, but I heard the same sound over and over again—*Tas*. Even my daughter, who'd lived among the Scots for months, didn't know what it meant. She was gasping for air, barely able to make a sound."

Aelgith stopped and swallowed. "We could hardly leave her there. She would have died from the cold before morning. At that time we didn't realize she'd been stabbed, or that she was soaked in blood, since it was so dark. I begged my daughter to help me carry her to at least the edge of the settlement where she might be found before she froze to death."

"Girl, what did you think when your mother asked you to carry her?"

Osgifu looked terrified. "I didn't want to. I wanted to keep running." Her lip quivered. Perhaps she was ashamed to admit that she cared more about saving her own skin than helping the fallen woman.

But it would have been so much better if they'd kept running.

"But you didn't want to disobey your mother?" asked Malcolm, in a much kinder tone.

Osgifu swallowed. "I was so grateful that she came to find me. I couldn't refuse her." She spoke so quietly that Margaret could barely make out her words.

"So you picked up the lady Beitris, who lay fallen and injured on the ground, and you carried her to the settlement?" asked Malcolm.

Aelgith nodded. "I took her head and my daughter took her feet. We knew where the settlement was even in the dark because two fires burned outside it."

Fires were set outside at night to keep wild boar at bay. While the boar were a popular hunting quarry and could make a tasty feast, they also had sharp teeth and were known to attack and eat children or the weak.

"We carried her to the edge of the ditch outside the settlement, and Osgifu pleaded with me to leave her there. By this time we'd realized she was bleeding, as you could smell the scent of her blood and we felt its stickiness on our fingers. She seemed to be bleeding from both front and back. She also hadn't breathed a word since we picked her up and she hung limp in our arms as if she were already dead."

Aelgith's face crumpled at the grim memory.

"If you thought she was already dead, why didn't you leave her and flee?" asked Malcolm.

Aelgith drew in a slow breath. "She was still warm. I

thought there was a chance she could be saved. What use would it be to save our mortal bodies if we abandoned this woman in her time of need and lost our immortal souls?"

Well said! Margaret inwardly praised her for introducing this line of thought. Someone concerned for the fate of her soul would hardly kill a total stranger for no discernible reason.

"So we carried her over the ditch, which wasn't a deep one. The light of dawn now hovered just behind the hills to the east so we could tell which building was the hall. We hurried to the back of it and left her right by the door there, then hurried away.

Malcolm frowned. "How was anyone to find her at the back door of the hall? Why would you risk entering the settlement and then not wake anyone?"

Aelgith faltered. Her lips trembled. "I was afraid, sir. Afraid for myself and my daughter."

"Did you realize that your clothes were soaked in blood?"

"I knew I had blood on my hands. They were sticky with it. We didn't discover the full extent of the staining until the sun rose higher in the sky."

The awful image prompted Margaret to close her eyes and say a swift prayer for poor Beitris and the passage of her soul to Heaven. What a terrible way to die—but at least she'd been in the caring arms of strangers and not left to perish alone on the cold moor.

"How did you expect to escape when you were stained with blood?" asked Malcolm.

"Since our cloaks had parted when we lifted our arms to carry the dead woman, the blood covered our gowns. Our cloaks had little blood on them. So as long as we kept our cloaks closed over our stained gowns, no one would know."

"And how did you intend to obtain new clothes?" asked

Malcolm, clearly curious. "Did you have money? Or did you intend to steal them?"

Aelgith hesitated. "I'd hoped to be able to wash our clothes at some point."

"In the dead of winter when the rivers have ice forming at their edges? And you would crouch naked over the stream while you did this?"

Aelgith's lip trembled again. "To be sure, helping this woman was a mistake that likely doomed us to discovery and capture."

"So you wish you'd left her to die alone on the moor." He stated it coldly.

"No!" Aelgith's eyes closed and her forehead crumpled. "I don't know. I do know that I didn't kill her, or harm a hair on her head, and neither did my daughter."

Margaret realized that she was holding her breath again. She exhaled gently and drew in a new breath, attempting to calm herself. Diarmad's face was rigid with anger as he stared at the two women as if they truly had killed his beloved wife.

"Did you know that the woman you carried was with child?"

"No," said Aelgith. "It was dark. I did notice it when we laid her down, though, since her cloak fell back to reveal her swollen belly."

"Murderer!" cried Diarmad. "Twice a murderer!"

"Silence!" barked Malcolm at Diarmad. "You were warned to mind your mouth and now shall pay with five of your best sheep."

Diarmad's mouth fell open.

Margaret blinked, glad Malcolm was seemingly willing to take against his nobles, if the need arose.

"Now I have questions for your daughter." Malcolm

looked at Osgifu, who stood visibly trembling from head to toe, face white. "You knew the lady Beitris, didn't you?"

Osgifu nodded stiffly, as if she worried that her head might fall off her shoulders. "But...but..." she struggled to find her voice.

"But what?" asked Malcolm, at least somewhat gently.

"It was too dark to see her features when we found her. I didn't realize who it was until we laid her down at the door of her hall."

Malcolm looked surprised. "But then you did know. You knew that the lady of Balbarnie now lay dead on the doorstep of her own hall, and you failed to raise an alarm?"

Margaret stiffened. This was indeed damning.

"If she'd breathed, my lord...if her body still quickened with any life at all—" said Osgifu. "But she was gone and I wanted to escape with my life."

"You were—you are—the property of the Earl of Fife." He peered at her. "His stolen property."

Margaret stared at her husband. She bit her tongue. King William had forbidden the sale of slaves out of England! These savage men would probably claim that they didn't buy them; they were legitimately seized spoils of war.

She drew in a measured breath, attempting to calm herself.

"I stole her," said Aelgith suddenly. "The fault is mine. She resisted leaving."

"Is this true?" asked Malcolm of Osgifu.

The girl nodded. "I was afraid. I didn't want to be hunted down. I thought we'd die out in the cold. My mother insisted that God would protect us."

"And you chose to obey your mother instead of your master?"

"I was so shocked to see her there. I'd thought I'd never see her again. If she could find me I thought anything was possible and perhaps the Lord would deliver me from captivity as he delivered the slaves from Egypt."

Margaret admired this new wise comparison, grateful that Osgifu had found her tongue and remembered her education.

"Did Mac Duff treat you ill, while you were in his household?" asked Malcolm, tilting his head slightly.

"No, sir. I had food and clothing and my duties were not too hard, which is all a slave can hope for." Osgifu's mouth trembled at the word slave. Clearly it was hard to call herself such. Born a noblewoman, she must have once hoped for a kind husband with a well-run estate and a brood of pretty children to dote on.

Margaret couldn't imagine surviving such a cruel turnabout of circumstance. She'd survived a variety of horrible surprises—her father's death and William's invasion being the two worst to date—but had never lost her noble status or the privileges and protections that came with it.

Could such a disaster happen to her, too, if her husband was killed and her brother taken prisoner—or worse? Could she and her sister and mother be dragged onto a ship and.... She snapped her attention back to the trial. Such doom-laden thoughts were a temptation from the Devil and had no place in her mind.

"If you're not hanged for murder, you'll be returned to the house of your master," said Malcolm coolly.

Margaret leaned forward in her chair, an outburst on her lips. She'd promised Aelgith that they'd free her daughter! She managed to stop herself just in time. Surely Malcolm didn't mean to keep the girl enslaved? Perhaps he was just bargaining for her life.

Osgifu's eyelids fluttered as if she were struggling to keep them open and her gaze fell to the floor again. Aelgith's face had tightened into a mask.

This is why I stole her! Margaret could feel Aelgith's protest as if she'd shouted it aloud. She didn't trust these Scots—she didn't trust Margaret—to win her daughter's freedom.

Margaret wished she could take her husband aside and try to drum some sense into him. Did he truly think it right that high-born ladies should be forced to sweep floors and scrub dishes for the rest of their lives? She diverted her energy into a quick prayer for forbearance and patience, two things she suffered a painful lack of at this moment.

"In my view, it seems unlikely that either of these two women—a frail and malnourished mother and her thin daughter who barely reaches her shoulder—could have inflicted the stab wounds that we found in Beitris's body." Malcolm looked directly at Mac Duff. No doubt Beitris's father's opinion weighed more than Diarmad's, since he was a more important chieftain and ally.

Malcolm turned his gaze on Diarmad. "Which leads me to find that my ally and neighbor, Diarmad Mac Aidh, may have committed the crime."

"This is an outrage!" Diarmad rose to his feet again.

"Mind your tongue, boy!" roared, Malcolm. His voice echoed off the walls and the ceilings and even off the swords and cups and plates and rang in the air for some moments. Diarmad had the decency to look chastened. "My wife and I examined your knife and found it to have blood on it."

"That was fr—" The words shriveled on his lips and Malcolm slammed his hand down on the table, causing all the cups and goblets to rattle.

"We also found rings of dried blood around your wrists, right where your cuffs would be, and traces of burned cloth in the brazier in your sleeping quarters. These items together suggest that you might have stabbed her and made efforts to clean yourself and destroy your clothes, and even wiped your blade with a cloth but neglected to wash the blood out of the carved design."

Margaret knew that only a fool washed a steel blade with water for it would surely rust as it dried. It was better to scrub it with a handful of wood ash.

"But now you may speak and plead your innocence if you wish. Just remember that God hears any lies you tell and will store them to weigh against you on Judgment Day."

Margaret approved of this reminder that his moral failings would catch up with him. However, if he'd murdered his wife he'd hardly be expecting anything but the fires of hell by now...if he even believed in God and the hereafter.

Diarmad rose to his feet. "Why would I kill my wife who was heavy with my child? Surely this is all I could wish for and the fulfillment of any man's hopes for the future." His voice shook a little, perhaps trembling under the force of Malcolm's gaze.

Margaret glanced at Enfleda to see her reaction to this. Sure enough, her face looked pinched and her lips narrowed to a hard line. She'd failed to fulfill her husband's dreams and secure her own future as his wife or even his widow, leaving her in a precarious position.

"In truth, your wife was fed up with you." Mac Duff's deep voice cut through the air. "She'd begged me to take her back."

Diarmad's mouth opened and closed like a fish on land, gasping for air. "And you killed her for the shame of it!" he cried, staring at Mac Duff. "An honor killing! Anything but accept her returning home in shame having failed in her marriage. Her last word was *Tas*, which means father in the Pictish language. Surely she accused her killer with her last breaths!"

This outburst silenced everyone in the room. Mac Duff himself looked too stunned to even protest.

Margaret looked at Malcolm, who seemed to be considering this new possibility. Then she looked at Enfleda, whose face had brightened considerably. Did Enfleda relish the prospect that her husband might now hang for the crime, leaving her free to marry her lover?

"Mormaer Mac Duff," said Malcolm calmly. "What did your daughter say to you about her husband?"

"She told me he was a madman who drank and raved and wandered about at night. She also said he had the brain of a squirrel and didn't have a thought in his head about anything except his food and his hunting." Mac Duff glowered.

"And what did you say to her when she asked to come home?"

"I didn't take her seriously. Women can go half-mad when pregnant, as I'm sure you all know."

Margaret flinched, as several people turned to look at her. She lifted her chin, indignant, not wanting to dignify the barbed comment with a reaction.

Malcolm crossed his arms over his chest. "So you told her to go back to her husband."

"I did indeed. I told her to mind her household and that managing her husband's moods and mischiefs was as much her duty as managing her cook and washerwoman."

"See?" cried Diarmad, newly animated. "He was furious with her! He didn't want her back. He must have sent someone to silence her."

Was this even a possibility? Margaret studied Malcolm's face. She couldn't be sure that he'd entirely ruled it out. It seemed unlikely in the extreme—to her—but she was still learning the mores and manners of these chieftains, governed by their ancient lineage more than modern customs.

Suddenly Enfleda spoke. "My husband would never do any such thing! After he sent his daughter back to her husband, I told him to calm himself and to pray with me for the success of their marriage and the blessed birth of their child."

Mac Duff now looked at his wife as if she'd lost her mind. "Shut up, woman, with your nonsense."

Audible gasps followed, and Margaret suspected that one came from her mouth.

"I'm defending you!" protested Enfleda.

"Not one man here thinks I killed my daughter," said Mac Duff. "Am I right?" He looked at Malcolm. Then he turned back to Enfleda. "I wonder if you had some reason to wish for Beitris to meet with misfortune."

"What? Why would I want that?"

Malcolm leaned back in his chair and cleared his throat. "It has been observed by some that you've been married to your husband for several years now, and despite your youth and vigor have yet to give him an heir."

Enfleda's mouth turned down and an ugly line appeared beneath her plucked brows. "I'm young yet and have patience and faith in the Lord that he shall give us a child."

Margaret stared at her husband, praying he wouldn't look at her. If he did, everyone there would probably know that she put this flea in his ear.

Malcolm continued. "I wonder if you thought to help the Lord in his work by encouraging another man to plant his seed in you."

Enfleda paled and Margaret watched her shrink into her chair. "What? Never!"

Mac Duff's face changed color entirely, growing beet-red as his bushy brows lowered. He turned to Malcolm. "Who, pray, do you suspect of sowing his bastard seed in my wife?" His voice contained more than a little of a growl or snarl, and one of the dogs near the fire responded to it, jumping to his feet and growling back very low and menacing.

Malcolm now looked at Diarmad, whose eyes widened under his gaze. "Never! I...I would never!"

"Methinks your guilt has spurred you to answer before I even asked the question," said Malcolm slowly.

Margaret realized she was holding her breath again. A burst of pride and satisfaction that her husband had taken her words to heart warmed her. She looked quickly at Aelgith and Osgifu, whose faces showed no expression at all.

Malcolm inhaled slowly. "We have heard that when Enfleda made a visit to the house of Diarmad and Beitris, she took advantage of an opportunity to slip away into the woods with him, and returned disheveled and flushed."

Diarmad flew to his feet—for the third time? Margaret was losing count. "Who said such a thing? I'll have his head!"

Margaret prayed that he wouldn't say it was Osgifu, the slave girl, who might be easily discredited now that she stood accused of murder and had motive to point a finger at someone else.

"I've heard enough!" roared Mac Duff. Suddenly he was on his feet, sword drawn. Diarmad pulled his blade from his sheath, and half the assembled company ducked under the table as their great swords banged together in an almighty clash.

CHAPTER 22

*S*creams rent the air and the sound of furniture falling, dogs barking and footsteps pelting across the wood floor half made Margaret want to cover her ears. The long swords flashed through the air and the company scattered. One young man crawled under the table and across the floor on all fours like an insect scuttling from a fire. Others rose to their feet and drew their swords, standing armed and ready, with their eyes on their king.

Malcolm sat still as a statue in his chair. Margaret expected him to call for guards to break them up. Surely he wasn't going to allow a fight in his hall? It took all her fortitude to follow his example and stay still in her seat.

"I'll have your head myself!" roared Mac Duff. Despite his age, which must be twice Diarmad's, he bested him almost immediately, drawing blood from Diarmad's arm as he knocked the younger man's sword from his hand and sent it clattering across the floor. He then pointed his sword into the younger man's chest. "Are you ready to die?"

"I did not call for trial by combat!" boomed Malcolm. To Margaret's surprise, his face showed amusement. "Though if

I had, it's clear that the Mormaer of Fife would easily win the honors." Malcolm leaned back in his chair as if viewing an enjoyable jongleur. "However such is not necessary since I did not suspect him for even one instant of murdering his daughter and I find the accusation points the finger of guilt at the one who made it."

Margaret realized she was gripping the arms of her chair. She took a moment to feel grateful that no one else appeared to be injured. The men who'd fled for cover now eased out of their hiding places and tried to resume their former seats without drawing attention. The young man who'd crawled under the table looked mortified...as well he might in this warrior culture.

"I should cut your head off right now, and it's only out of respect for our king that I'm restraining myself," growled Mac Duff.

"Your wife wanted me to kill her," said Diarmad, in a squeaky voice. He squirmed under Mac Duff's sword and the sharp point made a hole in his tunic.

"You dare to blame my wife for your evil deeds. I'll pierce your heart right now!"

"Stand down, Mac Duff," bellowed Malcolm. The force of his voice made Margaret flinch. She glanced at Enfleda—wait, where was Enfleda?

Several people were now staring at the place where Enfleda had been sitting before the fight broke out. Chairs and benches had tipped over in the melée and she realized that one still lay fallen on the floor.

"Where is my wife?" shouted Mac Duff.

His men rose to their feet, swords still drawn, and the tower guards all looked around. Margaret, gripping the arms of her chair again as if she might fall out of it, searched the room and saw no sign of Enfleda's pale blue gown or white veil.

"She can't have gone down the stairs, surely?" said Margaret to the guard nearest her. She looked from one staircase to the other. "She must be on this floor somewhere." Margaret rose from her chair, unable to sit still any longer. Mac Duff still loomed over Diarmad, who'd gone limp like a deer who realizes that he's about to be torn apart by the hounds and whose soul has half left its body in readiness.

Your wife wanted me to kill her. That was almost a confession. And everyone in the hall had heard it. But where was Enfleda? She'd started this whole chain of accusation and blame by stealing her own cross and accusing Aelgith of the crime. Margaret rose from her chair.

"My lady, please—" One of Malcolm's guards tried to stop her. Malcolm was now on his feet roaring at the guards to find Enfleda at once. They scurried about checking behind screens and bed curtains and running into the chambers.

"Was there anyone guarding the stairs during the fight?" asked Margaret, peering down one long run of steps. No one responded, which was an answer of sorts. "Go down and look for her! She may be in the woods by now."

She stepped to the side as guards, swords flashing, clumped and clattered down the stairs. How did they not see her leave the room? Then again, how did she not notice? The scuffle between Diarmad and Mac Duff seized everyone's attention and focused it to one point.

"Let the hounds scent her cloak!" cried Malcolm. "Chase her down and bring her here."

Mac Duff still stood over Diarmad. Malcolm ordered his two bodyguards to tie up Diarmad like a hog and leave him there on the floor. He told Mac Duff to sheath his sword and stand down.

"What was this miscreant cretin doing talking to my wife?" He kicked Diarmad, who squealed. "And why would my wife want him to kill my daughter?"

"Wait until the company is reassembled and we'll have all the answers we need." Malcolm spoke calmly.

Aelgith and Osgifu, all but forgotten amidst the tumult, clung to each other. Margaret's heart swelled with true hope for them for the first time that day.

From the hall, she could hear a great commotion of horses' hooves and shouts and dogs barking. *They're going to hunt her like a hind.*

Everything in her recoiled from this—not only because Enfleda was a woman, but perhaps also because she was English. Like Margaret she'd also been married, quite possibly against her will, to a man more than twice her age. Despite her revulsion for the ease with which Enfleda had accused two innocent countrywomen, she couldn't help a prick of horror at the prospect of this hunt.

She hurried to Malcolm, who stood with Mac Duff, looking down at Diarmad and saying something inaudible in hushed Gaelic. "Husband, surely such a company of men and horses and dogs is not needed to find one lone woman in winter. Please, call them off and send a calm company of guards to retrieve her. We'll never learn the truth of the matter if she's torn limb from limb."

He looked at her as if she were mad, then he turned to Mac Duff. "My wife has a soft heart."

"Better than a heart and soul of ice," said Mac Duff. "If she tupped this....thing—" He kicked at Diarmad, who lay trussed like a captured beast. "I'll have her torn limb from limb myself."

"God forbid!" said Margaret, before she could stop herself. "We are Christians and must follow the law."

"I am the law in my lands!" said Mac Duff. "Your husband granted me that right."

"My husband told me that your laws invoke fines and

penalties to avoid taking a life." She wished she knew the details, but perhaps they only existed in Mac Duff's head.

"There are times when taking a life is an act of mercy," growled Mac Duff, peering down at Diarmad.

"We must follow God's laws," said Margaret quickly.

"What would God have us do with such a fiend?" asked Malcolm, glaring at Diarmad. Margaret swallowed, pondering God's punishments…a generation wandering in exile? Her own family had suffered that much and more.

"Shall we nail him to a cross?" asked Mac Duff, with sudden good humor.

"No! And it's blasphemy to even suggest it." Margaret crossed herself.

"And what of my adulterous wife?"

"If your wife is found guilty she should receive the punishment due to a lady of her stature according to the laws of Scotland."

Mac Duff peered at Malcolm, head cocked. "What would we Scots do with such a wench, do you think? Stake her to a hillside to be fed to the wild beasts?"

"Do you really speak this way of your wedded wife before she's even convicted of a crime?" asked Margaret, too shocked to stop herself. "At least give her the chance to speak for herself."

"If she's returned in one piece I suppose she'll have the chance."

He cares for her so little. It almost seemed as if Mac Duff would prefer for his wife to be savaged by the hounds. No wonder she'd sought solace or safety—of a dubious sort—in the arms of another man.

She looked down at poor, foolish Diarmad; then reminded herself that he'd almost certainly attacked his pregnant and defenseless wife with a knife blade, plunging it into her as her blood sprayed over him. *What did I do to find myself in the presence of such evil?* Her hand flew to cross herself again.

She wanted to run away to pray, but didn't dare leave the hall. Aelgith and Osgifu's fate hung in the balance and they might have been put to death already without her intercession.

"Take heart," she said to them softly. "For I believe the truth is about to come out."

ENFLEDA WAS BROUGHT BACK into the hall within the hour and bound to a chair with rope. Much as she despised the woman, Margaret hated to see her like this, her veil snatched away and her dress torn. Her ice-blue eyes shone with panic rather than cunning. The jeweled gold cross still hung incongruously around her neck.

She studied Mac Duff's face to gauge his reaction to his wife's captivity and saw that he peered at her as if she were a mysterious sea creature dragged from the deep rather than a mortal woman.

Margaret had taken a moment in the confusion of her return to whisper words in her husband's ear. She'd whispered similar words of encouragement in the ear of Osgifu, who swallowed hard in response.

"Enfleda, wife of Mac Duff, your sudden departure from this hall, amidst accusations of infidelity and disloyalty, does not reflect well on you," said Malcolm calmly. He strode around the table, where the men had reassembled, and circled the chair where Enfleda sat. She now occupied the spot where Aelgith and Osgifu had stood. They'd been moved to one side.

Enfleda glared at him, probably to hide her terror. Her lips had narrowed into a tight line.

"The accusations made against you, which have been given weight by your flight, were offered by the slave girl Osgifu. She was a witness to you disappearing off into the wood with Diarmad Mac Aidh—" He glanced at Diarmad, who still lay trussed on the floor in obvious discomfort.

Enfleda's expression remained unchanged—hard as stone —as she risked a glance at her former lover.

"She said that you returned flushed and with bark on the back of your dress, as if he'd had his way with you up against a tree."

Margaret closed her eyes as the crude image hit her like a gust of hot wind. Was such vivid description necessary?

"What do you have to say for yourself?"

"Lies," said Enfleda quietly. "Why would I do such a stupid thing and with such a stupid man?"

"To get with child," said Malcolm calmly. "You knew Diarmad wouldn't reveal your secret since he was married to your husband's daughter. With his seed sowed in you, you might give your husband a son and secure your place as his wife. Without it, you might be cast out and...as has been observed, your noble father's fiefdom is no more and you have no home to return to."

Enfleda's expression wobbled. Again, Margaret felt a pang of sorrow or sympathy for her proud fellow country-woman, who'd been brought to this foul fate by the narrow circumstances she'd been thrust into.

Still, she could have chosen life as a nun if her husband cast her out. He'd surely not have refused to fund her enclosure in a convent. That would have been a better fate than the one she faced now.

"Is this true, Diarmad?" Malcolm kicked at him lightly with the toe of his leather boot.

"Yes," said Diarmad, unable to meet Enfleda's gaze even if he wanted to. "She told me to kill my wife."

Malcolm frowned. Margaret couldn't quite make sense of this part. Surely with her goal—a baby—achieved, Enfleda had no reason to wish harm to Beitris.

"I did not!" cried Enfleda. "Do you think I wanted to forsake the Mormaer of Fife to marry this fool? I admit I did...lie with him...but only to give my husband a son."

"Another man's son?" roared Mac Duff. "To be Mormaer of Fife? Are you mad?"

Enfleda looked down at the floor. "I wanted to give you a child and we'd tried for years to make one." Her voice sounded hollow and Margaret felt her loss and longing in it...the gradual realization that her aged husband would never make her a mother and that her days as his unloved wife were numbered.

"She loved me," cried Diarmad, from the floor. "She wanted to kill her husband and marry me."

"Nonsense!" Enfleda strained against her bonds as if she might rise from her chair and kick Diarmad herself. "He knew his wife wanted to leave him and go back to her father. She'd threatened to do it many times and he knew Mac Duff would blame him and possibly have him replaced as Thane of Balbarnie for his inability to manage his own household let alone his manor."

"I didn't know how urgent poor Beitris's pleas truly were," said Mac Duff, looking down at Diarmad where he lay on the floor.

"Beitris hated Enfleda and Enfleda knew it," snarled Diarmad. "Enfleda didn't want her husband's daughter back in her house, nursing and rocking a bonny babe. She knew Beitris would push her father to rid himself of his cold and barren wife. Enfleda begged me to be rid of them and to take her as my wife. She said she'd...take care of the old man."

"He lies!" shrieked Enfleda.

"How would you have killed me, woman?" Mac Duff

sounded more curious than enraged. "Would you have stabbed me in my bed or poisoned my ale?"

"I would never do such a thing!" Enfleda's words rang hollow.

Were they true? Did Enfleda plot to kill Beitris? Margaret couldn't be sure.

It was hard to imagine that cold, calculating Enfleda—wife of the second most powerful man in the kingdom—would want to be saddled with the night-walking and dim-witted Diarmad. And even if her husband did die, as his childless widow she might be married off to whoever his oldest son chose rather than a man of her own choice.

Margaret could no longer hold her tongue. "Enfleda was perhaps not the most loving wife to you, sir," she said to Mac Duff. "But I doubt she had anything to do with your daughter's murder. I think that Diarmad's shame at losing his wife and daughter back to her father's household—which would surely have happened sooner or later—prompted him to take her life. He may even have done the deed in the throes of his sleep-walking, where he wanders the halls unwitting."

Everyone now stared at Margaret as if astonished that she'd speak so boldly. *I'm the queen.* Surely she had a right to voice her opinion? And now that she had their attention—"And you can all see that Aelgith and her daughter Osgifu are entirely innocent of the murder, and in fact risked their own lives in an effort to save poor Beitris as she lay dying. That their efforts were futile cannot be held against them. If anything, their courage and kindness should be rewarded here on earth as it will surely be in Heaven."

A mix of terror and triumph hummed in her blood after this little speech. She braced herself for their reaction.

"My wife makes good sense." Malcolm's voice boomed across the hall, silencing the hum of whispers and murmurs.

"The two English women had no reason to murder Beitris, and should be commended for their kindness."

Margaret looked at Aelgith and Osgifu, who now clung to each other, still not daring to look hopeful.

"And who else but her husband—whose blood-boltered dagger and bloodstained wrists were evidence of his crime— had a motive to kill poor Beitris? I, Malcolm, King of the Scots, hereby sentence Diarmad Mac Aidh to die for his crime."

A howl emerged from Diarmad, where he lay trussed on the floor. "If I did it I was asleep and insensible! I would never kill my dear wife."

Revolted though she was by his crime, Margaret couldn't help a pang of sorrow for the young man. Had he truly murdered his wife, unwitting? Horror and violence had consumed the lives of every man up and down these islands, so there was scarcely a man who hadn't drawn blood on the battlefield. Her own husband's nightmares left him drenched in sweat and panting in their bed. Should they show him clemency if he'd committed the crime unawares?

A young man Margaret recognized as one of the guards approached Malcolm, and whispered in his ear. Malcolm frowned. "Bring him in," he said. "The priest has been found. The man who heard confessions at Balbarnie. We shall hear what he has to say on these matters."

The priest surely won't repeat what he's heard in confession. Margaret felt horror at the idea. Confession was a sacred trust. Still, he would have heard the confessions of both Diarmad and his wife Beitris, so if anyone knew what lay in their hearts, he would.

CHAPTER 23

For some reason, Margaret had expected a hoary old man of the cloth with a long gray beard and a weathered face. When he reached the top of the stairs, she was surprised to see a tall, dark-haired man with hollow cheeks and a haunted look in his gray eyes.

Haunted? He looked utterly terrified.

Instead of priestly robes, which varied considerably, she'd found, from plain black garments to gold-embroidered riches, he wore a monk's habit of rough brown sack-cloth, much stained, especially about the knees.

He startled visibly, jumping back a step, when he saw Diarmad bound and trussed like a captured hog on the floor.

"Your name, father?" asked Malcolm.

"I...I...I am Torcall...but I no longer claim the role or honor of priest. I am a simple monk."

"But you were the priest for the Mac Aidh family who lived at Balbarnie?"

Margaret watched his prominent Adam's apple rise and fall. "I was, sir."

"Why did you leave?"

"As God is my witness—and to my great shame—I found I cared more for wine and ale than for my calling after five years tending to this family."

Margaret peered at him. He didn't look like a drunk.

"Are you drunk now, Father Torcall?"

"I am not. But I am guilty of trying to lose myself in drink as well as prayer since I left that hellish place."

Mac Duff's mouth fell open. "Hellish? Why?"

The priest—or whatever he now was—looked at Mac Duff. "The family is cursed. No amount of prayers could lift the misery in them."

Mac Duff swallowed and—if she wasn't mistaken—his eyes glittered with unshed tears. Margaret's heart now ached for this grizzled father. His daughter had pleaded to leave her husband and come home to safety and solace...and he'd refused her. No doubt he'd thought he was doing his duty, upholding the honor of the family—

Malcolm cleared his throat. "Without revealing anything said to you in the sacred covenant of confession, do you think Diarmad capable of murder?"

The priest hesitated, risking a glance at Diarmad, who glared back at him. "He's a fool, my lord. But he has a strange cunning. He never confessed anything of murder to me—so I don't think I break my vows to say this—but his older brother died in a hunting accident and then shortly after that his father and mother grew gravely ill after eating a trout caught in the nearby stream."

"Did he eat the trout as well?"

"I was not present at the dinner, but the cook who prepared it and two serving girls also died."

Margaret blinked. Had Diarmad committed multiple murders to take control of his family's estate and fortunes?

"God's grief!" cried Mac Duff. "I admit I chose the lad as a husband for my daughter because he had already inherited his estates. There's nothing worse than marrying a girl off to a man who'll be older than me when he finally comes into his property. But to hear that he took his patrimony in violence and sin—" His rough countenance sagged. "My poor dear Beitris. I thought more of my honor than of her happiness. I delivered her into the hands of a monster, and made her stay with him until he killed her."

Margaret crossed herself. Her sympathy for foolish and half-mad Diarmad had evaporated entirely.

"May I cut his head off right here in your hall?" Mac Duff was already on his feet.

"No!" cried Margaret, unable to stop herself. "Our hall is new and a place of peace and I don't wish his tortured spirit to walk it at night."

Everyone stared at her. She turned to her husband, silently apologizing for the outburst.

"My wife is right. He shall die at the appointed place and time. But you shall have the satisfaction of doing the deed."

Diarmad, his hands and feet tied behind his back, let out a howl and then broke into sobbing.

Malcolm watched him for a moment, then looked back at Mac Duff. "And what would you wish to become of your wife?"

"She defiled herself with another man and I banish her from my halls."

Enfleda held herself stiffly, face carefully composed. The worst had now happened—the rejection and expulsion she dreaded.

"Niall, remove the cross from around her neck," commanded Mac Duff to a young man standing against a wall. "I shall give it to my next wife."

Now Enfleda did flinch. She stood still as a statue while the young guard lifted the gold cross from her neck. Margaret reminded herself not to feel too much sympathy, since Enfleda would have been happy to watch Aelgith and Osgifu go to their deaths for the theft of it.

"Where do you intend for her to live?" asked Malcolm.

Margaret didn't like Malcolm asking the aggrieved party to decide her fate. It invited the worst and most humiliating punishment imaginable.

Still, she held her tongue. Would she intervene if he asked for her to be burned alive or fed to wild beasts or some other savage punishment that this vindictive warlord might find lurking in his brain? Enfleda was cold and cunning but those qualities sprang from her sense of dignity and nobility. Her crime, lamentable and low though it was, arose from an effort to preserve her status as wife to a great lord. Margaret would not allow her to be sold into slavery or treated like an animal.

"She should be locked up in a nunnery," said Mac Duff after some moments' reflection.

Margaret sagged with relief. While this certainly wasn't Enfleda's vocation, it would provide her with a life of dignity and a measure of protection and she could at least pray for the passage of her tattered soul.

Malcolm nodded and murmured something to one of his guards, who led Enfleda away down the stairs.

Anxious that Aelgith and Osgifu not be forgotten amidst all this horror, Margaret risked speaking again. "I would like the two women from Hampshire to be released into my care."

She glanced at Mac Duff, expecting him to contradict her and claim the girl as his property.

I am your queen.

She projected all the regal dignity and majesty she could conjure as she met his gaze.

"The slave girl Osgifu is highly skilled with needlework. I'd like her to show my next wife how to make the patterns

255

of tiny stitches she employs," said Mac Duff, his chin lifted. "I wish to keep her in my household."

Furious, Margaret glanced at Malcolm. Malcolm leaned back in his chair. "I hope you shall rest at least a little easier now that your daughter's true killer has been found."

"I'll rest easier after my sword slices his damned head from his shoulders," growled Mac Duff, peering down at Diarmad. The condemned thane was making a lot of pathetic whimpering noises amidst his sobs.

Any sympathy that Margaret might feel for him was consumed in fury that Osgifu hadn't yet been pronounced free after her horrible ordeal.

She drew in a breath and spoke with conviction. "Since the Earl of Fife is staying with us for the Christmas feast tomorrow, I shall take the women somewhere to rest." In a worst-case scenario, perhaps Mac Duff could be convinced to find a place in his household for Aelgith. Then at least the mother and daughter could stay together.

She looked around, expecting someone to protest, but neither Malcolm or Mac Duff even seemed interested enough to object. She decided to depart the hall with Aelgith and Osgifu before anything else happened.

She rose from her chair on the dais and lifted her skirts, then stepped down to the floor. Carefully skirting around the prostrate Diarmad, she approached Osgifu and Aelgith and murmured for them to come with her. Grizel followed her like a shadow without being summoned.

On the stairs, Aelgith asked if they were going back to the jail.

"God forbid!" said Margaret. "I hope that Beathag will allow you to stay in her house until I can come up with a plan for the two of you." She turned to Grizel. "Do you think she will?"

"Yes, my lady."

Margaret knew that Beathag would hardly dare to say no to her queen, but she would compensate her well and send ample food for all of them.

"You've saved our lives," said Aelgith, once they were outside. The crisp winter air stung her skin. They walked down the well-trodden path to the village, wind whipping at their capes as they emerged from the shelter of the woods. "Though it pains me that my daughter is still a slave to that brute."

"I beg of you, do not try to take your fate into your own hands again," said Margaret gravely. "Put your faith in God and trust me."

"I promise you, my lady, I will put my life and my daughter's in your hands."

WHILE MARGARET WOULD HAVE PREFERRED the eve of Christmas to be spent in prayer to welcome the birth of Christ, the household descended into drunken revelry as the holy day grew closer.

Margaret had learned to pick her battles. While she might have persuaded her husband to hold off for a few more hours, there were at least three score other brawny adult men aching to toss back horns of wine and ale and sing and laugh and make merry. Even a queen's influence had to be used sparingly so as not to lose its authority altogether.

Margaret went to bed long before her husband, but prayed and stayed awake waiting for the chance to bend his ear with pleas for him to buy Osgifu's freedom.

When Malcolm did finally climb between the curtains, he was half insensible with drink and sleepiness. Her urgent whispers fell on deaf ears and he was asleep and snoring loudly before she'd finished speaking.

Seething with frustration, Margaret turned away from him. This was exactly why she didn't want to get married. Men could do whatever they wanted, whenever they wanted. As a wife it was her duty to put up with it.

In the royal courts of both Hungary and England, she'd heard too many women sigh and grouse about their wayward husbands. And men wondered why women craved the safety and security of a convent, where they were brides of the Savior of all mankind, who never crawled into bed drunk or beat them or took advantage of a serving girl in the buttery.

Not that her husband had done any of those but the first. She crossed herself quickly and thanked the Lord for that. A man of genuine belief, Malcolm took the vows of marriage seriously and attempted to live according to the Ten Commandments. She'd seen and heard of many—so many—who did not.

Calmed by these reassuring thoughts that her husband, while not perfect, was still a good man, she decided to put her faith in God regarding the fate of Aelgith and Osgifu. *Let his will be done.*

MARGARET AWOKE IN A PANIC. Would their Christmas festivities begin with Diarmad's head being violently removed from his shoulders? This could not happen on such a holy day. She felt in her bones that it was her duty to prevent such a horror.

Malcolm grunted when she shook him. "Is the house afire?" he grunted.

"When will Diarmad be punished?"

"When Christmastide is over," he said, suddenly lucid.

"You read my thoughts."

"I've come to know you well, my love." He pulled her into his arms.

"We shall wait all twelve days before…."

"All twelve, my love. Rest easy. No heads shall roll during our Christmas feasting…even if my brother Donald Ban bays for the sport of it." He chuckled at his own joke.

"Where is Donald Ban? I was expecting him yesterday."

Malcolm nuzzled against her ear and whispered. "I sent him on an errand yesterday. I thought his presence in the hall during the women's trial might be disruptive."

Margaret's heart swelled with gratitude—and love. "You are truly a great and kind man, my lord." Did she dare risk pushing for Osgifu's freedom? Of course she did. "But what of the poor slave girl's fate?"

He pulled back a little. "I see you still don't trust me."

"I do trust you," she said doubtfully.

"Then prove it."

CHAPTER 24

*T*he household rose before dawn for the Christmas morning mass. Grizel braided Margaret's hair and pinned her veil by candlelight. The tower echoed with the hushed rustling and clanking of people rising to celebrate the birth of Jesus.

The assembled company gathered outside the tower and Malcolm and Margaret led the walk down the hillside from the tower to the church below. The usually freezing chapel had been abustle since Matins and braziers warmed the nave. Candles shone in every corner and green boughs and garlands of pinecones and mistletoe and embroidered ribbon swagged the arches and columns.

Margaret and Malcolm led the procession up to the altar, where they knelt on thick cushions and bowed their heads. Peace filled Margaret's heart during the service. Despite the tumult and disaster of the last few years, she was still alive, her family safe, and men still gathered to celebrate the birth of Christ.

Fervent prayers for the coming year, as well as the

coming days and even hours, crowded her mind and moved her lips.

As she and Malcolm turned and led the assembled crowd out of the chapel, she glimpsed Aelgith and Osgifu, standing in the back corner with Beathag, their hands pressed together in prayer.

She'd begged these two women to put their trust in her... would she be worthy of it?

A SUMPTUOUS FEAST awaited them on their return to the hall. All the delicacies withheld during the long Advent period sat steaming on the table: roasted fowl of all sizes, thick slabs of beef, sliced thinly and drenched in rich gravy, pork cooked so tender that it flaked when the knife pierced it. Rich sauces made with preserved autumn fruits, butter and herbs and heady aromatic spices filled jugs and bowls interspersed between the meats. Rolls and pastries fresh from the ovens sat piled high on silver platters.

Margaret's stomach—delicate at the best of times and more so now that she was with child—recoiled from the warring aromas. She and Malcolm took their seats in the middle of the high table.

She did her best to eat, for the health of her baby and to show appreciation for the hard work in the kitchens and the bounty they'd been blessed with. Mac Duff sat at her left and she even managed to engage him in conversation about hunting, which was clearly his favorite subject.

After a long and somewhat tedious conversation about stag ruts, she asked a question that burned in her mind. "How do you speak such good English and French as well as your own language?" Like her husband, his rough warrior exterior hid a mind seasoned by education.

"Don't tell anyone, my dear, but we're all raised to be king in this land."

"Like my brother," she said, truthfully. "Should my husband rest easy when his mormaers harbor such visions of grandeur?"

"Your husband can rest easy as long as he keeps William from ransacking our lands." Mac Duff tore into yet another pheasant leg like a wolf attacking its prey. "For I think we all fear having to bow to the Norman."

Margaret suspected that the very barrenness of this land kept William from wanting to expend too much energy on it. "Tell me, why does my husband still insist on incursions into Northumbria now that William claims it? Surely that only pokes at the bear when he'd be better left to lick other people's honey from his paws."

"Sometimes, my dear, attack is the best form of defense. Your husband knows this better than any man."

ONCE THE FEASTING was over and everyone sated, they sat and listened to a bard sing a long and—to Margaret—mostly incomprehensible story about people sailing across seas and fighting and sailing across seas and fighting and... Finally it ended and Malcolm summoned the company to walk down to the wooded hill to the town.

It took some time for everyone to don their cloaks and Margaret wondered what Malcolm intended to do with them all on this sunny but bitterly cold winter's day. As they emerged into the open plain she saw a strange pageantry unfolding in one of the sheep fields. A line of cows and horses, even some sheep and dogs, decorated with ribbons and greenery, greeted them. Each animal was held by an attendant, most of them men draped in their plaids, some with garlands over their shoulders or sprigs tucked into the clasps of their cloaks. Some were held by girls, all of them pretty, with their hair unbraided and falling over their shoulders.

"What is this?" whispered Margaret to Grizel.

"The gift-giving," the girl whispered back to her.

Malcolm marched up to the line of animals. One of the horses, a large black beast with a long mane and a thick white blaze along its nose, pawed impatiently.

"For my dear friend Mac Duff, I gift three war horses, well-trained in the art of fighting."

Mac Duff approached the black horse and held out his hand for the horse to sniff. The horse nuzzled it gently, then let out an approving snort and tossed its head, flourishing its thick mane. "Aren't you a beauty," said Mac Duff. The other two horses were dark bay in color, a matched team, both with black-feathered feet and imperious expressions.

"I give you five fine head of cattle, three in milk and two with haunches to feed your entire company for a month." Three girls led the milk cows forward, and two men handled the beef cattle.

Smaller boys and girls then led the sheep forward. Thick with winter wool, their black faces almost crowded into invisibility by it, the sheep looked confused and tried to hide behind each other, making the children giggle.

Then a boy of about fourteen led the two dogs—hounds with long shaggy hair, forward. Mac Duff approached them and again let one sniff his hand, then petted its head. "Fine animals, are they sons of your Fincar?"

"Aye, they are," said Malcolm. The satisfied smile on her husband's face told Margaret that he enjoyed this gift-giving almost as much as the recipient. She knew enough about breeding and training to be aware that years of careful husbandry had gone into each of these animals.

All kings took great pride in the breeding of their horses, but Malcolm extended that pride in creation to these other animals that helped to sustain life in this harsh land with its unyielding soils and long winters.

Mac Duff turned from surveying his new animals. "My dear friend and trusted and revered King, you have outdone yourself with this gift. I fear I cannot repay your generosity."

"You can risk your life on the battlefield for me again," quipped Malcolm.

Margaret stiffened. She hoped he wasn't planning another foray south. Could they at least catch their breath after the last debacle?

Malcolm continued. "And there is one gift I crave, that you have the power to give. The girl, Osgifu, who is your captive by right."

"The girl is yours, my friend."

Margaret's heart swelled with joy, and she realized that she'd clapped her hands together. She smiled at Malcolm. He'd planned this all along, and it must have taken considerable arranging and no small sacrifice from his carefully tended stock. Unable to resist, she approached her husband and kissed him on the cheek, which made him smile awkwardly. Mac Duff guffawed with laughter.

The festivities continued with Mac Duff leaping on one of his new war horses—with no tack whatsoever except the red rope leading it—and managed to turn it in circles and gallop it back and forth across the field with calm expertise.

"See?" said Malcolm, to Margaret. "I told you to trust me."

"You could have told me you were planning this." She'd certainly have slept better and enjoyed the morning service and the long feasting more if she'd known what awaited them afterward.

"That would have ruined the surprise."

"It's a very expensive gift," she marveled.

"Mac Duff is a very important ally. He fights as well as he rides and his men are loyal to him and to me. That is priceless."

~

AFTER THREE MORE DAYS OF feasting, Mac Duff returned to his winter home at Cupar with his new prize animals and his captive for disposal in his own time and on his own terms. Enfleda was packed off to a convent somewhere in Cumbria. She'd left for the long, punishing journey on a donkey with only two guards to escort her and a letter of introduction from both Malcolm and Mac Duff, promising payment for her care and a command for her immediate enclosure.

Enfleda wouldn't have to become a nun. As an adulteress she might not even be allowed to. But it wasn't unusual for women to live out their lives in the safety of a convent according to the patterns and rituals of the sanctuary. Margaret was glad that she'd at least have a chance to atone for her sins and be afforded a life of dignity appropriate to her birth.

Speaking of which...she waited until Mac Duff had left before inviting Aelgith and Osgifu to take up residence in the hall. They were not servants, or peasants, certainly not slaves. They needed time to heal from their ordeal before she could find a more permanent situation for them.

Aelgith had benefited from a convent education similar to her own and they now shared happy hours of conversation on various subjects. The servants rubbed balm into Aelgith's sore feet and prepared nourishing meals to rebuild her strength. Now they sat stitching before the fire after an excellent dinner.

"It was Opus Anglicanum that saved our lives," said Aelgith. "When we were brought to Northumbria I gave the lady of the house some tips to save a piece of needlework she was fumbling. She had me take it over and I soon put Osgifu to work on it."

Aelgith's needle flashed in and out of the delicate work in her hands. Gold thread shimmered in the candlelight and her delicately wrought leaves and flowers looked almost alive.

"I thought Mac Duff would keep me forever, just for my stitches." Osgifu worked on a long piece of gold-trimmed ribbon that would ornament the altar cloth for the new abbey church. "Though my skill kept me working inside and not freezing out on a moor with a flock of sheep. Enfleda was jealous of my skill and kept trying to pass my work off as her own. She's too impatient to make her stitches neatly."

Margaret had learned the delicate art of making the rich and extravagant needlework known as Opus Anglicanum at the knee of Queen Edith, wife of the Confessor. Edith was an avid needlewoman herself and purchased the finest silk and gold and silver threads to make vestments for even the Archbishop of Canterbury.

Aelgith already looked ten years younger. Grizel had concocted a blend of wine and herbs to lighten her hair to match the golden ends of her braids that persisted from her old life. The lighter color blended the sprinkling of grays and brightened her complexion. With the hollows of hunger already filling in under her cheeks and eyes, and her skin softened with sheep grease, she looked like a different woman.

"How old are you?" asked Margaret, marveling at the transformation.

"Thirty-six," said Aelgith, head bent over her stitches. "I had my son at sixteen and dear Osgifu at twenty-two."

Margaret's heart ached for her losses. "Your son was still young when William took Hampshire."

"Sixteen, but he wouldn't stay home even though I begged

him to. And his father reasoned that they were fighting for our kingdom and our very lives." She sighed. "My husband was a brave man and a kind one. I wish we'd been granted the grace to grow old together."

Margaret pondered that—once healed—Aelgith could still marry again, to a widower who already had children that needed raising and wasn't looking for more. Such men did exist. "How do you wish your life to unfold now?"

"I hardly dare look past the morrow," said Aelgith quietly, hands stilling over her stitchery. "I'm afraid to even dream in case my hopes are snatched away." She looked at Osgifu, now bent over her elaborate stitching. "My hopes lie with my daughter. But can she even hope for the ordinary comforts of life—a husband, a family, a home? Our people are exiles and being driven like geese across the countryside."

"Except that geese can fly away," said Osgifu suddenly.

"Not if their wings are clipped," said Aelgith. "Only wild geese have unclipped wings."

"It's a shame humans can't live wild," mused Osgifu.

"I think that was your mother's plan for the two of you," said Margaret gently. "That you'd be foraging for berries in the forests of Hampshire."

"We'd get wet in the rain," said Osgifu with a shy smile. "I'd rather be stitching Opus Anglicanum."

"Osgifu is too young to marry," said Margaret. "I know many girls are married off at her age but I'll always be grateful that I wasn't. Now that she's safe under my roof she can resume her education and mature into a woman at a measured pace."

"Do you think we'll ever be able to return to England?" asked Aelgith.

"I asked myself the same question when we first arrived here. My brother still harbors hopes of sitting on the throne and holding court at Westminster." She spoke low. His ambitions were well known but it still felt somehow…danger-ous…to speak them aloud. "But my life lies here in my husband's kingdom."

"Are you not worried that William will invade?" asked Aelgith quietly.

Was it treasonous to speak the truth? "I am. How could I not be? But whatever happens, we must adapt and survive. We've come this far. We have the strength of our faith and hope for the future."

"And a great quantity of this beautiful gold thread," said Osgifu, looking up from her stitches. "I feel like I'm in a folk-tale where someone is spinning straw into gold."

Margaret laughed. "Wait until you see what's arriving on the next ship from Flanders. We shall have you arrayed like a princess in patterned silks. I intend for the nobles of our court to be the peers of any in Westminster."

"Good luck prying the smelly plaids off any of these Scotsmen," said Osgifu with a smile. "Even Mac Duff himself sleeps in his more often than not!"

"Ah, I shall not try to change their culture and customs too much," said Margaret. "Just to add some refinement and perhaps a little sparkle." She lifted her stitching, a small purse she intended to wear on her belt to carry her precious Black Rood. The gold thread shimmered in the candlelight. "To honor the glory of God and the Kingdom of the Scots."

THE END

AUTHOR'S NOTE

Every British pupil has the date 1066 emblazoned in their brain. The fateful year when William the Conqueror invaded and overthrew England changed everything: language, laws, social structure and land ownership. The Anglo-Saxon ruling class was displaced and disinherited almost overnight. Those who survived the initial onslaught had to scramble to find their place in the new social order and adapt or perish. My fascination with this era led me to Queen Margaret of Scotland, who navigated these choppy waters with such grace she would be declared a saint less than two centuries after her death.

We have a first-hand account of Margaret's life and character written by Bishop Turgot, who knew her well. While some dismiss his biography as a sort of hagiographical puff-piece, there are elements in it that no one would want in their PR packet. It seems obvious to modern readers, for example, that she struggled with anorexia. Her forceful personality shines through in her insistence on debating with powerful clerics, with her royal husband acting as her translator. Her possibly obsessive and excessive acts of self-abasement and charity—washing the feet of hundreds of paupers and feeding orphans with her own spoon— mark her as eccentric in an era when noblewoman were expected to sit quietly at their needlework. These aspects of her personality contrast intriguingly with her insistence that the Scottish court be expensively decked out in the latest imported fashions— which they must also be prepared to donate to paupers at a moment's notice. I was particularly fascinated by Turgot's account of her sending spies to seek out English captives being held in cruel bondage and paying to free them.

While there are a variety of contemporary and near contemporary sources on this era, they often contradict each other. Examples include conflicting accounts of where Malcolm spent his youth in exile, what happened to Ingibiorg, the mother of his first two sons, even whether Malcolm could read. I like the theory that Malcolm spent his youth in the court of Edward the Confessor, where he would have had a rich education and exposure to the mores of Edward's Norman-influenced court. Malcolm reportedly visited Westminster after his 1058 conquest of Scotland, and met the young Margaret. It's suspected that Edward even promised her to him at that time, when she was about thirteen, and that she begged to continue her convent education instead. Popular legend has Margaret's family washing ashore in Scotland after a storm derailed their attempted flight back to Europe. I prefer the theory that they fled north to belatedly fulfill the decade-old promise as they struggled to salvage the wreck of their hopes that Margaret's brother Edgar Aetheling would be king of England.

Building a picture of this period in medieval Scotland meant letting go of preconceptions. There were no stone castles, for example! While Iron-Age round brochs still dotted the land-scape, there had been little to no stone construction since the Romans abandoned Scotland. The towers of popular imagination were a Norman introduction. Malcolm built what may have been the first one around the time that Margaret and her family entered his life. The ruins in Dunfermline—which may be from a later rebuild—are known as Malcolm Canmore's tower to this day.

Rather than being the ancient rulers of Scotland, Malcolm's royal ancestors had in fact invaded from Ireland, bringing their Gaelic language and customs and defeating the Pictish people who'd ruled before them. Malcolm's kingdom was smaller than present-day Scotland: The Norse Earls of Orkney ruled the Orkneys, the Hebrides and the mainland north of the Dornoch Firth; the Norse Lords of the Isles controlled the Western Isles and much of modern Argyll and Bute; While Malcolm III had at least nominal control of Cumbria, the Lothian area was still a battleground between England and Scotland and much of it was considered to be Northumbria in this era. Kings, clerics and many nobles would have had at least some command of several languages, including English, Latin, French, Norse, Danish, and Gaelic, which rivaled Latin as the literary language of this time.

I look forward to exploring and imagining Margaret's world and her attitude toward it in this series of mysteries. The title character of my *Ela of Salisbury Medieval Mystery* series was a wealthy widow with eight children in the prime of her life. I was drawn to Ela because she defied stereotypes of medieval women by securing and holding the roles of castellan and sheriff in an era when that was almost unheard of. Margaret would also go on to have eight children, but she outlived her husband by only one day and thus spent her entire life married to a king and living in the fishbowl of the royal court, with all the challenges that implies. I remain fascinated by how these intelligent, educated and powerful women managed to negotiate the limitations and expectations of their eras to command the admiration of their contemporaries and to leave their mark on history.

If you have questions or comments, please get in touch at jglewis@stoneheartpress.com.

OTHER BOOKS BY J. G. LEWIS

The Ela of Salisbury Medieval Mystery Series

This series features a real historical figure—the formidable Ela Longespée. The young Countess of Salisbury was chosen to marry King Henry II's illegitimate son William. After her husband's untimely death, Ela served as High Sheriff of Wiltshire, castellan of Salisbury Castle, and ultimately founder and abbess of Lacock Abbey.

AUTHOR BIOGRAPHY

J. G. Lewis grew up in a Regency-era house in London, England. She spent her childhood visiting nearby museums and riding ponies in Hyde Park. She came to the U.S. to study semiotics at Brown University and stayed for the sunshine and a career as a museum curator in New York City. Over the years she published quite a few novels, two of which hit the USA Today list. She didn't delve into historical fiction until she discovered genealogy and the impressive cast of potential characters in her family history. Once she realized how many fascinating historical figures are all but forgotten, she decided to breathe life into them again by creating stories for them to inhabit. J. G. Lewis currently lives in Florida with her dog and her horses.

For more information visit www.stoneheartpress.com.